DIVINE INTENT

L.L. TAYLOR

PREFACE

"Hi, Dani. This is Tina at the clubhouse. Your mom was supposed to pick Mason up at four o'clock, but we haven't heard from her."

Dani looked at her watch. It was 5:25.

"There's no answer at the house, and we close in five minutes. She's never late. We're a little worried."

That trace of foreboding Dani had been feeling all day crept back.

Dani did a quick U-turn and headed for the Sunnyside Clubhouse. She reached for her phone and dialed her parents' number. No answer.

A moment later, Dani's phone rang again...*unknown caller*. This time the reception was poor and all she could hear were fragments of a woman's voice.

"Mom? If you can hear me, don't worry, I'm picking up Mason. We'll meet you at the house." The line went dead.

-- -- -- -- --

It was 6:12. Dani was four blocks from the Shaw's house when she could see the glow of the rotating blue and red lights in the fading early evening sky.

Dani's heart was racing as she neared her parents' home on Butler Avenue.

"What did Amanda do now?" she wondered aloud, feeling a mixture of panic and anger.

As she turned the corner onto her parents' street, Dani could see half a dozen police units, an ambulance, two news vans parked near and around her parents' house—and Amanda's car in the driveway. As she drove closer, distraught familiar faces came into view as neighbors gathered in small groups.

The groups began to separate, creating a path for Dani's Jeep. Dani could hardly give the gas pedal enough pressure to move forward. She didn't want to. She was afraid of what she might find when she reached the driveway.

The invading response vehicles blocked the entire street. Dani could no longer drive forward. She had nowhere to go.

Just then, a police officer began walking toward Dani's Jeep.

"Ma'am, we have an emergency situation, you're going to have to turn your vehicle around."

Dani pushed the gear shift into park, opened the door, and sprang from her seat, unconsciously leaving the vehicle running.

"This is my parents' house!" she shouted, "What's going on?"

Several police officers heard the commotion and began walking toward Dani and the officer standing beside her.

"What's going on?" she screamed again as she began running toward the double French doors just beyond the covered entryway to the house.

One of the officers approached Dani and forcefully grabbed her by the shoulders, directing her toward him.

"Ma'am, there's been a shooting." Others gathered around as the officer continued. "We've dis—"

"Is everyone all right?" Dani asked in a barely audible whisper.

"I'm sorry to say, we've discovered four deceased individuals," Dani's legs began to give way, "an unidentified man and woman, as well as the owners of the home, Randall and Britta Shaw."

Dani collapsed as her knees buckled beneath her.

CHAPTER ONE

The pelting hail sent shock-waves across Dani's shoulders as she footed her way through the oblivion of cars lining *The Daily Journal* parking lot. The SUVs and Hummers were out in droves as the early morning weather report had predicted the last snowfall of the season this afternoon in the inconspicuous little town. With its nineteenth century buildings that lined Main Street, to its old-fashioned prosperity, what Glenbrook lacked in big city sophistication, it made up for in small-town camaraderie.

Dreary-weather spring days always gave Dani a sense of foreboding; today was no exception. Arm's length from the driver's side door, she shook free the loose pebbles of hail from her jacket and climbed into the familiar leather bucket seat of her cherry red Jeep Wrangler. As the frozen rain ravished the top of the vehicle, Dani started the ignition, turned the heater on full blast and rested her forehead against the cushioned steering wheel.

As she had already done at least a dozen times that day, Dani prayed that God would take away the lingering uneasiness that had been distracting her all day. Then, as quickly as the prayer escaped her thoughts, the warmth of the heater began to permeate the Jeep. The hail swiftly dissipated and was replaced with a gentle unassuming rainfall.

Dani could feel her body relax as the mesmerizing tune of the falling rain seemed to unlock a distant memory of brisk autumn days at the home in which she had grown up nestled among the valleys and pines at the base of the Sierra Nevada mountains. Back then, autumn was her favorite time of year. As a child, she would become giddy as the looming thunder clouds rolled in, followed by the gentle trickles of rain. She especially looked forward to the first storm of the season. At the first distant roar of thunder, she would open her bedroom window, close her eyes, and lose herself in the fragrant aroma of the precipitation on the surrounding sun-dried grass.

Adorning her ruggedly-worn-slightly-too-small hiking boots and void of socks, Dani would forget to tie the laces before hurrying out the front door to her secret place in the open meadow that lay just out of sight of the modestly landscaped front lawn. She knew that if she timed it just right and approached with the silence of a cat ready to pounce, she would get a glimpse of the deer nibbling on the sweet juicy apples that invaded the ground below the fruit-ravished trees, before the elegant creatures bedded down for shelter from the impending storm.

Plucking a glossy Gala from a low-lying branch, Dani would wipe the apple clean with the sleeve of her blouse and begin dancing and singing among the tall meadow grass whose tops reached the bottom of her bony, suntanned knees. She would spin in circles as her calico print cotton skirt brushed the pedals of the wild daisies that reached toward the open sky above. It wasn't long before she would be drenched to the bone from the now cutting rain falling around her. Tromping through the newly formed puddles of muddy water, she'd slowly make her way back home, savoring the smell of the smoke from the wood-burning stoves from across the rolling hills and mountainsides.

Her mother was all too familiar with Dani's rainy-day antics. When the rain would come and Dani was nowhere to be found, Britta Shaw knew her daughter, muddy boots and all, would at any moment come bursting through the front door, jet up the stairs with soaked clothes trailing behind her, and immerse herself in to a steaming tub of water, shrieking with a mixture of glee and martyrdom agony as the scalding liquid stung her frigid skin. Britta learned to be prepared. Dani knew she could depend on her mom to have the porcelain heaven ready to engulf her chilly, eight-year-old little frame. To Dani, the warm encompassing water was like snuggling between her mama and daddy under their feathery down comforter on a frosty winter night. If only life was still so simple and carefree as it was fifteen years ago. If only...

Startled back to reality by the annoying honk of a car horn, Dani lifted her tired head, packaged up her little childhood fantasies, placed them in a neat little box, and stored them in a back corner of her mind to be opened on another day—at another time. And of course, Dani was certain, there *would* be another day and time.

As Dani began backing out of her parking space, she heard the sound of brakes shrieking immediately behind her. Travis, in his shiny blue BMW, had narrowly missed plunging into the Jeep's passenger side door.

"Sorry 'bout that, Dan," Travis shouted through the small slit in his driver's side window. "Why don't you let me take you to dinner and make up for scaring ya' like that?"

Both Dani and Travis knew his proposal was merely a rhetorical prompting that had elicited the same response a thousand times before. "I'm not interested, Travis." Dani drove away, disgusted at

Travis' incessant flirting, and yet strangely flattered at the same time.

From the day Dani met Travis Jakobs, *The Journal's* editor in chief, there was an instant and forbidden attraction. In fact, Dani had even contemplated turning down the position as *The Journal's* restaurant columnist and food critic rather than allow herself to be put in a vulnerable work environment with an outwardly flirtatious married man. But in the end, Dani decided her commitment to Christ would give her the strength and discipline not to fall victim to Travis' advances. Dani was stronger than that. After all, she had spent most of her life as a homeschooler whose activities centered around her family and the tight-knit church community of which she had been a member since she was an infant. Some exposure to the "real world" couldn't hurt. In fact, one of Dani's favorite professors at the private Christian college from which she graduated always emphasized the need for Christians to step outside the boundaries of one's own little world in order to reach those who didn't know Christ. Dani couldn't think of a better place to do just that. She could put her education to use, and at the same time serve as a godly example and witness to people like Travis Jakobs.

Halfway home and deep in thought, Dani nearly ran a stop sign as she headed toward her condo on the south side of town. The rain had picked up, and Dani struggled to see out her windshield through the downfall that was now showering the streets. The volatile weather slowed the usually fifteen-minute afternoon commute to a snail's pace. She began thinking about the last two years she'd spent at *The Journal.* She loved her job as food columnist and critic.

The food was great if not for the few extra pounds she'd put on over the past twenty-four months, but writing was her passion. Even if all she wrote about was the intricate flavors of the Crab Bisque served at the Echelon or described the tantalizing taste of the perfect combination of mustard and horseradish on the grilled Reuben special from Tony's Café, Dani could make any meal—any restaurant—sound as though it was fit for a king.

Fresh out of college, Dani had applied for the position as food critic at *The Journal* on a whim. She hoped to find work in her hometown, but knew the likelihood of finding full-time employment in the writing industry in Glenbrook, population less than 29,000, was slim. The editor of *The Journal*, Stan Montgomery, liked her resume and the intern work she had done at the university and was impressed with her writing samples. He eventually asked Dani to come in for a "trial run" as he called it. Her assignment was to write an eight-hundred-word column about the newest burger joint in town. The place happened to be one of about six hundred stores in a chain spread across and exclusive to California. It was quite a challenge for Dani to take an average, mundane restaurant and make it appear extraordinary. But extraordinary is what Big & Juicy became. The title is what first caught Travis' eye, "Fast-Food Socialism." But the intrigue didn't stop there.

Dani began her article:

You won't find it at McDonalds. Burger King doesn't have it. And one would certainly never see it at Jack in the Box. No, I'm not referring to the best fast-food burger around. I'm talking about people—complete strangers—sharing the same table while gorging on juicy burgers and greasy fries.

Big & Juicy truly does take one back to the fifties. Aside from it's menu, which is limited to the fifties' drive-in restaurant items; burgers, shakes, and fries, and the respective paraphernalia including photos of old Chevys, Big & Juicy is the only place in America where you'll find people who have never met one another co-mingling during lunch, not merely to be social, but with a hidden agenda—they simply want dibs on the unsuspecting stranger's table.

Even families aren't exempt from this phenomenon. Mothers send their toddlers to the booth with the elderly couple enjoying an afternoon outing or the ex-con recently released from the Pen. Fathers send their sons to the table with the ballerinas dressed in pink tutus. Husbands gladly leave their wives to fend for themselves. On one occasion, when there wasn't a seat in the house, I witnessed a little old lady exiting the restroom with French fry grease dripping from her lower lip. Apparently, the seats in there were better than no seat at all. Customer behavior is simply inexplicable.

But, ahh, perhaps there is a reason for this unadulterated mayhem! Could it be that if one desires to actually sit down to eat one's meal, one has no choice but to resort to this not-so-common method of social agenda? These unprecedented phenomena could be constituted as latent aggression as a result of the never-ending line of people, which runs half a block down the street, all with two goals in mind— get a burger and get a table! I don't care if you get there when the doors open each day at 10:30, there is already a line. It's similar to attending a rock concert. People seem to come from miles around, days before, (or at least the night before) to pitch tents or host tailgate parties in an attempt to get "the good seats." Guests of Big & Juicy often send co-conspirators in ahead to get dibs on a table before the priceless seats are swept up by the selfish guests in the front of the line. It's truly amazing. The tables are full before the first order hits the register! God forbid you're dining alone and have to use the restroom in the middle of your meal. A half-eaten burger and a handwritten note on the trademark Big & Juicy napkin reading, "In the restroom…will return shortly" is no guarantee that your food, let alone your table, will still be available when you return. And that's not even the worst of it!

Once someone spots an unoccupied table and hurdles beneath guests legs, leaps over plant partitions, and does a full body skid for a seat, it is clear that they have truly embarked upon an investment. Now, one might ask how a Formica table with an attached hardback rotating chair, much less one that does not even belong to the current occupant, might possibly be considered an investment. Well, I urge you to

7

consider the following scenario: Y2K. An earth-consuming technical breakdown has destroyed a third of the world's population as a result of plane crashes, train derailments, and alleged alien abductions. All technical systems are down and water systems have failed. Even the rivers, streams, and lakes have been polluted with nuclear contamination due to military fallout and worldwide chaos and anarchy. All of which were predicted to inevitably take place at the onset of Y2K. Now imagine that you have the only gallon of fresh drinking water left within a ten-mile radius. What that gallon of water could get you! Need I say more?

My suggestion to those of you who've yet to experience the Big & Juicy phenomenon and are contemplating venturing out in to this delectable jungle is that you come well prepared. You won't get far without an expensive, top-of-the-line pair of running shoes, a good book—preferably one with a minimum of six sequels, a soft pillow for those much needed and expected catnaps during your long wait, and last but not least, a comfortable transportable patio ensemble. These highly recommended items along with a scheduled weeks vacation from work are essential for a successful dining experience at Big & Juicy—an experience which is sure to leave you with a satisfied palate and bonded friendships that will last a lifetime.

Dani could recall coming into the newsroom the morning her article appeared in print. High fives to the new girl from some.

"Way to get fired before you're even hired," from others.

"Lookin' to get blackballed, are ya?" shouted sarcastic sympathizers.

In sheer humiliation, Dani had made a sharp left for the break room. Nearly in tears, she attempted to pull herself together before once again feeding herself to the lions and throwing herself at the mercy of the king of the jungle himself—Stan Montgomery. What a fool she had made of herself. So much for bringing new, creative blood to the table. That was it. She'd go face the music then look for another job, preferably as far away from this unforgiving little town as she could.

Hopefully, her initiation into the glamorous media world would not follow her from town to town, city to city. Maybe she could get a job with the local quilting guild writing their monthly newsletter—if she was lucky.

Dani headed straight for the door that lead back into the crowded production room with an unbridled determination to hold her head high. It was then that she had first laid eyes on Travis Jakobs. He was ruggedly handsome as he walked through the break room door. He stood six feet three inches tall, was in his late thirties, had a muscular build, and piercing blue eyes.

Dani's eyes seemed to simultaneously dance with excitement at the instant attraction she felt, and shatter with disappointment as she glimpsed the wedding band on Travis' left ring finger. Not that she was looking for a relationship. She knew that God would bless her with the right man at the right time. Too bad this wasn't him or it. "Don't listen to those hecklers out there. They're just jealous that a rookie straight out of school could come in here and impress the pants off Stan Montgomery. Montgomery is a hard man to please." Travis' eyes searched Dani from head to toe openly admiring what he saw. "I've never seen the man laugh so hard over a political cartoon, let alone a food column."

"You mean he liked it?"

"Yeah, he liked it. He loved it. Big & Juicy might not, but Montgomery doesn't care. Your column is already the talk of the town. That's what Montgomery wants. People reading. People talking. He's already got readers emailing in commenting on the 'spunky' new angle." Travis was slowly shaking his head with a mischievous grin on his face while mumbling something under his breath.

"What?" Dani demanded.

"Brains, beauty, *and* spunk. You're gonna have the guys lining up at your door in no time at all."

Dani looked at him with a naive, girlish smile. "I doubt it," she protested.

"Oh, you can count on it. In fact, would you give me the honor of being the first to write your number on my heart? That way it'll be with me wherever I go," he coaxed.

"Give me a break. Maybe that dorky charm works on your generation, but my generation of women is far too sophisticated to fall for your empty antics. Besides that,"— she glanced down at his left hand—"that wedding ring doesn't help your case any." But it was too late. As much as she tried to convince herself otherwise, Dani already had a crush on this pathetically adorable and completely unattainable man.

"My wife and I have a very open and honest marriage. She does her thing. I do mine."

"No thanks. I'm not interested." She lied. That would prove to be the first among many "I'm not interesteds" in the years to come.

"We'll see. It's simply a matter of time, and I'm a very patient man." Travis gently brushed up against Dani as he turned and headed for the door. "Oh, by the way, Montgomery wants to see you in his office. Something about a permanent position."

Dani squealed with excitement as Travis left the room. She could hear him laugh as he walked away. She hoped he didn't think she was excited about their conversation. She wasn't. She was excited to be landing her first real job as a news reporter—even if it was just food news. There was no way she was going to allow a married man to intrigue her senses any further than he already had. Never.

Dani was lost in thought when she was startled by the familiar honking of a horn from the car behind her. The light had turned green and it seemed, even in this quaint little town, everyone was in a hurry to get home. She giggled aloud when she came to a minor traffic jam just outside the parking lot of the Big & Juicy.

"Guess my column didn't hurt their business any," she commented aloud.

Closer to home, Dani thought about her cozy little two-bedroom condo. Her job at *The Journal* afforded her the privilege and finances to buy her first home last spring. She'd been fixing it up ever since. She loved everything about her humble little home. The quaint little neighborhood made for the perfect setting for a young single woman. Garbo's, the city's most exclusive golf course and country club, bordered the east side of the condominium complex. On the westside was a little strip mall with uppity establishments like Capelli's Salon and Day Spa, a twenty-four-hour women-only fitness center, and, of course, Dani's obsession, Caroline's Coffee House.

Located at the back entrance of the complex was a coded metal gate that allowed tenants to enter Oak Park. The park's name was fitting, as when one descended from the hillside leading down to the playground the vibrant colors of the red, yellow, and orange leaves on oaks below painted the landscape as far as the eye could see.

Dani preferred to get her exercise by running the trails that sprawled throughout the park. Oak Park held a pristine beauty and peace about it that drew Dani, and it seemed many others, to its grassy knolls and voluptuous shade trees. Dani would often sit under an enormous oak with her laptop, finding inspiration by simply watching the children play and couples strolling hand in hand, or throwing a stick or two for the friendly neighborhood canines to fetch. Her favorite times at the park were spent with her six-year-old cousin, Mason. Dani would push Mason on the swing until his feet reached the leaves on a low-lying oak. Mason would always beg to go higher.

"Higher, Dani, higher!" he would holler looking back to make sure Dani was still there.

"You're going to disappear into that tree one of these days," Dani would shout. "You're one brave little man."

"You do it, Dani," Mason would always challenge. "Bet you can't get as high as me!"

Dani would fix her fanny on the swing next to Mason and start pumping her feet as fast as they would go. Mason would try his hardest to pump faster than Dani, but Dani's long legs were no match for Mason. He couldn't seem to get his legs pumping at a consistent pace with the sway of the swing. In no time at all, Dani and Mason would be neck and neck, disappearing into the branches at every forward thrust and simultaneously descending back down as laughter filled the playground.

Dani always felt like a little girl when she and Mason had their swinging wars. But Mason loved it. Dani loved Mason. She had grown to love him in a way that she had never expected. Maybe it was the unstable life he had lead, maybe it was his endearing smile, or perhaps it was the way he said her name; as though she was his best friend. She didn't know why her love for him was so strong that it almost hurt her heart; she simply knew that she loved the precious little boy.

Mason's mom was Britta Shaw's kid sister and Dani's aunt. Amanda McCullough was thirty-five years old when she gave birth to Mason. She told the family that Mason's daddy was a two-timing loser, and when he heard she was pregnant, he had driven off in a drunken rage. His car twisted itself around an ancient oak out on Highway 174. Amanda said he never had a chance.

Amanda herself had become a heroin addict beginning when she was seventeen. Despite a half dozen short jail terms and as many court ordered attempts at rehab, the drugs consumed Amanda. The courts had requested that Britta and Randal Shaw obtain guardianship of their nephew while his mother served a four-month jail term for drug-related probation violations.

Dani's mom and dad agreed as they had done so many times before. After all, Mason was a good little boy who simply needed some love and someone to help him understand what a special and valuable boy he was. Besides that, they had not only become accustomed to Mason's long stays with them, but they enjoyed having him as part of their everyday lives. They did everything within their power to ensure that Mason did not disappear into the labyrinth of the foster care system.

When Amanda was released on probation four months later, she left Mason with Randy and Britta and took off with some guy she had met while serving her sentence. It was almost a year before the Shaws heard from Amanda again. It was on Mason's sixth birthday.

Randy, Britta, and Dani were throwing a pirate-themed birthday party bash for Mason along with five of his closest buddies from Mrs. Rhodes's kindergarten class. Mason had made plenty of friends during his few months at Sunnyside Elementary, but he knew he couldn't have them all at his party. He had decided that he couldn't give his five buddies invitations at school because his other friends would have hurt feelings. So he came up with a plan.

"Auntie Britt," he had exclaimed one day. "You better call Rocky's mama, Jacob's mama, Nicholas' mama, Jessica's mama, and Chelsea's mama and tell them about the party. But don't forget to tell them it's a secret because I don't want Theo and Jason and Kaitlyn and Colin and all my other friends to be sad that they can't come."

That's the way Mason was. He was always thinking about everyone else. If he saw someone crying—even if it was a perfect stranger—he would gently walk up to them and wipe their tears away. In his precious childlike way, he would say to that person, "Don't cry. Jesus loves you all the way to heaven and back."

His aunt Britta had repeated the same aphorism to Mason one night shortly after he came to live with the Shaw family when he had woken in the night crying uncontrollably. He said he was afraid that his mama was coming to take him away and that she was going to leave him alone in the dark room at the hotel. He didn't want to be alone.

Britta had cuddled her nephew in her lap that evening and began to tell him about Jesus. She had promised Mason that Jesus was always with him and that whenever he was scared, all he had to do was ask Jesus to take his fear away. She told him that wherever he went and whatever he did, Jesus would always be right there with him and that He would protect Mason.

"Why would Jesus do that for *me*?" Mason had asked.

"Because He loves you so very much."

"Does He love me as much as you and Uncle Randy and Dani and Mama love me?"

"Mason," Britta had said, "Jesus loves you so much that He gave His life for you. He loves you all the way to heaven and back."

"With sugar on top?"

"Yes. With sugar on top."

It was that night that Mason decided it was his mission in life to make sure no one was ever sad or scared again. He wanted everyone to know that Jesus loved them too.

Over the past eight months, Mason had grown from an introverted, shy, aggressive little boy into a loving, kind, and affectionate young man. He was completing his homework every afternoon, became a spelling whiz overnight, and gained the self-worth he had lacked most of his young life.

He was such a blessing to the Shaw family. It was difficult to imagine their lives without him in it.

That day at the party, with Amanda standing at the front door, they knew their lives were about to change once again.

That's what Amanda did. She would leave Mason with the Shaws for months on end and then just show up one day, gifts in hand, saying she was clean and sober and ready to take Mason back.

The Shaws had no right to refuse. After all, Amanda was Mason's mother, and she loved him the best way she knew how. Unfortunately, her best wasn't ever enough. She loved her drugs too much to give Mason the love he deserved. Nevertheless, the courts always gave her the benefit of the doubt and would send Mason back to his mother.

This time was different though. Amanda's recent absence prompted the courts to give permanent custody of Mason to the Shaws. They determined that Amanda's history of drug use and her refusal to commit to a treatment plan would prevent her from making the lifestyle changes that were necessary to provide a healthy living environment for Mason.

Amanda had been outraged when Britta explained the judge's ruling. Her current boyfriend Rob, didn't help the situation at all. High on drugs and reeking of alcohol, Randy had asked Amanda and Rob to leave so as not to scare Mason's birthday party guests with her erratic behavior. He asked Amanda to come back when she was lucid and sober. They would talk then.

Stumbling and nearly falling to the ground before Rob grabbed hold of her arm preventing her from hurdling face first onto the concrete, Amanda brushed a limp oily strand of hair from her eyes and threatened in an eerily monotone voice, "You'll pay for this."

Amanda's threats were not unusual. It was always the drugs talking; she never followed through. But from that day on, Amanda and her new friend were not giving up. They made threatening calls nearly every night to the Shaw's home. Sometimes, it was Amanda. Other times, it was Rob. It was always the drugs.

Dani had talked to her mom about filing a restraining order to keep them way. But when Britta went to the courthouse, the clerk explained that unless someone has committed a crime, there was nothing that could be done. Even tape recorded calls could not be used as evidence of a threat unless the other party was informed that they were being recorded.

Randy and Britta were not terribly concerned. Mason's school was aware of the situation and knew never to allow Mason to leave the school with anyone other than Randy, Britta, or Dani. Amanda had made her threats before, and sooner or later, she'd tire of it all.

-- -- -- -- --

Dani was two blocks from the gated entrance to her condo when the familiar chirp of her cell phone interrupted her thoughts. It was Sunnyside Clubhouse. Mason attended the after-school program on Mondays, Wednesdays, and Fridays while Britta volunteered as a counselor at a teen crisis center in the town of Whitley, a thirty-minute drive from Glenbrook.

Mason must have left his backpack at school and Miss Tina wants me to pick it up, Dani assumed.

"Hello. This is Dani."

"Hi, Dani. This is Tina at the clubhouse. Your mom was supposed to pick Mason up at four o'clock, but we haven't heard from her."

Dani looked at her watch. It was 5:25.

"There's no answer at the house, and we close in five minutes. She's never late. We're a little worried."

That trace of foreboding Dani had been feeling all day crept back. "I'm sure everything's okay. She's probably just stuck in traffic and left her cell phone at home as usual. I don't even know why she has that thing. It doesn't do her much good setting on her desk at home." Then as an afterthought, Dani said, "Or maybe she's counseling with a client, and she hasn't been able to interrupt the session to call to say she would be late." *That must be it*, she thought.

"I'll be there in ten minutes."

Dani did a quick U-turn and headed for the Sunnyside Clubhouse. She reached for her phone and dialed her parents' number. No answer.

A moment later, Dani's phone rang again...*unknown caller*. This time the reception was poor and all she could hear were fragments of a woman's voice.

"Mom? If you can hear me, don't worry, I'm picking up Mason. We'll meet you at your house." The line went dead.

-- -- -- -- --

"Hey, little man," Dani announced as she entered the delightful little classroom adorned with colorful leaves created from construction paper.

"Dani!" Mason exclaimed as he abandoned the markers and coloring books sprawled across a small table and ran toward Dani, throwing himself into her arms.

"Where's Auntie Bwitt?" Mason wondered aloud. Mason could not pronounce his Rs so he generally replaced the R sound with the W sound. The speech impairment caused Mason to sound younger than his age. But he had been working diligently with his speech and language teacher, Mrs. Lee, on proper pronunciation.

Each night, after Britta would read a bedtime story and say prayers with him, Mason would choose fifteen words that included the R sound and say them very deliberately. Mason was his own hardest critic. He wouldn't say good night until each word was pronounced with perfection. He was very proud of himself.

"I mean Auntie Brritt." Mason repeated with a serious determination.

Dani grinned. "Auntie Britt had to work late. We'll go home and get dinner started for her."

"To your house or me and Auntie Britt and Uncle Randy's house?" Mason asked.

"Your house, silly," Dani chuckled. "That way, it will be all ready for Auntie Britt and Uncle Randy when they get home from work."

"Grab your backpack and say goodbye to Miss Tina."

When they reached the car and were safely buckled in, Mason asked, "Can we make spaghetti, Dani?"

"I'll bet we can." Spaghetti was Mason's favorite. Britta fixed it almost every Friday night. "Can I help boil the noodles?"

"If you're very careful," Dani replied.

"Cool." Mason tried to sound like one of the third graders at school. "I always help Auntie Britt with the noodles. She says I do a gweat job."

"Oh, I know you do. I've eaten your noodles lots of times, and they are the best!" Dani replied as they drove toward her condo so she could change her clothes before going to her parent's house. She wanted to be comfortable watching their Friday night movie together.

-- -- -- -- --

Dani was pulling the key from the deadbolt on the front door of her condo when Mason plowed his way in ahead of her. Just as she was setting her briefcase and a stack of papers onto the mahogany hall tree, her cell phone and home phone began to ring almost simultaneously.

She fumbled with her cell phone, dropping it to the ground as the battery cover went flying.

"Darn it," she said in frustration.

She reached for the telephone setting on the kitchen counter.

"Hello," she said with a tone of exasperation.

"Dani?" the voice questioned.

"This is Diana Whittlesey. I've been trying to reach you at work and on your cell phone." Diana was Britta and Randy's next-door neighbor.

"Diana, how are you?"

Without hesitation, "Something's wrong at your mom and dad's house," she said in a shaky voice. "You need to get over there right away."

"What do you mean 'something's wrong'? What happened?" Dani asked with a controlled, yet concerned voice.

Without further explanation, Diana continued with a distressed tone, "You need to come right now, Dani. The police are here."

"I'm on my way!"

Dani reached for Mason's hand as she headed for the door.

"Hey! Where we goin?" Mason asked.

"I've got to go do something, little man. We're going to see if you can stay with Miss Cilla and George just for a little while." Dani loved the Gordons. They were an elderly couple who lived two doors down from her. They always loved to see Mason and cared for him whenever Britta was in a bind and needed a sitter.

Their nearest grandchildren lived in Santa Monica, nearly a day's drive away. Though their families would come to visit several times a year, the Gordons missed their grandchildren terribly. When Mason would come to spend the night with Dani, they would always bake cookies to bring to the Gordons. The Gordons, in turn, spoiled Mason rotten.

He was their substitute grandson.

"Yeah! I can play with B."

"B" was short for Brittany, the Gordon's three-year-old shih tzu dog.

"I'm sure B would love to see you. But we've got to hurry."

With only a vague explanation, Dani asked the Gordons if Mason could stay with them. They graciously agreed and Dani was out the door apologizing for the spur-of-the moment intrusion as she hurried to her Jeep. "I'll be back in just a little while," she said, trying to disguise her concern. "Be good, little man!"

Dani waved good-bye to Mason as she drove away.

"ISDLY," Mason hollered. ISDLY meant "I Sure Do Love You". They had made it up when Mason was only two years old. Every time they would leave each other, they would always end their good-bye with their favorite acronym.

"ISDLY too." Dani's voice faded as the jeep disappeared around the corner.

It was 6:12. Dani was four blocks from the Shaw's house when she could see the glow of the rotating blue and red lights in the fading early evening sky.

Dani's heart was racing as she neared her parents' home on Butler Avenue.

"What did Amanda do now?" she wondered aloud, feeling a mixture of panic and anger.

As she turned the corner onto her parent's street, Dani could see half a dozen police units, an ambulance, two news vans parked near and around her parent's house—and Amanda's car in the driveway. As she drove closer, distraught familiar faces came into view as neighbors gathered in small groups.

The groups began to separate, creating a path for Dani's Jeep. Dani could hardly give the gas pedal enough pressure to move forward. She didn't want to. She was afraid of what she might find when she reached the driveway.

The invading response vehicles blocked the entire street. Dani could no longer drive forward. She had nowhere to go.

Just then, a police officer began walking toward Dani's Jeep.

"Ma'am, we have an emergency situation, you're going to have to turn your vehicle around."

Dani pushed the gear shift into park, opened the door, and sprang from her seat, unconsciously leaving the vehicle running.

"This is my parents' house!" she shouted, "What's going on?"

Several police officers heard the commotion and began walking toward Dani and the officer.

"What's going on?" she screamed again as she began running toward the double French doors just beyond the covered entryway to the house.

One of the officers approached Dani and forcefully grabbed her by the shoulders, directing her toward him.

"Ma'am, there's been a shooting." Others gathered around as the officer continued. "We've dis—"

"Is everyone all right?" Dani asked in a barely audible whisper.

"I'm sorry to say, we've discovered four deceased individuals," Dani's legs began to give way, "an unidentified man and woman, as well as the owners of the home, Randall and Britta Shaw."

Dani collapsed as her knees buckled beneath her. Her mind seemed to fade in and out of consciousness as she heard only fragments of how the investigators believed the events unfolded according to a news reporter standing only yards away.

The unidentified female victim appeared to have shot the two residents and the unidentified man before turning the gun on herself.

A neighbor had become concerned when she noticed that the gray Volkswagen, belonging to

Amanda, had been parked in the driveway since early morning.

The neighbors to the right and left of the Shaw house were familiar with the troubles the Shaws had been having with Amanda and her friend Rob, and they had taken it upon themselves to be watchful of suspicious characters in the neighborhood or anything that appeared to be out of the ordinary.

When, by four o'clock, Diana Whittlesey noticed that Amanda's car was still parked outside the house, she asked her husband to go over to see if everything was in order.

Mr. Whittlesey had found the door ajar and two bodies lying face down in the foyer.

When police arrived they discovered the bodies of Britta and Randy Shaw in the adjoining kitchen; Randy slumped over the dining table, Britta lying on the floor in a pool of blood. Mrs. Whittlesey told the police that she suspected the two unidentified bodies were those of Amanda McCullough and her boyfriend, whom she and her husband knew only by the name of Rob.

Dani's stomach churned. Her heart sank. She burst into mindless sobs. Dani was inconsolable. Her mom—her best friend. Her daddy. How could she live without them?

Nothing would ever be the same again.

CHAPTER TWO

The three days since her parents' death had been brutal for Dani. Media from throughout the state had ascended upon Glenbrook like a vulture diving for its prey. It seemed the entire population of Glenbrook attended the graveside services to show their respects. To many, it was as if they had lost a member of their own family. Everyone mourned for the tragic loss of life. Hearts were broken; a small town's innocence lost.

Perplexing stories of a drug addict's rampage and a torrid family feud spread across the state like wildfire. Every hotel room in town was occupied by members of one media outlet or another. Even some callous Glenbrook residents took advantage of the media parade by renting out spare bedrooms in their homes to news reporters for a small fortune. No one was immune to the uninvited attention the media had brought to the otherwise nameless little town.

But amid the whispers and exaggerated tales, it quickly became business as usual for the citizens of Glenbrook. Though, no longer was it the spirit of camaraderie that urged them on, but rather, a spirit of fear. How could this happen in their quiet, mundane, white picket-fenced community? How could this happen to *them*?

A plethora of friends and acquaintances and even well-meaning strangers appeared at Dani's condo following the murders to offer heartfelt sympathy and awkward expressions of comfort. No one knew quite what to say. Most simply embraced Dani and told her how much she was loved. Women from the Shaw's tight-knit church congregation took turns bringing meals to Dani and Mason. But most of the food went untouched.

Poor little Mason. In the blink of an eye, he had lost nearly everyone he had come to love so dearly. He didn't understand it all. He knew only that his family was never coming back, but that he would see them again in heaven someday. The thought of heaven comforted him; the thought of being alone frightened him. But he knew he had Dani. He would always have Dani. Dani would always have Mason.

-- -- -- -- --

It was four weeks before Dani was emotionally ready to return to *The Journal*. Mason had returned to school the previous week and seemed to be coping relatively well. The school had taken numerous measures to address the issues that arose from the tragedy. They had brought in a psychologist to make available to the children who had questions and fears about what happened. The day before Mason returned to school, the principal, Mr. Geary, arranged a school-wide assembly, addressing some of the children's major concerns.

The children wondered why Mason's mommy would do such a thing. Where was Mason's daddy? They wondered if their mommies and daddies could get hurt too.

A little boy raised his hand. "My mommy says Mason's mommy was sick," he said. "Is that why she hurt those people?"

Another little girl asked with a childlike innocence, "Who is going to make Mason his lunch for school now?"

Others wondered if Mason was going to move away. They didn't want him to.

Mr. Geary answered the children's questions very delicately with the help of the new psychologist, Mr. Buggs. All the children laughed when the principal introduced them to the new school counselor. When the children's questions had been answered, Mr. Buggs talked about how important it was to just be a good friend to Mason. He explained that it was critical not to say hurtful things and that teasing or jokes about what happened would not be tolerated.

"If there is anything else you need to talk about or if you just have a question, you can come see me any time," he said. "Just ask your teacher, and you'll be excused to come to my office." Mr. Buggs assured the children.

The next day, Mason was back in school. He was afraid to get out of the Jeep and walk into class alone, so Dani held his hand tightly—as much for Mason as for herself— and looked straight ahead as she headed in the direction of Mrs. Rhodes' classroom.

While Dani knew that people's concerns were well-meaning, she dreaded the pitiful looks and hushed whispers as she passed vaguely familiar faces in the school yard. Everyone knew more than she wanted them to know. Dani didn't want to have to talk about it. She didn't want to have to think about it. Not right now.

Mason kept his eyes glued to the ground until he reached his classroom. As he and Dani walked through the door, Mason's eyes met Mrs. Rhodes. He dropped his backpack and ran toward her, hurdling himself into her arms. He buried his face in Mrs. Rhodes well-padded shoulder. Mrs. Rhodes simply hugged him for the longest time. When Mason finally pulled his face away, his teacher gently brushed the bangs covering

Mason's right brow and quietly said, "I'm so glad your back, Mason. We've all missed you terribly."

At that moment, Mason's best buddy, Rocky, came bursting through the classroom door. "You're back," he hollered in jubilation. "Come play foursquare with us!" Mason looked at Dani then back at Rocky. "Ah wight." He reluctantly agreed.

Ever since the death of his family, Mason had reverted back to replacing the R sound with the W sound again. It was as though he couldn't focus enough to say his words correctly. Or maybe it was his way of trying to stay a little boy in a world that seemed to demand he grow up before he was ready—before any child should have to. Either way, his therapist had said that it doesn't matter. He would have to cope with this tragic experience on his own time and at his own pace.

Mason walked toward Dani with glossy blue eyes. Dani bent and cupped Mason's face with her soothing hands, "ISDLY, little man."

He leaned his mouth toward Dani's ear. "ISDLY too, Dani," he whispered. Mason nearly squeezed the breath out of Dani as he hugged her goodbye.

Dani sat silently in her Jeep and watched as various aged elementary school children shuffled off to their respective classrooms. To her surprise, a tiny tear rolled gently down her cheek. Immediately, she was overwhelmed by a memory from her past. The day, the moment of that heart-wrenching memory flooded her mind. She tried to resist it, but the memory invaded her.

It had been a cold damp day like today nearly six years ago when she was told, what she thought at the time, was the worst news of her life. She had spent most of her teenage years suffering with debilitating menstrual cramps each month. At first, she thought it was normal. But when she was eighteen, the pain became unbearable. Dani's mom had hesitated to bring her to see a doctor because she knew Dani was committed to abstinence until marriage, and she didn't want Dani to have to experience a pap smear before it was necessary. Dani didn't want to either. How humiliating. But something had to be done. The family practitioner had researched different avenues for easing the discomfort, but nothing seemed to help. Dr. Kendall recommended that Dani see a specialist. There was no other choice.

The gynecological specialist knew immediately what the problem was—what was causing Dani so much pain. She had endometriosis, and the scarring in her uterus had become so severe from the prolonged condition that she would likely never have the ability to carry a baby to term. Even at eighteen, the news had been devastating.

All she could remember ever wanting was to be a wife and mother. She wanted lots of kids—seven or eight of them. How could God do this to her? She had always been a good girl and made good choices. What had she done to deserve this? The doctor explained that it wasn't anything Dani had done, but that the condition was hereditary. In fact, Dani's mother, Britta, discovered she had endometriosis when she was a young girl. Britta was able to carry Dani for nearly seven months before her uterus became unable to accommodate the baby's weight. Arriving nearly nine weeks early, weighing a slight four pounds two ounces, with her intricately formed fragile petite frame, Danielle Lynn Shaw arrived into the world. Randall Shaw had been the first to hold his precious baby girl. Britta and

Randy kept a twenty-four-hour vigil over Dani's incubator that would become her substitute womb for her first three weeks of life. They would caress her miniature hand and quietly sing songs to her as she lay helplessly connected to a breathing machine. Then after twenty-two heart wrenching days, Dani lay contently in her daddy's arms as her parents introduced her to her new home. The next five years brought four heartbreaking miscarriages for Britta. The scarring had become too severe to carry another baby to term. Dani became Britta and Randy's pride and joy.

Dani remembered the doctor explaining that endometriosis is a disorder in which bits of tissue from the inner lining of the uterus grow inside a woman's body, outside of the uterus. As though reading from a textbook, the doctor went on to explain that during a normal menstrual cycle, the ovaries produce hormones that stimulate the cells of the uterine lining—the endometrial cells—to multiply and prepare for a fertilized egg. These cells swell and thicken. If a pregnancy does not occur, this excess tissue is shed from the uterus and discharged from the body. But in a woman with endometriosis, patches of misplaced endometrial tissue implant themselves on organs outside of the uterus, such as the ovaries, fallopian tubes, and bladder.

These cells also respond to the ovaries' hormonal signals by swelling and thickening. However, these cells are unable to separate themselves and shed from the tissue to which they have adhered. They sometimes bleed a little and then heal. This happens repeatedly each month, and the ongoing process can cause scarring. It also can create adhesions. The rest became a blur. The last thing Dani remembered the specialist saying was, "Adhesions are web-like tissues that can bind pelvic organs together…" This was the case with Dani. The adhesions in her body were so severe that the likelihood Dani could ever carry a child to term, even with hormone therapy and surgery, was very slim.

Dani recalled that day like it was yesterday. The doctor had been patronizing; talking to her as though she was a child, but telling her things no child should have to hear.

Now, sitting in her Jeep, the emotions Dani felt—the anger, the disappointment, the self-pity—it all came back to her at once, as it had done so many times before.

No, she wasn't going to do this again. God had other plans for her life. But why couldn't it include having children? She loved kids. She would be a wonderful mother. Why had God given her such a desire, then destroy the ability to fulfill that desire in the blink of an eye? Dani knew she didn't have the right to question God's motives. She knew He was just and that He loved her as only He can love. But sometimes it was hard to accept that she would never become a mother. That she would never experience the joy of creating a uniquely precious little person with the man she loved. She knew she would never hold her newborn baby to her breast to nourish his little body. It was almost unbearable to think about. She prayed that God would provide some purpose to fill the emptiness she felt.

The echoes of the school bell sounding startled Dani back to the present. She found herself with hands clutched to the steering wheel, knuckles white from her commanding grip. Tears filled her eyes as Dani cried out to God to help her stop hurting.

She didn't know how long she'd sat motionless in the confines of her Jeep, but when Dani looked around, nearly all the hustle and bustle of parents dropping their children off for school and teachers racing to beat the bell to their classrooms had dissipated.

Her grasp on the steering wheel loosened as Dani felt the warmth of the sun peek through the morning clouds. She looked upward to find a sea of blue sky replacing the grey gloom that had welcomed in that humid Wednesday morning. As the clouds parted above, the darkness began to fade from her heart. Dani was ready to face her day with a newborn fervor.

-- -- -- -- --

Just as Mason had courageously done with his classmates, it was Dani's turn to face her colleagues and the inevitable myriad of sympathetic offerings. Over the past weeks, Dani's main source of support came from friends from the small Christian fellowship she had been attending. She felt close to them all. Her pastor was a humble man whose past was a secret to no one. He loved to say, "If God can forgive me, he can forgive anyone."

Bo Avery was the most authentic man Dani had ever met. He had lived a difficult life and had made, at his own admission, some inexcusable choices as a young man. The right corner of Bo's mouth would quiver in his attempt not to cry each time he would talk about his past. Never before had Dani known someone so truly grateful for his salvation and what Jesus Christ did on the cross for him. Bo knew, beyond a shadow of a doubt, that when Jesus was on that cross, gasping for His last breath of air, His last thoughts were of

Bo...and every other "Bo" that had ever been and was to come.

Bo was the type of pastor that not only taught about the Word of God, but he actually lived it. Of course, he wasn't perfect, but he was honorable and kind, and most of all, he loved Christ with everything in him. Dani thought to herself, if ever there was a man whom she admired most in this world—besides Jesus and her daddy—it would be Bo Avery. He was an admirable man whom Dani knew committed the first thought of each day to Jesus and fell asleep at night with his last thoughts of his precious Savior as well. He never said it, one just knew it.

The recent weeks had planted in Dani an obvious sense of loss and abandonment, an overwhelming sadness, an inexplicable sensation of guilt and an unbridled anger that seemed to grow as the days wore on. As time went by, Dani began to isolate herself from even her closest church friends. Mason and Mr. and Mrs. Gordon seemed to be the only people Dani had any desire to associate with. Though well-meaning, her church family served as constant reminders of the life she once had. She had never grown terribly close to anyone at *The Journal*, so it wasn't difficult to hold them at bay. The only colleagues she ever really spoke with were Travis and Stan.

Stan called occasionally under the auspice of concern, though Dani thought his concern was more for the future of her column than for her well-being. Then again, she had become terribly cynical and suspicious of people and their hidden agendas. In truth, she knew deep down that Stan was a good man whose motives were likely genuine.

Dani wasn't sure what his intentions were, but whenever Travis called, she found herself drawn to his soothing voice. It wasn't so much the words he said that made her melt, but the way he said them. He was always so compassionate and understanding. He didn't just listen when Dani unloaded, but he actually heard her. On the two occasions he stopped by Dani's condo, he comforted her like a brother might do. He would never leave her house or hang up the phone without saying, "Call me if you need anything…anything at all." Though she would never ask, it comforted Dani to know that Travis meant it. Day or night, she could pick up the phone and he would be there for her—she believed that with all her heart.

With those few exceptions, Dani was angry at everyone—at her parents, at Amanda, at the media, at herself, but most of all, at God. She never expressed her feelings of anger to Pastor Bo because she felt guilty for having them. Theoretically, Dani understood that God hadn't done this to her, but accepting that there was a lesson to be learned and a purpose within God's will for what happened was beyond Dani's ability right now. There was no understanding, no forgiveness, no faith—just anger in Dani's broken heart.

But life had to go on. And it did.

On her first day back to work, Dani parked her Jeep in her usual parking space at *The Journal*. Her mind was willing her to move, but she remained motionless; the only sound was that of her racing heart. Her knuckles were white as they grasped the black leather steering wheel. Five minutes had passed before she could physically remove her hands from the grip of the wheel and force her feet to the spongy, newly black-topped ground below. *I can do this.* She could feel her body begin to shake as she gathered her briefcase and a stack of papers she had been working on from home. Stan Montgomery had called her two days after her parents' death and told her that she could take as much time as she needed. If she wanted to keep herself busy, he had a pile of editorials that needed some attention.

She had gone to the office one evening after most of the staff was gone for the day. With a slightly cracked voice, Stan had said to Dani, "It's good to see ya', kid." He had handed her the stack of editorials. "Now get outta here." He winked. It was a side of Stan Montgomery she had seldom before seen. But maybe his usual impassive, insensitive front was merely a way of maintaining respect and control over an often excessively independent staff. Maybe the bottom line wasn't really all about money as was Stan's motto.

In the days following her parent's death, Stan's coverage of the event was tastefully reported, and he refused to allow *The Journal* to exploit such a horrific tragedy that arguably struck so close to home. He respected Dani's privacy and her need to mourn and made sure the rest of the staff did as much. He had threatened the entire staff in his unique Stan Montgomery way. "I hope none of you intend to make a name for yourself at Dani's expense. It won't be tolerated." No more words were needed. Everyone knew that their jobs were at stake. No one would do that to Dani anyway. Over the past two years, they had all come to respect Dani and admire her for her hardworking nature and her ability to never get mixed up in the internal office affairs.

Today would be more difficult for Dani than the first day of her new job when she was tossed into the lion's den. This time, she wouldn't simply be the new kid on the block.

This time, she would be the pathetic, wounded freshman starting a new school after a long summer break. It took everything that was in her not to turn around and bolt. But Jan Singleton, Stan's administrative assistant, had already seen Dani coming. Dani would eventually have to face the inevitable.

Dani walked through the front doors with her head held high.

"Hi, Dani, glad to have you back." Jan tenderly smiled.

"Hey, Dani, good to see ya," came another voice.

"Dani. Thank God you're back. Montgomery had Spencer writing your column. With the way he writes, even McDonald's could lose business," awkwardly joked one of the marketing staff.

"You're real funny," Spencer countered. "Happy to have you back, Dani."

"Thanks, guys," she said. "It's good to be back."

Dani had made it to her office without a hitch. She slammed the door behind her. Whew! *Now how are you holding up* or *is there anything I can get you?* She simply needed to be left alone—to settle back in to her old routine. But Dani realized nothing would ever be routine again.

-- -- -- -- --

As she began to lose herself in her thoughts for what seemed like the thousandth time that day, Dani was startled by a tap on her office door.

"Come in," she managed to get out.

"Hey, beautiful." It was Travis.

As much as she hated to admit it, she was happy to see him. Even if his flattery didn't hold much weight, it felt good to be noticed. "Hello, Travis."

"You're looking better than ever," he said, inspecting her from head to toe. "I've really missed you."

Strangely and for the first time, Dani was thankful that Travis was focusing on *her*, not her situation. As Travis stood in front of her desk, Dani noticed how ruggedly handsome he truly was. His distinct jawline gave him the sophistication of an experienced man of the world, but his full, pouty lips reminded her of a shy school boy; Travis was anything but. Dani couldn't help but be flattered by his attention.

"It's good to see you too, Travis." She meant it.

"Boss wants to see you." He grinned. "Can't blame him." Ignoring Travis' obvious flirtations, Dani sighed.

"Thank you, Travis. I'll be right there."

"Better not keep him waiting." Travis teased as he exited her office.

Dani stood, straightened her skirt, and cleared her throat. "Here goes nothin'," she said aloud and headed for Stan's office.

"Good morning, Dani." Stan leaned back in his desk chair, arms crossed over his chest. "It sure is good to have you back—it really is."

"Thank you, Mr. Montgomery. It's good to be back."

"Enough of that Mr. Montgomery stuff. It'll be Stan from now on, understood?"

"Yes, Mr. Mont…Yes, sir." Dani smiled coyly.

"My father used to tell me, 'fall off the horse, better get right back on,'" he said. "Are you ready to do that, Dani?"

"I think so," Dani replied hesitantly.

"You *think* so? Either you are or you aren't."

"Yes, sir. I'm ready to work. I need to work."

"Good. I knew I could count on you." Stan continued, "Listen up. Giovanni's, off of Old Highway 49, is achin' to have you write a review for them. Business is down, and they've been waiting for you to get back because they seem to think you've got the magic touch. I offered up Spencer, but they turned him down flat. I've reserved you a table for tonight at six."

"I'll be there," Dani replied with confidence. "Oh, wait a minute…"

"What is it, Dani?" Stan asked.

"Um. It's nothing. I'll have the article on your desk by noon tomorrow."

How could Dani have forgotten about Mason? She had planned to pick him up from Sunnyside Clubhouse at 5:15. Perhaps Mr. and Miss Cilla could take care of Mason for an hour or two. Dani headed back to her office and pulled the Gordon's number from her Rolodex. "Hello, Miss Cilla, this is Dani."

"Hello, dear, how are you doing? Is everything all right?"

"Yes, Miss Cilla, everything is fine. Except, I'm kind of in a bind. I have to work this evening, and I know it's short notice, but I was wondering if you might be able to keep Mason for a couple of hours."

"Oh, dear, I would love to. But George and I go down to Springhill Convalescent on Monday evenings and read to the elderly folks."

Dani chuckled to herself. The Gordons were in their late seventies themselves.

"I understand, Miss Cilla."

"I would be glad to any other time, Dani. You know how George and I love your little Mason." Miss Cilla smiled to herself. "And, why, my little Brittany, she just adores Mason too."

"I know. Mason looks forward to seeing all of you too. I'm sure I'll work it out somehow," Dani resigned. "Thank you anyway."

What was she going to do? Maybe she would just have to take Mason with her to the restaurant.

At five o'clock, Dani was out the front door of *The Journal* and headed for the Jeep. Fifteen minutes later, she headed for her condo with Mason buckled in the backseat describing his exciting day at school. She drew Mason a warm bath and threw on a quick change of clothes.

"Can you wash your hair by yourself tonight, Mason? We've got to hurry and get cleaned up so we can go to dinner."

"Couwse I can, Dani. What we gonna' eat?"

"How about your favorite?"

"Spaghetti?" Mason squealed.

"Of course," Dani exclaimed.

They both grew silent. Each knew the other was thinking about the last time they were to have spaghetti dinner together as a family. Tears came to Dani's eyes. She walked over to the bathtub and kissed Mason on the forehead. "I love you, little man." Spaghetti would never taste the same again.

"Me too, Dani." Mason dabbed bubbles on the tip of Dani's nose.

"Okay, kiddo, get your fanny moving!"

That was the first of many nights Dani and Mason would spend immersed together in her work.

The following morning, Stan Montgomery praised Dani for her "Dani style" creativity. Dani was back! At least as much as she could be for the moment.

-- -- -- -- --

The weeks turned into months as Dani and Mason attempted to live as normal a life as possible. On several occasions, Annabelle, the secretary at Sunnyside Elementary, had called Dani in to pick up Mason. Though he had adjusted relatively well to his return to school, some days it was all just too much for Mason. He had been seeing Mr. Buggs on an almost daily basis, as well as his crisis counselor at the local domestic abuse center twice a week.

As a result of Mason's inability to cope, Dani was missing a lot of work. She even started taking Wednesdays off from work to help in Mason's classroom. Dani would help with art projects and writing assignments. She would sometimes read to the children and play games with them on rainy days. Mr. Buggs had suggested that it might make it easier for Mason if Dani stayed close by for a while.

Stan assured Dani that her absence wasn't a problem, but Dani could tell by his tone of voice, he wasn't being altogether forthcoming. She knew Stan didn't intentionally sound irritated, but it was clear her absence was becoming an inconvenience.

On one occasion, when Dani was called in to pick up Mason, he had been very quiet and withdrawn during the ride home. Dani decided to take him to get ice cream at the Sweet Shoppe on the corner of Main and Church Streets. As they strolled hand in hand, Dani asked Mason what was bothering him.

Mason was reluctant at first. "Delana says her mommy isn't her birth mommy." He continued, "She says she didn't grow in her mommy's tummy. She was adopted." "Does that bother you?" Dani inquired.

"No. But where did she come from if she didn't grow in her mommy's tummy?" he asked.

"Well," Dani contemplated, "when a mommy has a baby, she wants what's best for him. Sometimes, if she can't give him the things he's going to need as he grows up, even though it may make her very, very sad, she decides to let another mommy and daddy take care of him because she wants *him* to be happy."

"So that's why Delana's birth mommy gave her to her other mommy and daddy?" Mason asked.

"I think so," replied Dani. "And because Delana's new mommy and daddy had so much love to give to her."

"Does that mean that Delana's birth mommy didn't love her?"

"No, Mason. It means that Delana's birth mommy loved her more than anything else in the world. It means that Delana's happiness was even more important to her birth mommy than her own happiness," Dani tried to explain.

"So her birth mommy let Delana's new mommy and daddy adopt her because she wanted her to be happy?"

"Well…yes." Mason was silent.

They walked another block. "Whatcha thinkin' about, little man?"

"Dani?" Mason stopped walking.

Dani crouched down and looked straight into Mason's eyes. "What is it, kiddo?"

"Did my mommy love me?"

"She loved you very much, Mason."

"Did she want me to be happy?"

Dani's heart was breaking. She pulled Mason to her and cupped his little face in her hands. "Of course, she did."

"Do you think *you* could adopt *me*?"

Dani's eyes filled with tears. "Would that make you happy?"

"Uh, huh!" Mason exclaimed.

Dani thought for a moment. "Nothing would change you know?" Dani continued. "You would still have your same room. You would still have to go to school. I would still work at the newspaper. All of that would stay the same."

"That's okay," he said. "'Cause then you would be my mommy."

"Mason, Amanda will always be your mommy, and she'll always be with you in your memories."

"I know," he said. "But then I can tell my friends that I grew in my first mommy's *tummy*, and I grew in my second mommy's *heart*."

A tear streamed down Dani's cheek. This precocious little boy had become the love of her life. It was unreal to believe she could love someone so much. But she did.

"We'll see what we can do about that, little man." Dani stood with her hands on her hips. "Now let's go get ice cream!"

-- -- -- -- --

Dani waited a week before contacting an adoption attorney. She wasn't quite sure how to go about adopting Mason, so Dani called Delana's mom for some advice. Although the circumstances were different because Delana's birth mom had contacted them through an adoption facilitation center and was not blood related, Delana's mom thought her attorney might be able to help Dani.

Deborah Klein was already familiar with Dani's name when she called to make the appointment. Who wasn't? Deborah was more than happy to meet with Dani to discuss her options.

Dani scheduled an appointment with Deborah for noon the following day. The two women discussed the inevitable legal red tape they would have to plow through. All in all though, it looked like it would be a straightforward, clean-cut adoption.

Deborah had asked about Mason's biological father. Dani explained that he had passed away right around the time Mason was born. He had never known his father.

"Was there ever a paternity test done on Mason and his father?" Deborah asked.

"I don't know." Dani had never thought to ask Amanda that question.

"Then we'll have to place a public notice of adoption in the local and surrounding papers."

"What for?"

Deborah saw the look of panic on Dani's face. "Don't worry, Dani, it's just a formality." Gathering several papers strewn across her desk, Deborah was nonchalant. "You already said Mason's father is deceased. It's just a necessary step in any adoption process." She continued, "Assuming we don't run into any roadblocks, you'll be Mason's legal mother before the end of the year."

It all felt so strange and surreal to Dani. Only six months ago, she had been a carefree, happy-go-lucky recent college graduate with relatively few responsibilities. Now, in less than twelve weeks, she was going to be a mother to a six-year-old little boy. This certainly wasn't what she had planned for her life. But Dani was grateful that she had Mason.

-- -- -- -- --

The holidays came and went without so much as a snow flurry. It had been a mild winter so far, and Mason couldn't wait until the first snow day.

Dani and Mason spent Christmas morning cuddled up in their new jammies and watching all the old Christmas movies Dani had loved as a child. They each made a list of all the things they were thankful for and then sang happy birthday to Jesus. Instead of the usual honey ham and scalloped potatoes that they had enjoyed together as a family in years past, Dani and Mason decided to start their own tradition of spaghetti and sourdough bread.

"Aren't you tired of spaghetti yet?" Dani asked Mason.

"No," he said. "It makes me think of Auntie Bwitt and Uncle Wandy."

"It makes me think of them too." The holidays had been difficult for Dani. Mason too. There wasn't a lack of visitors coming to see Dani and Mason at the condo, but it seemed nothing could fill the void in their hearts.

"Hey, little man," Dani exclaimed. "Do you know why today is so special?"

"Uh, huh. 'Cause it's Jesus's birthday!"

"You're right! Do you know why else it's so special?"

"Why?" Mason looked puzzled.

"Because tomorrow I get to become your second mommy!"

Mason squealed. "Yeah!" He jumped on Dani's back and the two wrestled and laughed until they were both in tears. Unlike so many of the tears they had cried over the last several months, these were tears of joy.

Tomorrow was the beginning of a whole new life for Dani and Mason. All they had was each other, but that was all they needed.

CHAPTER THREE

It was the day after Christmas and most of the shops in Glenbrook's miniaturized version of the business district were closed. Glenbrook wasn't like big cities where Christmas was merely another day. In fact, most people in Glenbrook didn't just celebrate Christmas day, they celebrated Christmas week beginning Christmas Eve and continuing through the New Year. But the extra vacation days weren't simply in celebration of the holidays, rather they were in preparation for the traditional football marathon beginning on January 1. The New Year's Day games weren't just a pastime for Glenbrook sports fanatics, they were an obsession. The season turned into one long holiday for many of the residents of this beat-of-your-own-drum town. But at least the government offices were open for business. That was all Dani cared about today.

After today, Mason and Dani would officially belong to each other. They were scheduled to meet Deborah in the judge's private chambers to sign the papers at 11:00 a.m. Mason could hardly contain his excitement. Neither could Dani.

Dani had taken Mason to The Kid's Corner, a quaint little children's boutique in downtown Glenbrook, the previous week to pick out an outfit to wear to the adoption ceremony at the courthouse. He had carefully chosen just the right red, white, and blue striped tie to wear to the document signing. Mason wanted to look just right for the judge. He looked like a miniature little man on his first day at the office with his navy slacks and crisply pressed white-collared shirt.

With his big blue eyes and deep auburn hair, Mason was simply irresistible.

Dani was nervous. She wore black tapered slacks with a cropped matching suit jacket. The sage-colored blouse she wore brought out the emerald glow in her eyes. She pulled her hair back into a French twist with a loose ebony lock falling gently over her left cheek. The 1/2-carat diamond studs that her daddy had given her years ago for her high school graduation complimented the ensemble just perfectly. How she missed her daddy. He would be so proud of her today. He would probably have given Dani some speech about the seriousness of the responsibility she was taking on. He would then make some kind of joke to prevent himself from crying. But then again, if he were still here, none of this would be happening. It was all so surreal to Dani.

All morning, she had been feeling that familiar sense of foreboding—the same one she had felt the day her parents died. The same apprehension she had felt so many times before and since. As she had always done, Dani said a quick prayer that Jesus would remove the anxious feelings and help her have faith. Of course, she was feeling uneasy. After all, this was going to be a life-changing experience for both. Dani determined that nothing was going to ruin this day. Nothing.

"It's time to go, little man," Dani shouted to Mason from the kitchen. "Did you get enough to eat?" Dani finished gulping down her third cup of coffee.

"I couldn't eat all my ceweal, Dani. I'm too excited."

"Me too, kiddo!" She giggled at Mason's childish anticipation.

"This is gonna' be my vewy best day evew!" Mason squealed. "Oops…I mean ve*rrr*y best day eve*rrr*."

"Even better than when we went to Disneyland?"

"Yeah."

"Even better than last summer at Water World?" Dani probed.

"Way better!" he exclaimed.

"Even better than that day I made you try asparagus?" Dani teased.

Mason giggled. "You'we silly, Dani. That was yucky"

"Well then, let's get going!" Dani and Mason raced for the door. They could no longer contain their excitement.

-- -- -- -- --

Deborah Franks planned on meeting Dani and Mason a few minutes early to make sure all the final paperwork was in order before they met with the judge. It was already 10:45 and Deborah hadn't shown up yet. Dani and Mason had been waiting for at least a half hour already.

Dani had turned off her cell phone so they wouldn't be interrupted in the judge's chambers. She hoped Deborah hadn't tried to call. It was getting late; maybe she had better call Deborah just in case.

Dani pressed the power button on her cell phone. There were six calls from Deborah, which had all come within the last thirty minutes. Dani's heart sank. What could be so urgent?

Just as Dani dialed her password and attempted to retrieve her messages, Deborah came plowing through the lobby doors.

Dani leaped to her feet. "What is it?" She could see by the look on Deborah's face that something was wrong.

"We need to talk, Dani." She took Dani's arm and guided her toward a small conference room. "Mason, I need you to sit right here for a little while so Dani and I can talk. Can you do that for me?"

"Uh, huh." Mason looked unaffected by the tension that instantly filled the hallway corridor.

"We'll be right in this room if you need us, little man. I can even see you through the glass panel in the door." Dani pointed toward the small room.

Deborah and Dani closed the heavy door behind them as they entered the room. Through the glass panel, Dani could see Mason driving his yellow Camaro Hot Wheel along the back of the lobby chairs.

"We've got a problem, Dani." Deborah continued, "Remember how we were legally required to post a Notice of Adoption in the local newspaper?"

"Yes."

"The purpose of that notice is so absent fathers who can't be located and may or may not know that their child's mother is planning on placing the baby for adoption have ample opportunity to contest an adoption if he so desires."

"But Mason's father is dead." Dani was confused.

"Right. Well, that's what we assumed. But I got a call this morning from a man claiming to be Mason's father."

Dani's heart sank. It wasn't possible. "He's lying. Mason's dad died years ago." Dani scrambled to collect her thoughts. "Everyone in town knows about what happened. This is just some kind of a sick joke."

"I don't think so, Dani. The man sounded legitimate." Deborah continued, "The guy said he's been searching for Amanda and Mason for a while. After he heard...well... what happened, he knew he had to do something."

"He must want something." Dani started pacing. "I have some money saved. It's only about $6,000, but that's probably a fortune for some druggie like him."

"I don't think he wants money. He sounds like a guy who's got his act together." Then, as if in disbelief, "Dani, three weeks ago, he picked up everything he owned, transferred his job as an assistant pastor at a church in Southern California and moved his family to Glenbrook. They've finally settled in and now he wants to see Mason as soon as possible, Dani. And he really wants to meet you."

"No way!" Dani was angry.

"Dani, if he can prove that he's Mason's father and wants custody of him, we've got a serious problem."

"How does he prove it?"

"Through a paternity test. They take some of Mason's blood and some from this guy and then they can determine whether or not they are father and son." Deborah knew how much Mason and Dani meant to one another. But something told her that this was only the beginning of a long, difficult road ahead for them.

"And if he is Mason's father?"

"Unfortunately, Dani, he stands a good chance at getting custody."

Who else was God going to take away from her? What was He trying to teach her? Dani couldn't take it if she and Mason were split up. There had to be something they could do.

-- -- -- -- --

The next few days consisted of dozens of phone calls to and from Dani's attorney, subtle explanations to Mason and sleepless nights. Dani hadn't known what to say to Mason. She didn't see the purpose in telling Mason about a man who may or may not be his father—in all likelihood, he was not. So she came up with an explanation about the judge not being able to do the adoption as scheduled. Mason had been disappointed, but was still filled with anticipation for the adoption to take place and to become Dani's little boy.

Mason had started back to school after a two-week winter break. The first day of school of the new year, the children adorned new clothes, fresh haircuts and much anticipated new toys they had received from moms and dads, grandparents, and distant aunts and uncles for Christmas to share for show and tell. Mason had planned on bringing the adoption certificate to show his classmates, but instead, brought the photo album Dani had made him for Christmas. The album had pictures of Mason and his mom, as well as photos of Mason with Britta and Randy and Dani. It even included photos of the Gordons and their canine friend, B.

Although Dani had gone overboard and spoiled Mason with too many toys and games and clothes to count, the memory album was Mason's favorite gift. He slept with it under his pillow every night. Each evening at bedtime, just before prayers and story time, Mason and Dani would look at each page in the album. Mason would always ask the same questions about when the picture was taken, who had taken it, and where they were when it was taken. Dani would tell him the same stories over and over about the day or the special occasion the photo was taken. Mason always closed his eyes and smiled, as though he were reliving the experience even if he was too little to remember.

Since the day at the courthouse when the adoption plans fizzled, Mason seemed to gradually withdraw. Dani's dismal attempts to reassure Mason that the postponement was just temporary seemed as pathetic to Dani as they probably were to Mason. Dani knew Mason could hear the concern in her voice no matter how hard she tried to disguise it. Mason was a bright boy. He knew there was something she was not telling him.

During the first week after school resumed from the winter break, Dani had been at work attempting to write her column when she received a call from Annabelle, the school secretary. Mason was having a difficult time and had spent most of the day in Mr. Bugg's office. Mr. Buggs had tried to get Mason to express his feelings through sand therapy, but to no avail. Mason couldn't focus and refused to talk to Mr. Buggs about what was going on in his little mind. Mason had asked if he could go home. Mr. Buggs felt that it would be a good idea if Dani came to pick Mason up and take him home. When Dani arrived at the school that afternoon, Mason burst into tears and threw himself into her arms. It took everything Dani had to keep her own tears from flowing. Dani had carried Mason to the Jeep that afternoon with his face hidden in her shoulder.

The following week, as Dani and Mason were snuggled up on Mason's bed looking through the photo album for what was probably the hundredth time, Mason became very quiet.

"What's up, little man?" Dani questioned gently.

"Were Auntie Bwitt and Uncle Wandy your mommy and daddy?" Mason asked in his familiar altered speech.

"Yes, they were, Mason," she said. "They'll always be my mommy and daddy."

"And my mommy will always be my mommy even though she isn't here, huh?"

"Yes. Always."

"Dani?" Mason probed. He turned his head and looked straight into Dani's eyes.

"Hmm?" That familiar sense of foreboding instantly washed through Dani.

"Do I have a daddy?"

Dani was dumbfounded. She prayed for God to give her the words to say.

"Everyone has a daddy, Mason." Dani dreaded what was coming next.

"Then who is my daddy?" He said with his inquisitive big blue eyes staring up at her.

Dani hesitated, "I'm not sure, little man."

"Has my daddy ever met me?" he continued.

"I don't think so, Mason."

"Does my daddy know where I live?"

"I don't know. He might."

Mason lay there in silent thought. Neither he nor Dani knew quite what to say next. Dani broke the silence.

"Would you like to meet your daddy?" Dani managed to ask.

"Would it make you sad?"

Dani's heart sank. Mason must have overheard the telephone conversations with the attorney that had taken place over the past weeks. Dani had been so consumed with how the emergence of Mason's father would affect her; she hadn't even thought about what it might do to Mason. She had never even considered the possibility that Mason might *want*, or even *need*, to meet his father. Her heart began to race.

"As long as you're happy, Mason, then I'll be happy too." Dani managed with a lump in her throat.

"Do you think my daddy would want to see me?" Mason was unrelenting.

"Of course, he would want to see you. How could he resist this cute little face?" Dani tickled Mason under his chin. They both giggled. "I'll see what I can find out about your daddy."

"Maybe I look like him," Mason pondered aloud.

That night, when Mason and Dani said bedtime prayers together, Mason prayed for his daddy. He asked Jesus to make his daddy really nice and really strong, and he prayed that his daddy would be a fireman. Mason's expectations were high. Dani silently prayed that his heart would not get broken. She prayed that her own heart would survive what was ahead. If she lost Mason, she would have nothing— no one.

Dani sat and stared at him as Mason drifted off to sleep. She couldn't bring herself to leave the unsullied bundle lying next to her to retreat to the comfort of her own bed. Her tears fell silently as Dani gently stroked Mason's silky hair. She tried to pray, but her prayers were interrupted by the plethora of thoughts and scenarios that raced through her mind. The last time Dani glanced at the clock, it read 3:33. She finally crawled out of Mason's bed and retreated to her own.

After a surprisingly restful, albeit short, night's sleep, Dani awoke with an unexpected clarity. Even among her fragmented, interrupted attempt to pray last night, God still heard her. He had given Dani an inexplicable peace as she awoke that early January morning. She knew what she had to do.

-- -- -- -- --

"I want to meet him, Deborah."

Dani had spent the first two hours that morning in her makeshift home office doodling in her address book, trying to muscle up enough courage to call her attorney. "I need to meet him and make him understand what it would do to Mason if he were taken away from the only person in his life that he can still count on."

Whether Dani was aware of it or not, Deborah knew that Dani's desperate attempt to convince Mason's father that he was doing the wrong thing would be as much for Dani's sake as it was for Mason's.

"As your attorney, I'm glad to hear that you're willing to meet with this man, Dani," Deborah said. "It will make it much easier than waiting for the courts to force it to happen.

"And as your friend, Dani, I truly admire you for being so strong. You and Mason have been through so much. I don't think I could have been so strong at your age. For God sakes—even at my age," Deborah said with a nervous chuckle. She'd been curious about Dani and her ability to look at the positive side of things since the day they met. The only time she had witnessed even a tinge of hopelessness in Dani was the day at the courthouse when she learned of the existence of Mason's father. Most clients would have gone ballistic. But not Dani. She would always say to Deborah, "Everything happens for a reason." Although at times, Deborah guessed it was merely Dani's way of trying to cope. She wondered if deep inside, Dani was falling apart. If she was, at least she was keeping it together on the outside. Wherever Dani found her strength, Deborah thought, even if it was in Jesus as her client claimed, Deborah envied Dani. Dani had something that Deborah wanted. What that "something" was, she wasn't certain.

"I'm not as strong as you think, Deborah. Sometimes I think I might lose it at any moment," Dani said with a typical tone of humility. "Somehow God just gets me through it one day at a time."

"I admire your faith," Deborah said with an authenticity in her voice.

"It's the only thing that gets me through, Deb." Dani often wondered about Deborah's faith. She always seemed so confident; so in control. But lately, Deborah seemed less sure of herself; always questioning Dani about her beliefs. Dani was always happy to share her beliefs with Deborah. Yet, she often felt underqualified to be witnessing to this professional woman who was nearly three times Dani's age. Her words never seemed to come out quite right. She would have a point in her mind that she'd want to get across, but she'd fumble over the words and never felt like she was making it clear to Deborah what she was trying to share.

-- -- -- -- --

In true Mason fashion, he kept reassuring Dani that even if his daddy was really nice, Mason could never love him like he loved her. Even though Dani would never express her insecurities to Mason about him meeting his biological father, at almost seven years old, Mason was exceptionally intuitive. He was such a sweet, sensitive boy.

Unfortunately, he hadn't inherited those traits from his mother. But in Amanda's defense, it was probably the addictions that caused her to think only about herself, never anyone else. Her life had been a constant drama. Nothing was ever her fault. It all started when she was a sixteen-year-old sophomore in high school. She'd gotten mixed up with the wrong crowd. The first time she went to a party—or at least she claims—someone had spiked the punch. That night, she had been arrested on a DUI and sent to juvenile hall. As a result, she had lost her license for two years. But that experience was just the beginning of a downward spiral that eventually destroyed Amanda's life and the lives of so many people who loved her.

"Dani, why aren't you listening to me?" Mason asked with a concerned look on his face.

"I'm so sorry, little man. I was lost in thought." She gave him a reassuring pat on the knee.

"What were you thinking about?" he asked curiously.

So as to not cause Mason sadness, she chose her words carefully. "I was just thinking about your mommy and about how much she loved you." Because Dani knew that even with all the pain that Amanda had caused and all the people she had hurt, a mother never stops loving her child. And in those rare instances when she was sober, Amanda could be a good mother. Those instances, unfortunately, had been few and far between. Inevitably, Amanda would end up in jail or show up at the Shaw's front door in the middle of the night after having been beat up by a boyfriend. It was always "the last time." It never was though.

Eventually, Amanda and her so-called friends began pushing. Her addictions deepened and her self-worth dwindled down to nothing. Amanda had confided in Dani once. She told Dani that she knew in her heart she had let Mason down; she had let everyone down who loved her. Amanda had said she no longer felt worthy of their love. Dani tried to tell her, but Amanda simply could not accept that there was nothing she could have done to stop them, especially Mason, from loving her. Time after time, they'd shared with her about Jesus and His salvation. Once in a while, Amanda would even attend church or go to a Bible study with the Shaws. But she just never seemed to clear her mind enough to hear God speaking to her. As an afterthought, Dani pondered, maybe she had. One never knows where another's heart truly lies. The only one who truly knew Amanda's heart was Jesus. Perhaps, Dani prayed, Amanda had given her life to Christ on her own terms, in her own way, and none of them had known.

Strangely – even after all Amanda had done to destroy her family – Dani smiled at the thought of seeing Amanda in heaven one day. She envisioned the day when she would see all the people she'd loved and lost; her parents, her grandparents, sweet Mrs. Jane from down the street, the church members who had gone to be with the Lord over the years, Amanda.

Yes, she hoped she'd see Amanda too.

"Dani! Do you think he will?" Mason asked, exasperated.

"Forgive me, little man. I've just got a lot on my mind," she said. "Do I think who will…do what?"

"Do you think my daddy will like me?" he said with concern in his voice.

Dani looked down at Mason's precious, worried little face. He looked as though he was going to cry.

Dani pulled her Jeep to the side of the road. She turned off the engine; she wanted his full attention. She reached for Mason's tiny hands and held them tightly. "Mason," she continued with a crack in her voice. "Your daddy loves you so much that he moved here from hundreds and hundreds of miles away just so he could be with you."

"But he doesn't even know me. How could he love me already?" Mason asked Dani.

"He loves you already, because he knows that Jesus made you. Jesus knew how much your daddy would love you," she said, squeezing his fragile hands.

"Nana used to tell me that Jesus loved me before I was even in my mommy's tummy. Did my daddy love me before I was in my mommy's tummy too?" he continued.

"Oh, Mason," She assured, "we all loved you before we ever knew you. God designed every one of your fingers, your cute little toes, your big blue eyes, even that little freckle on your nose…He designed them to make you like nobody else. He gave you things that might make you look like your daddy, like your nose, and things that make you look like your mommy, like your shiny auburn hair. But, Mason, Jesus created only one of you. And when He did, he decided that He would bring you into *our* family. He blessed *us* with you."

With an innocent pondering, "Did He even know that I was gonna lose my front tooth last week?"

"Yep." Dani laughed. "He did."

Dani continued, "Then when He decided He was going to let us be your family, God gave us so much love in our hearts for you, that we had to share that love with other people. People like your daddy. Only, you know what?" she asked rhetorically.

But Mason quickly responded, "What?" with his big blue eyes anticipating her answer.

The innocence in his expression made her smile. "We didn't have to share our love for you with your daddy," she said. "Because he already had more love for you than he could have ever imagined."

With a toothless grin, Mason looked thoughtfully out the passenger seat window. The two sat in silence for a brief moment. Then Mason turned back toward Dani and said, "Then I already love my daddy, too."

The lump in Dani's throat made it impossible for her to speak. She simply cupped his cheek with her hand and kissed him gently on the forehead.

Then, without hesitation, "Are we ready to do this, little man?" She needed his reassurance now.

"I'm ready!" he said bravely.

-- -- -- -- --

Dani and Mason sat in Deborah's elegant office with its walnut bookcases and matching desk waiting anxiously for David Fowler's arrival. Even Deborah was nervous. It had been only two weeks since she had broken the news to Dani—David Fowler was, in fact, Mason's biological father. Dani had protested, not wanting to believe it. "The tests are wrong. He can't be Mason's father," she'd argued.

Deborah had explained that the test results proved David's paternity with 99.99 percent accuracy. The chances that someone else was Mason's father were one in more than twenty million. The tests weren't wrong. Dani had been devastated and was terrified to break the news to Mason. But unlike Dani, Mason had accepted the news in stride. He had already determined in his mind that David was his daddy. Dani could tell that although Mason tried to hide his excitement at having a daddy in order to preserve Dani's feelings, his curiosity was difficult to disguise. It broke her heart to realize that this innocent little boy was intuitive enough to consider how Dani might be affected by the unfolding events. It occurred to her that Mason was handling the situation much better than Dani herself.

It was true. Dani had been thinking only of herself and how David's intrusion into their lives would affect *her*. She had been completely oblivious of Mason's feelings and how it might affect *him*. She was ashamed at the realization of her own selfishness. She'd determined that very day that she would be more conscious of Mason's feelings. But, she had assured herself, it would be a cold day in hell before she'd let some pill popping, ex-druggy take Mason away from her. She was not going to let that happen.

As the three waited for David's arrival, it was Mason's childlike innocence that served to ease the tension. "Ya' know what would be weally cool?" Mason asked.

"What's that, little man?" Dani tried to set aside her uneasiness.

"If my dad has a pet dinosaur," Mason offered as though he were talking about a pet dog. Deborah and Dani laughed. "You know dinosaurs don't exist anymore, goofy!" Dani exclaimed.

"I know," Mason countered. "But it still would be weally cool!"

Dani reached over and ruffled Mason's hair. Wanting to look just perfect for his first time meeting his dad, Mason licked the palm of his hand and smoothed his bangs forcing the disheveled pieces back into place.

It was hard to determine how it would all play out. Deborah's brief conversations with David Fowler had been pleasant, and he seemed to be genuine in his desire to be a father to Mason. But Deborah had seen this more times than she cared to remember—ulterior motives were often a driving factor. In David Fowler's case, it could be about the notoriety that the drama of the Shaw's death could bring him. He could be looking for money—an inheritance that the Shaws may have left Mason. He could simply be acting out of vengeance toward Amanda even in her death. God only knew what David's motives were. But Deborah's gut instinct told her that David was authentic—that he truly wanted to be a father to his son. Deborah's heart was heavy for her client. Dani had lost so much already. She wondered how Dani would survive if Mason were taken from her. Whatever happened, though, Deborah had determined that she would fight to the end for Dani. She had become more than a client to Deborah, she'd become her friend.

A gentle knock on the door startled all of them. They looked at one another as if unsure of what to do next. Deborah was the first to stand. She smoothed her sophisticated black pencil skirt and walked toward her office door. Surprised by her own anxiety, she hesitated briefly before grasping the door knob and turning it slowly to the right.

She took a step back as the door opened. The look of terror on the man's face actually made Deborah feel sorry for him. She held out her hand to him. "You must be David. I'm Deborah Klein. It's a pleasure to meet you."

David willed his hands to stop shaking as he reached for Deborah's. "Thank you for taking the time to meet with me," he said. "I'm sorry I'm late. I've been pacing the hall outside your office trying to muster the courage to come in," he admitted.

Deborah let out a nervous laugh. "Please come in. We've all been pretty nervous too." She waved her arm toward a high-back antique chair upholstered in a pale pink chiffon fabric. Next to the high-back set an identical chair separated by a mahogany end table. Across from the trio of furniture sat Dani and Mason on what was clearly, even to the untrained eye, a stylish relic to be admired. But David didn't notice the elegant décor. His eyes were trained on Mason as he awkwardly fumbled in his seat, trying to get comfortable.

Mason stared at David in silence. He appeared to be in awe of his father. Dani, on the other hand, avoided David's gaze altogether. She couldn't bring herself to look him in the eyes.

Deborah knew she had to say something to break the ice. But before she could say anything, David's voice broke the silence. Leaning forward and resting his elbows on his knees. "Hi, Mason," he said in barely a whisper. "I'm David."

Mason stood up, took two steps forward, and offered his hand to David. Surprised at Mason's self-assuredness, David took Mason's hand and shook it as though he were being introduced to a business associate.

"It's vewy nice to meet you." Mason sounded more like a man than a six-year-old child. "But do you think I could call you Daddy instead of David?" he asked casually.

David chuckled. "It would be my honor," he said with a crack in his voice.

For a brief moment, Mason stood there examining David's face. David returned the curiosity. Then, as if he'd known his father all his life, Mason leaned forward and hugged David. The tears that had begun to form in the man's eyes could no longer be contained. David wept as he held his son in his arms.

Dani, too, could no longer control her emotions. Watching the touching encounter between father and son sent tears streaming down her face. The anger and resentment that had been building up for weeks dissolved in an instant. This *was* Mason's father. The identical dimple in their right cheek and unwieldy cowl lick over each of their left eye, to their inherent emotional connection and inexplicable instantaneous commonality with one another confirmed to Dani what she'd been so reluctant to accept. As she sat watching them behind streaming tears, she could no longer deny the inevitable; a bond had already been created that could never again be broken—by time, distance or circumstances.

CHAPTER FOUR

The meeting with David at Deborah's office had gone better than any of them expected. Dani was hopeful that meeting Mason would curb David's curiosity, and he would choose to become a mere temporary presence in Mason's life. Today would reveal a lot about the Fowler's intentions. Dani and David had spoken only once since the meeting nearly a week ago. David wanted Mason to meet his wife and their two children. Mason was excited to discover he had a little brother and baby sister. He wasn't sure how he felt about David's wife, after all, he already thought of Dani as his mom. Nonetheless, Mason couldn't wait to meet his new family. As they drove the 3.7 miles from Dani's condo to the Fowler home, Mason and Dani sat silent in their own thoughts.

The Fowlers lived in a new, but modest development on the south side of Glenbrook. Most locals referred to the area as South County. It was a beautifully landscaped neighborhood with a community playground nestled among freshly planted maples and tall pines that clearly existed before the development was built. Someone took precious care not to disturb the natural growth that had accumulated. At the far end of the playground was a man-built pond with a cascading waterfall just large enough for toddlers to wet their toes and a flock of ducks to call home. It was quaint. It was peaceful.

At 562 Danby Circle, there stood a double-story house with a two-car garage located at the end of a well-maintained cul-de-sac. The surrounding homes were nearly identical, only the colors ranged from ivory to light brown and somewhere in between. The

Fowler's home was somewhere in between. A maple tree, which stood in the middle of the right side lawn, was a vibrant green and had a redwood bench encircling it. The walkway leading to the front porch was lined with purple and yellow pansies.

Dani decided to park her Jeep out near the road instead of in the driveway. Earlier that week, she noticed a small amount of oil leaking from underneath had left an oily puddle in her parking space at the condo. She didn't want to blemish the Fowler's otherwise spotless paved drive.

She and Mason sat there staring at the house, the engine still running as if the Jeep might take off on its own at any moment. Dani knew she had to be the adult. *God, please get us through this.*

"This is it, little man." She ruffled Mason's hair.

Mason reached in the backseat and grabbed the two small gifts he had chosen for his new little brother and baby sister. When Mason had discovered that his daddy had two more children, he asked Dani if she would take him to the Dollar Store so he could use the money he had saved and buy them each a present.

Dani and Mason had spent nearly an hour looking for just the right gifts. In the end, he had chosen for his four-year-old brother, Samuel, a plastic Tyrannosaurus rex that made a loud roaring sound with the push of a button on its underbelly. For Kylie, his six-month-old baby sister, he'd picked out a plush rainbow-colored stuffed caterpillar.

Mason had wrapped both gifts with meticulous intention, making sure each one was perfectly packaged. Kylie's gift was wrapped in pink paper with multicolored flowers and a purple bow on top. He had wrapped Samuel's present in a camouflage gift bag with olive green tissue paper.

"Do you think Samuel will like his dinosaur, Dani?" he asked nervously.

"I know he will, Mason. Don't you worry."

With a deep sigh, Dani opened the driver's side door, and with shaky knees, made her way around to Mason's side of the Jeep. Mason jumped out with gifts in hand. Together, they began walking toward the front porch. Their collective pace slowed as they approached the front steps. Mason reached for Dani's hand. She gave his a tight squeeze. "You're doing great, little man. No worries," reassuring herself as much as Mason.

Dani reached for the doorbell, but before she could press the buzzer, the door opened—slowly at first. She looked down to see a miniature round face with wide eyes staring up at her from the narrow opening. The boy stood about three feet tall with chocolate-colored puppy dog eyes. His hair was a golden blonde with bangs that were stiffly gelled pointing toward the sky. As his gaze traveled from Dani's face to Mason's, the look of apprehension on his face faded into a look of delight. He reached his arm forward and extended it toward Mason as if to shake hands. Gift bags clutched in his hands and still close to her side clinging to Dani's arm, Mason offered his hand to the boy. With a firm grasp, the boys shook hands like two miniature men.

"Hi. My name's Samuel," the boy said. "My bestest friends call me Sam." The manly introduction was quickly overshadowed by the innocence of the boy's voice.

"I'm Mason," he said nervously and questioningly looked up at Dani.

Dani wanted nothing more than to ease Mason's nerves, but she was a wreck herself. In her futile attempt at pretending that today was just another day and there was nothing unusual about their first encounter with the Fowlers, Dani crouched down to the boys' eye level and held her hand out to Samuel.

"I'm very happy to meet you, Samuel," she said. "My name is Danielle. My best friends call me Dani."

Samuel smiled from ear to ear. "That's a pretty name. Can I call you Dani?" he asked in anticipation.

Taken aback by Samuel's precociousness, she hesitated briefly. Then, inherently, "I would like that very much," she said.

The boy's grin widened, revealing for the first time a dimple in his right cheek, identical to the one on Mason's cheek—and David's too.

Just then, the door opened wider. On the other side was David Fowler. He placed one hand on Samuel's shoulder and leaned forward to shake Dani's hand with the other. She extended her arm and awkwardly returned his welcome. David's smile was warm and welcoming.

Averting his gaze away from Dani, David looked down at Mason with a sort of contented resignation. "I'm so glad you and Dani are here, Mason," he offered. "Everyone is very excited to meet you."

Straightening his stance, "They awe?" Mason asked as if surprised.

David chuckled. Then in a gentle, soothing voice, "Of course, they are," he assured Mason. "They're in the backyard. Come on in."

David stepped to the side and motioned Dani and Mason into the house.

Running ahead of them, Samuel headed down a long hall toward the backyard. "Come on," directing his attention toward Mason. "We can play in my sandbox." Samuel's hurried stride caused the rest of them to pick up the pace.

Samuel was the first to step on to the back patio, followed by Dani and Mason, hand in hand, and then David.

Immediately, a petite woman who couldn't have been more than five feet two headed directly for Dani. With a baby on her left hip, the smiling woman reached toward Dani, pulled her close, and embraced her as though the two were old friends.

Dani awkwardly returned the hug reaching up with one arm and maintaining Mason's tight grasp with the other hand.

"Dani," the woman said, "I am so happy to meet you." There were tears in the woman's eyes. "I'm David's wife, Tracie."

The two women's eyes locked for a brief moment, with an odd sort of comprehension. "And this is Kylie," she said, smiling sweetly at the little girl on her hip. Chewing on a colorful icy teething ring, the little girl's nose wrinkled behind an irresistible little grin.

Mason clung to Dani's side again, but this time his grasp was slightly less rigid than before. Mason was behaving uncharacteristically shy, avoiding eye contact with everyone except Samuel.

Recognizing Mason's uneasiness, without skipping a beat, Tracie squatted down to meet Mason's gaze. "Whatcha' got there, Mason?" eyeing the gift bags.

Still averting Tracie's eyes and without a word, Mason offered his delicately wrapped treasures to his new stepmother. "Here you go," Mason announced shyly.

"This is beautiful," Tracie praised. Holding up the delicate pink gift bag, Tracie deduced, "Let me guess, this one must be for Kylie? Pink is her favorite color." The corner of Mason's lip proudly curved upward as he tried to conceal a smile.

The rambunctious little Samuel had been so riveted by his new big brother that he hadn't noticed Mason had come bearing gifts. "Wow!" he exclaimed, bouncing up and down. Dani couldn't help but gleam at his enthusiasm.

Suddenly, Dani realized that David had been silently standing on the sidelines watching the events unfold. "Whoa…hold on a second, Sam," David said, stepping toward a small table in the corner of the patio. "Don't you want to give Mason *his* surprise first?"

Samuel raced past David, nearly toppling the table over, sending a shabbily wrapped gift plummeting to the ground. Unconcerned about the condition of the package's contents after the two-and-a-half foot plunge, Samuel swooped it up and jetted back toward Mason.

"I got you somefing too," he announced, pleased with himself. A smidgen of excitement danced in Mason's face. Moment by moment, he was beginning to loosen up.

As Samuel offered his prized gift to his new brother, Tracie handed the camo-wrapped gift bag to Samuel.

To all their surprise, Mason, wide-eyed and animated piped up. "I know, let's open them at the same time!" he exclaimed.

Agreeing with Mason's brilliant idea, Samuel could no longer control his curiosity. He had to know what the cool-looking package contained. "Yeah!" he screeched. "Good idea!"

Simultaneously, the boys dropped to their knees and began tearing at their respective packages, each racing to beat the other, displaying it for all to see. To everyone's amusement—mostly the boys—the gifts were identical Tyrannosaurus rex dinosaurs standing upright on its hind legs with scales protruding from its spine.

"Cooool," the boys said in harmony, both overjoyed at their gifts. The three adults laughed, mimicked by baby Kylie who inadvertently dropped her teething ring to the ground. *Leave it to a child to lighten the atmosphere*, Dani thought.

Rising to his feet, Samuel hollered, "C'mon, Mason, I have a Triceratops...a Velociraptor...an Astrodon—*he* has big teeth shaped like stars...a Saltopus..." Still listing his cherished collection of prehistoric creatures, Samuel's voice faded as he sprinted toward a wood-framed sandbox in the far corner of the yard. Having shed all semblance of timidity during the previous moments of playfulness, Mason was right on Samuel's heels.

"How about some raspberry iced tea?" Tracie offered, motioning for Dani to have a seat.

"Please." Dani's throat was dry. A glass of ice-cold tea was just the thing she needed.

Before heading to the kitchen to retrieve the icy drinks, Tracie casually handed Kylie to Dani, as if she were a close-knit family member. Awkwardly, Dani rested Kylie on her lap balancing the six-month-old in a sitting position. Inquisitively, the baby spiraled her limber body around squirming to see the curious stranger holding her. Even less inhibited than her rambunctious big brother, Kylie pulled at Dani's dangling cross necklace. Mesmerized by its polished shimmer, the baby tugged on the piece of silver directing it to her mouth. Without thinking, Dani's motherly instinct kicked in, and she calmly pried the necklace from Kylie's miniature hand, replacing the makeshift toy with the stuffed caterpillar squeeze toy that Mason had bought for his baby sister.

Dani and David sat in uncomfortable silence anxiously waiting for Tracie to return. Both watched as Mason and Samuel animatedly shared stories and compared tennis shoes.

Earlier that day Mason had expressed his enthusiasm about becoming a big brother to a four-and-a-half-year-old. "I'll teach him how to write his name, just like Auntie Brit taught me how to write mine!" he had proclaimed to Dani during one of their previous discussions. Then as an afterthought, he'd speculated aloud, "I wonder what his name is."

Just as Dani contemplated what she might say to break the unnerving silence, Tracie returned with three tall glasses of iced tea, two juice boxes with straws protruding out of the top, and a sippy cup filled with what looked to be apple juice.

"Hey guys, how about some juice?" she shouted, handing Dani a glass of tea. Caught in their fantasy dinosaur land, the boys were oblivious to Tracie's promptings. Kylie reached for the familiar Winnie the Pooh sippy cup, dropping her new toy to the ground in order to free her hands.

As the adults sipped their tea, they engaged in frivolous small talk. They watched the boys play together as if they were old buddies. When Kylie began to get fussy, Tracie excused herself to lay the baby down for a nap. Again, the conversation between Dani and David became awkward. They talked about the unseasonably warm weather. They talked about the state of the economy. When Tracie returned, they talked about Kylie's sleeping habits. They talked about the joys of having children, which sent a chill through Dani. They talked about the Fowler's neighborhood and the impending growth that was expected during the next few years. They talked about the upcoming local elections. They talked about everything—except what was really on their minds.

Finally, unable to contain her curiosity at David and Tracie's apparent apathy, Dani interrupted David mid-sentence. "I'm sorry," she exclaimed. "I don't understand why we aren't talking about what's really going on."

Dani stood up, and in stark contrast to her usual passive temperament, she looked David squarely in the eyes. "What are your intentions?" she demanded. "You come into our lives and threaten to destroy my family and then you sit here and talk about the weather!"

Though the boys were far enough away that they could not hear the conversation between the adults, Dani muffled her anger in a hushed tone. She looked in the direction of the sandbox. For the time being, the boys were lost in their imaginary prehistoric world.

Turning again to face David, she didn't hold back. "I don't get it! Why, after all these years, did you decide to do this now? Why not when Amanda was alive? You had to have known that Amanda was incapable of taking care of your son. What father, in his right mind, would allow his child to be raised by an admitted drug addict?"

With a look of shame on his face, David lowered his head in silence. Tracie looked panicked. She didn't know what to say—to Dani or to David.

Dani continued her hushed rampage, "The two of you are acting like this is no big deal. You act like you're living in some kind of 'Leave It to Beaver' make-believe world. You live in your perfect little white-picket-fence home, with your perfect little family and their perfect little clothes. I'm sure you have a perfect job and perfect friends and a perfect reputation!" she said with venom.

Slightly embarrassed by her unbridled outburst, Dani leaned in closer toward David, "Tell me," she began. "How does someone so perfect get caught up with someone like Amanda, get her pregnant, and then just walk away?" Dani's words were harsh and even as she said them, she'd regretted it.

David reached toward Tracie and comfortingly squeezed her hand in his. "Dani, please sit down," he said. She did as he asked.

Though she'd tried hard not to cry, the tears began to flow. Tracie leaned toward Dani as if in an attempt to comfort her, but Dani crossed her arms in a dismissive manner and looked away. Tracie realized that Dani was not ready to be comforted—at least not by her. Tracie sat back in her chair and looked at her husband, her eyes desperately pleading.

"As many times as I've rehearsed this in my mind, I'm at a complete loss for words," David nervously wrung his hands together. "I don't even know where to begin."

Dani wanted to scream, *I don't care where you begin! Just leave us alone! Let us walk out of here so that we never have to see you again!* But the words would not come. So she said nothing.

"When I met Amanda, we were both heavy into the drug scene. I don't know how long she'd been using. I had been for a long time. We met through mutual so-called 'friends.' We had a brief relationship and split up after a couple of weeks. I don't even know if you could technically call it a relationship. We were both always high and so caught up in scoring our next hit that I don't remember most of the time we spent together." Dani appeared uninterested in David's sob story thus far.

Conscious of his pathetic attempt to rationalize the events that had unfolded so many years before, David said, "I'm not making excuses, I'm just trying to explain what happened."

Pausing for just a moment, David continued, "Anyway. We split up and I took off. I had no idea she was pregnant." David's eyes began to tear. "The first time I learned about Mason was when he was six weeks old. Amanda had applied for welfare, and they were coming after me for child support. By this time, I had been in jail for the umpteenth time on drug-related charges and had been in a court-ordered drug recovery program in the Bay Area for almost three months. About ten days after I found out about Mason, I was released and I headed straight back to town."

David turned to look at Mason playing obliviously in the sandbox. "When I saw him for the first time and held him in my arms, I instantly fell in love. He looked so much like me. There was no denying he was mine. But he had Amanda's auburn hair. He was the cutest little thing." David's reminiscent smile quickly faded. "But that was the first and last time I ever saw him.

"I would call Amanda and beg to see Mason. We would make arrangements for me to see him, but she would never show up. Finally, I couldn't find her anywhere. She'd left town with some guy and no one knew where they had gone. At least that's what her 'friends' were saying. I sent child support payments to a P.O. Box in town every month and someone always picked them up and cashed the checks. Even Social Services would not tell me where she was. They said their interest was in making sure 'the child' was properly provided for." David emphasized the child as if the social workers viewed children as numbers or files, rather than the innocent children they are.

David went on, "I staked out the post office, but she never showed. She must have been having someone else pick up the support payments for her. I even raked up enough money to hire a private investigator to find her and Mason. But I ran out of money before he could find them."

David reached for Tracie's hand again. He lovingly wrapped his large hands around hers. "I was finally clean and sober and living a decent life. I had gotten a pretty good job in Southern California—well, as good as an ex-druggie with a criminal history can get—but I couldn't get Mason out of my mind. I started going to a faith-based recovery program to try to deal with it. From that, I began going to a really great church with some incredible people. Then I met Tracie." David swallowed hard. "Then I met Jesus."

With a tone of humility, David said, "She knew about Amanda and Mason from the beginning. She didn't judge me. She wasn't insecure about my desire to find Amanda and Mason. In fact, she encouraged me to keep looking for them. A few months later, we were married. We began looking for them together. It seemed like every night one or both of us were online looking for…something. We weren't even sure what last name Amanda had given Mason or even what her last name was. Then life just kind of happened. Tracie was pregnant with Samuel within a month after our wedding. Three years later, Kylie came along."

David saw the questioning in Dani's eyes. "We never stopped looking, Dani. I promise. In fact, it was late one night, we had just put the kids to bed and went to try another online search. We were sitting next to each other on the couch when Tracie typed Amanda Shaw in the search engine. We had searched her name a thousand times before, so we didn't really expect to get any promising results. But there is was." David hesitated.

"There *what was*?" Dani asked, confused.

David looked at Tracie as if reluctant to continue.

"What, David? What was there?" she asked, more adamantly this time.

Another minute passed before David continued, "It was an article about your parents' death."

Once again, they all grew silent. Only the boys' distant laughter could be heard.

David's sympathetic voice broke the silence. "I never meant to hurt you. All I know is that God doesn't make mistakes. Your parents' and Amanda's death was a tragedy. It doesn't make any sense at all. But I also know that God knows what He's doing. Everything that happens, happens according to His will. It wasn't a mistake that we found that article that night. And it wasn't a mistake that God brought all of us together."

Dani was listening, but only hearing what she wanted to hear. David was inadvertently forcing her to relive the memories that she'd been trying so hard to forget. At the same time, a strange, contradictory sense of peace came over her. David was speaking about God…about trusting in Him…about His will. There was something about them that made Dani trust them. Could that be it? They were kind and loving and seemed to be good, authentic people. They had welcomed Dani and Mason with open arms even though Dani was behaving less than benevolent. If Mason was going to be torn from her life, she supposed, these people would at least teach him about Jesus. She fought back feelings of cynicism and anger.

Seeing that David wasn't quite sure what to say next, Tracie pledged, "We don't want to take him away from you. We just want to be a part of your lives. Mason deserves to know his father. He deserves to be *loved* by him." David was grateful that Tracie was doing the talking now. He was never any good at talking to women, especially in difficult situations.

Dani's voice still filled with bitterness. "Then why did you wait until the day before I was supposed to adopt him to contact my attorney?" she asked accusingly, her eyes searching Tracie's face.

"It was just a coincidence. David had been struggling with how to approach the situation. He didn't know where to begin. Did he call you? Did he show up at your front door? Did we contact our own attorney? We just didn't know what was best. We had decided not to be impulsive, but to trust in God's direction. We had been praying and praying for weeks since finding out about your parents' death. We talked to the head pastor at our church before we left Anaheim, then again with the pastor at our new church here in town. We knew there wasn't going to be an easy solution. In the end, we felt like God was leading us to contact your attorney. It seemed like the best way for everyone."

Tracie leaned forward. "We are so grateful that you agreed to meet with us." Pleadingly, she said, "We can make this work, Dani. I know we can."

-- -- -- -- --

The next few weeks and months flew by like a whirlwind. The courts had ordered two months of supervised visitation as a transitional period for everyone involved. At first, Dani accompanied Mason during every visit he had with the Fowlers. The supervised visits turned into unsupervised weekend sleepovers for Mason. Dani had tried to convince the court case worker that it was too soon for Mason to have overnight visits without Dani's presence, but in the end, the courts had agreed with the case worker's recommendations.

Mason had adjusted well to his place among the Fowler family. Even Dani eventually became content with the role she played in both Mason's life and the life of the Fowlers.

At first, Dani had wanted to dislike the Fowlers— to hate them for trying to take from her the only thing she had left in the world that mattered—Mason. She had entered their home—their lives, defensive, pretentious, angry. She had left there humbled, accepted, and vulnerable. They had been kind and welcoming; nothing like she had imagined, or rather, *wanted* them to be. She wanted them to be demanding, ruthless, deplorable people so that she could hate them—but they weren't any of that. Instead, as hard as she fought it, they had made it so easy to fall in love with them. Yet her heart and mind battled feelings of both love and hatred.

Dani didn't feel the jealousy she had expected. Her inherent need to maintain an odd, if not displaced, sense of loyalty to her own family's memory was overshadowed by an inexplicable sense of belonging.

She became accustomed to spending her Sunday afternoons with the Fowlers. She looked forward each week to not only spending precious time with Mason and his new family, *his family*, but gorging herself on the mouthwatering meals that Tracie whipped up. In fact, Dani had come to treasure every moment she spent with Mason and, to her surprise, the Fowlers. From the beginning, even with all the awkward and emotional turmoil that first few weeks brought for all of them, Dani had quickly connected, first with Samuel and Kylie, then with Tracie, and even David. Mason's connection with them was instant.

Dani had formed a special bond with one of David's good friends from the church, Buck Jennings. People who knew Buck referred to him as Uncle Buck—he wouldn't have it any other way. His wife of more than forty-five years had long passed away, and he now lived alone in a modest home just around the corner from the Fowlers. Having quickly formed a special friendship with the Fowlers—first through the church, and then as neighbors—Uncle Buck was a regular fixture at their Sunday night get-togethers.

Uncle Buck had no children of his own upon which to shower his love and attention and long ago took it upon himself to become the official "Adoptive

Uncle" of all who knew him. The parishioners at David and Tracie's church, The Crossing, loved Uncle Buck and took him under their wing. The women in the church would take turns cleaning his home, washing his laundry, and delivering his meals. The men were just as smitten by the gentle old man and made sure to keep Uncle Buck's lawn mowed and his gutters free of leaves.

In reality, though, Uncle Buck was more than proficient at taking care of himself. One night, after one of their traditional Sunday evening get-togethers, Uncle Buck was chatting with Dani as David and Tracie put the kids to bed.

"You know something, Dani? I don't really need everyone fussing over me. I'm perfectly capable of tending to my own needs. I'm actually being very selfish," he admitted. "I love the company. If it weren't for people bringing me dinner and mowing my lawn, I'd be a lonely old man."

Buck was an unassuming man who lived a humble life. Though he was the owner of a very successful nationally recognized publication known as the *Humanitarian*, he usually bought his clothes at discount stores and did his grocery shopping at the local food outlet.

Buck and his late wife, Annie, built the *Humanitarian* from the ground up. The two met as journalism majors at Golden Gate University in California. Married a year later, they scraped pennies to turn their collective dream of owning their own publication business into a reality. It hadn't taken them long to build a reputation of integrity and honest reporting.

The primary focus of the *Humanitarian* was to seek out the disenfranchised and otherwise forgotten facets of people within the United States. Through their reporting and subsequent rhetoric, they forced government and the entities there within to open their eyes to the travesties that a complacent society had inadvertently loosed upon America. They then made a call for action. The impoverished, the abused, the sick, the hungry—none were immune to the welcome mayhem that befell them when the *Humanitarian* made it their mission to bring a disadvantaged people's plight to the forefront of the American society.

The family burn barrel adorned the cover of a Fall 1979 issue of the *Humanitarian*. Beneath the headline, the subheading read, "The New American Dinner Table." The cover photo showed a shabbily-dressed man warming his hands from the fire of a rusty old oil barrel, with his wife and two small children standing close by as they eagerly rummaged through the remains of a wrinkled-up McDonald's bag.

The issue had caused uproar. It forced political party against political party, government against the church. Every facet of society placed blame on another for letting the American people down. The *Humanitarian* took a once-forgotten culture and single-handedly turned it into the most momentous and relevant cause of the decade.

It had been Annie Jennings who wrote the compelling article. It was more than her words that told the heart wrenching story of the hungry and homeless. But it was the photos—the sunken-eyed infant lying motionless in her mother's arms as her blank gaze staring somewhere off into space; it was the vision of a desperate father wearing a makeshift suit, exiting the dilapidated front entrance of the corner mini-mart after his fourth fruitless job interview; it was the hopeless mother searching a dumpster in vain for something that might represent her family's next meal—it was these photos and so many others that told the story. It could not be ignored, nor would it.

Annie had won a Pulitzer that year for her coverage on the homeless in America. It was the first of many awards the *Humanitarian* would receive for its charitable and altruistic efforts.

Though Uncle Buck no longer played an active role in the daily functions of the *Humanitarian*, he remained the board president and chief advisor. Dani knew that it was Uncle Buck who still made the important decisions, but Buck was too humble to admit it.

Sitting on the front porch across from the beautiful wrinkled face of this precious man, Dani realized that as the months wore on, though she had come to care deeply for the Fowlers, Dani had formed an inseparable bond with Uncle Buck. Dani and Uncle Buck spent many Sunday evenings, after the kids and even David and Tracie had gone to bed, sitting on the Fowler's front porch sharing stories. Dani mostly listened to Uncle Buck's tales of childhood mischief, college pranks, and confidential sources. When he would talk about Annie and their marital adventures together, Buck's eyes would first glaze over, and then he would slowly close them as if reliving the memory all over again.

Dani had grown to admire Uncle Buck, not only for his Godly wisdom and unfaltering faith, but for his humble nature. Buck was a man of incredible accomplishments, yet material belongings meant nothing to him. He had a way of making people feel better. When one left Uncle Buck's presence, they had somehow become a better person. In a few short months, Uncle Buck had become a vital part of Dani's life and had filled an empty space in her heart.

This Sunday, as small tendrils of curls brushed across her face, Dani smiled as she passed by Uncle Buck's house and rounded the last street corner before turning into the little cul-de-sac that housed the Fowlers and several other families that were so similar, yet so very different from Tracie and David and their little family. Dani mentally questioned herself, "Were they really so different from one another? Perhaps the little families with the 'Leave It to Beaver' appearances were bridled with their own dark secrets and familial dysfunctions." Dani found it ironic that the families, whom on the surface appeared the most "normal," were often the families most rooted in pain and secrecy.

Dani parked the little red Jeep in her usual spot out on the street in front of the grassy lawn that adjoined the house next door to the Fowlers. She paused for a moment, feeling content before hopping down from the lifted Jeep onto the pavement below. She reached for the chocolate cake resting on the back seat.

Together, Mason and Samuel had designated Dani the official "dessert fairy." They had decided that nobody could bake a cake or pie or cookies like Dani could. So each week, Mason and Samuel would put in their requests for the next Sunday's dessert. Their favorite was a decadent chocolate-chocolate chip-cake sprinkled with powdered sugar. Dani had tried to talk them into something different this time because they had had the same dessert three out of the past six weeks. But the boys could not be convinced. They had their hearts set on "the best cake in the whole wide world." Dani smiled to herself as she anticipated their delight when she walked in with the decadent cake which, this week, had gummy worms sprinkled on the side.

As usual, Dani opened the front door gently and announced her presence with a, "Knock, knock." She took pleasure in the role she played in the Fowler's family. Her presence was always welcome; she felt it, and she knew it.

"Dani!" Tracie hurdled from the kitchen with Kylie on her hip. She gave Dani a warm, welcoming hug and kissed her on the cheek. "I'm so glad you're here." She handed Kylie to Dani with one arm and took the cake from Dani with the other hand. "Will you please take her for me? I'm going a little nuts." Tracie kissed Kylie on the tip of her nose and said, almost rhetorically, "I think Kylie has more spaghetti sauce on *her* than I have in the pan." She wiped away a small speck of marinara that had dried on Kylie's little barefoot. As Dani positioned Kylie on her left hip, the precocious baby, in true fashion, reached for Dani's cross necklace and began dangling it between her fingers.

Grinning over her shoulder before disappearing into the kitchen, Tracie hollered, "Auntie Dani needs some practice anyway."

Dani felt a tinge of pain, but managed, "At the rate I'm going, Kylie will need parenting practice before I do."

Tracie was aware that Dani would likely never have children of her own. Dani had shared her story with Tracie several weeks after they first met. Still, Tracie was always so positive. She'd said to Dani, "God has incredible plans for your life, Dani. You need to trust in that. He is a God of miracles." She had said it without judgment or condemnation, but rather, with an unadulterated faith. "You'll have children one day. Maybe not in the traditional way, but I have no doubt that one day you'll be a wonderful mom."

CHAPTER FIVE

The winter season seemed to go on forever. Usually by late March, Glenbrook was experiencing some glimpse of spring. But the first welcoming pink budding cherry blossoms were nowhere to be found this year. Most of the town residents still had their snow shovels and bags of rock salt leaning against the house near their back door just waiting for the next snowfall. While the winter had not brought with it a particularly large amount of snow, it fell often and in small amounts, staying just long enough to absorb the mud and dirt from the well-worn county roadways before the fresh white crystals blanketed the ground again, giving the quaint little town a Thomas Kinkade appearance.

More than once over the years, Dani had mused to herself that during the biting winter months, her quirky little town often looked as though Mr. Kinkade himself had stood at the intersection of Broad and Maple Streets and painted the ancient Victorian homes, cobblestone sidewalks, and smiling faces into existence. But today, as Dani made her way through town, waving at the familiar faces opening up storefronts and sipping hot lattes at the corner bakery, she snickered aloud, "It all looks so perfect, so innocent. But we know better, don't we?" as though speaking to someone in the passenger seat of her sporty little Jeep. But Dani was alone; no one to hear the brewing bitterness she was feeling that day.

During the months that had passed since the Fowlers first invaded her and Mason's life, Dani had gradually begun to think that the welcoming the family had given her and Mason was simply a facade. A ploy they had created to prevent Dani from fighting for custody of Mason. And it had worked. And now it seemed they were slowly drawing Mason deeper into their family unit and pushing Dani out. She had expressed her concerns to Buck. He thought Dani was being sensitive to the natural bonding that was taking place between Mason and his new family. Maybe that was the problem, Dani thought to herself. Maybe the Fowlers were now Mason's *new* family, and Dani was no longer needed. Dani was feeling disconnected with David and Tracie—and even Mason—and began to distance herself. Maybe it was a self-preservation mechanism; maybe the Fowlers did, in fact, have ulterior motives. In any event, Dani was feeling vulnerable and alone over the past few days.

These days, Dani's only place of refuge seemed to be *The Journal.* She had given up her Wednesday evening Bible study and instead started attending a self-help meeting that Tanya, a longtime acquaintance and the director of sales at *The Journal,* had recommended. Tanya had recently divorced and was determined to get rid of all the "baggage" she carried around with her before getting into another "dysfunctional relationship." She had told Dani that the self-help classes and the books they recommended had been her saving grace. She said she was learning to "put herself first" and that she was done giving so much of herself and not getting anything back in her relationships.

Dani didn't completely agree with Tanya's points of view. After all, Dani had spent her entire life in a godly home with Christ-centered values. Her parents had been the most generous and giving people she had ever known. They spent their lives putting others first; giving up their holidays serving food at the shelter, using their vacation time from work going on mission trips, sharing Jesus with the residents at the local senior homes. Their kindness and service to others was endless. Dani had admired them so. Self-centeredness had certainly not been a part of their character, and Dani had inherited the same selfless qualities. But after weeks of patronizing Tanya, telling her that her schedule was too busy to fit it in right now, Dani had given in and agreed to attend a meeting with Tanya.

At the end of the first meeting, in true Dani fashion, she had offered to bring cookies the following week, locking herself into, at the very least, a one more week commitment. After that, she and Tanya, almost without failure, made a weekly event of it. They would first go to dinner, alternating who would choose the restaurant and then drive to the meeting together. Dani had even begun enjoying a glass of wine during their Wednesday night outings. If nothing else, Dani relished the camaraderie she was developing with Tanya and her new friends at the "meeting."

Even then, Dani spent most of her nights alone searching online employment opportunities. She didn't know what she wanted to do or where she wanted to go, but she knew she needed a change. The last few months had left her discontented with her job—with her life. The discontentment only worsened by the day. The more she threw herself into her work at *The Journal*, the more restless and unsettled she became.

Dani's half-hearted attempt at reading her Bible always seemed to be interrupted by thoughts of Travis Jakobs, of Mason, of her parents, of work, of Travis Jakobs. Why was she feeling so drawn to him? For the first time in her life, Dani was contemplating throwing caution to the wind; doing what *she* wanted to do, not what she was *supposed* to do, or what everyone else thought she should do. Maybe Tanya was right. Maybe Dani needed to start putting herself first.

-- -- -- -- --

As Dani neared *The Journal* and pulled into one of the few remaining parking spaces near the building's rear entrance, Travis came thundering in, driving his spiffy new navy blue convertible BMW with tan leather seats. Though his black Oakley sunglasses hid the expression in his eyes, Travis' arrogant, overconfident attitude was evident even in the faint smirk he wore as he gazed at Dani.

Travis couldn't help but notice that Dani had been dressing unusually provocative lately. Her typical mid-calf length skirts had risen to about three inches above her knees. Her suits appeared more tailored, showing her petite, yet curvy figure and accentuating her tiny waistline. She even started wearing eyeliner; her emerald green eyes having a hypnotic effect on Travis. Had she made the changes for him? Had he simply imagined the flirtatious way she flipped her hair as she left his office yesterday? Hadn't he caught her staring at him more than once over the past weeks?

For nearly three years now, Travis had used every trick in the book trying to seduce Dani. Other women were standing in line to get a taste of what Travis had to offer, but not Dani. She had always been straightforward with him, at first, politely, if not bashfully accepting his compliments. Later, feeling secure in her job and the role she played within the organization, telling him she was uncomfortable with a married man making advances toward her. Travis had backed off slightly. But it seemed to him lately that his subtle remarks were being well-received by Dani, if not welcomed. Travis knew that Dani was vulnerable. She had been through more in the last year than most people have to endure over a lifetime. Still, Travis was not one to turn the other cheek when opportunity came knocking. And his instinct was telling him that the knocking he was hearing was getting louder by the day.

"Hey, Dani. How's it going?" he hollered over his shoulder as he clumsily gathered his briefcase and a pile of papers from the passenger seat.

"Well, it's good to see the sun peeking through the clouds for a change," she said casually.

As he hurried to catch up to her, Travis openly admired Dani, starting at her tiny ankles and thin, muscular calves all the way up to the long, flowing ebony hair that fell gently over her shoulders framing her electrifying emerald eyes. "You're dressed to kill today, Dan. Got a hot date?"

Dani blushed. "No. I just thought it was about time I started making myself a little more presentable. Talent can only get a girl so far," she said naively.

Travis raised his brow, and with a grin, he said, "What kind of talent are we talking about?"

"I'm talking about *writing*, Travis, being a talented writer." Her gaze caught the mischievous look in his eyes. He was exquisite. His square jawline was accentuated by what appeared to be an ever-present five o'clock shadow. Dani couldn't help but notice the dimple that appeared on Travis' right cheek whenever he smiled. He was rugged, but at the same time, sophisticated. She had never really noticed just how appealing Travis was.

Dani was enjoying the attention she was getting. It was completely innocent after all. At least that's what she told herself.

"You definitely have talent, Dani. I've been impressed with your writing since day one," he said. "But it would be a cryin' shame to let all that beauty go to waste."

"I'm sure I'm not the first girl you've said that to, Travis." It was more of a question than a statement.

"You're the first *woman* I've said it to, Dani." His voice was deep and direct. He gently placed his hand in the small of her back as their pace slowed, and they simultaneously stopped and faced one another. Their eyes met. "You're not just a cute kid anymore, Dani. You're an extremely attractive woman, who has no idea what you can do to a man with those piercing eyes and bashful little smile." He looked away, sounding vulnerable, "What you do to me…"

Dani was flattered. She felt like a schoolgirl experiencing her first crush. There was an uncomfortable silence between the two as Travis lifted his head and, once again, their eyes locked. "I…Travis…I…"

Just then, Sarah James, the newly hired eighteen-year-old high school intern came rushing out the door and nearly plowed down Travis and Dani. "Mr. Jakobs." She giggled. "I mean, Travis, your eight o'clock is here. I didn't want to bother you, but he arrived early and has been waiting for almost a half hour." She looked at Dani, gave her an annoyed head to toe, and flipped back around. "I'll let him know you'll be right with him," she announced to Travis over her shoulder as she bounced back into the building.

Watching Sarah in that moment, Dani realized that Travis was right. Long gone was that innocent little girl who walked into *The Journal* nearly three years ago, fresh out of college, with nothing but a degree and dreams of taking the world by storm. Though barely in her mid-twenties, Dani suddenly became acutely aware that the cards life had dealt her over the past six months had come hurling in like a hurricane. And in the aftermath, with nothing left standing, maybe, just maybe, an entirely new, stronger, sturdier, better-able-to-withstand-the-elements person would arise.

-- -- -- -- --

Dani couldn't get Travis off her mind. For two weeks now, the two stole innocent, yet strangely intimate glances as they passed one another in the hall. They'd brush up against each other as they reviewed the following day's layout in the print room. His hand would graze hers as they both reached for the same coffee mug in the break room. Dani told herself that it was all just innocent flirtation. That nothing would come of it. The day after the "parking lot incident," as she privately referred to it in her mind, an enormous bouquet of long stem pink roses adorned her desk when she returned from lunch. The card simply read, "I couldn't let all that beauty go to waste." She smiled to herself. While taking in the aroma of the freshly cut flowers, she and Travis shared a knowing glance as he strolled casually past her office door.

At three in the morning, the production unit of *The Journal* was bustling with activity. The Friday edition was hot off the press and being loaded into a myriad of delivery vehicles surrounded by the dull hum of engines warming and exhaust pipes spewing a mix of liquid air and carbon monoxide. For the production line, the day was half over as the results of their hard work throughout the night would be promptly delivered to driveways and mailboxes, and as dawn broke, the awaiting hands of curious Glenbrook residents.

For Dani, her workday was coming to a close. Since her parent's death, Dani had made a habit of coming in to the office after or before business hours. At first, she was simply trying to avoid the sympathetic, awkward encounters with her coworkers—*How are you adjusting, Dani? Is there anything I can do for you? You should take some time off…go on a vacation.* All were well-meaning attempts to encourage and comfort, but Dani felt as though their efforts to help were more of an intrusion, impeding her ability to process the roller-coaster of emotions she was feeling. She knew she should be grateful for their support, but instead, their futile efforts irritated her.

As the months passed, though, Dani had come to realize that death impacts people in strangely profound ways— that everyone reacts and copes differently. Some try to avoid the subject altogether; others seem to want to talk about it incessantly, still others say nothing, yet their eyes speak volumes. Though Dani finally comprehended that her colleagues truly did care for her well-being, she had come to cherish the quiet late-night or early-morning hours and became accustomed to the silent solitude of working alone. At least, that was what she told herself. However, more than once, Dani had questioned her own motives.

While most of the writers and salespeople were settling in for their work day, Dani was just finishing hers. She did everything she could to avoid running in to Travis. Even their brief encounters sent Dani into a panic. What started out as a school-girl-like crush had grown into a full-blown infatuation. Day and night, he consumed her thoughts. She knew that her feelings were irrational, silly, wrong. She also knew that she couldn't allow herself to be alone with him. The temptation was too strong. The innocent flirtation in which she freely participated with him before her parent's death, had now become a dangerous game.

Every day she battled her conflicting desire to give in to Travis' advances and her own conscience. She had to constantly remind herself that he was a married man with two children. Travis had often told Dani how miserable he was. How, if it weren't for the children, he would be long gone. But then Dani would see them together. Candace would stop by to have lunch with him. Or she would bring the children in to show their daddy an art project they had made at school. They always seemed so happy. Then Dani would remind herself that things were rarely as they seemed—that clearly Travis' unhappiness was masked by a facade of normality and stability. It was all just for show. At least that was how Dani justified her unrelenting fantasies about a future with Travis.

He had promised her that he would leave his wife "in a heartbeat" if Dani would only agree to be with him. She imagined the two of them married, living in a home of their own. Working together, traveling together, dreaming together. Raising Mason together. They would have his children three days a week. On their weekends with his kids, they would take family trips. Maybe a weekend at the ocean, a road trip to the Redwoods—snowboarding in the winter, camping during the summer. She could cut back her hours at *The Journal* and focus on being a wife and mother.

Though she couldn't have children of her own, she would be a good stepmother. It all sounded perfect.

Though Dani had been avoiding Travis for months now, the constant e-mails and little notes he left on her desk continued to fuel her desires. But why was she avoiding him? After all, she'd always possessed an unremitting integrity and held herself to a high moral standard. She knew the difference between right and wrong and, no matter how difficult, she had usually chosen the *right* way of doing things. But she had to admit that lately, right and wrong had become less black and white. Still, what would be the harm in stopping by his office on her way out just to say good morning? He had been so consoling, so supportive during the weeks and months following her parents' death. She had needed his comfort, and he had been there for her. At the very least, she owed him her friendship.

As the usual hustle and bustle of the morning began to permeate the cubicles and private offices of the newly renovated brick building, the aroma of fresh brewed coffee pervaded the air. Dani leaned back in her cozy brown leather chair, rested her legs on the antique cherry wood desk, closed her eyes, and allowed the pungent fragrance to flood her nasal passages. "Mmm..." she murmured to herself. Coffee was one of those things that smelled much better than it actually tasted. As hard as she tried, even as a college student, she never acquired enough of a taste for coffee to jump on the venti-nonfat-no foam-four pumps chai latte bandwagon. Really, she could do with it or without it. But the scent was always so inviting. She sometimes wished she were a coffee drinker or, for that matter, a smoker or a wine connoisseur. Some source of tangible comfort that would allow her to escape life, if only for a fleeting moment.

Only recently had Dani come to understand the alcoholic's need for a drink, the addict's compulsion for another hit. Perhaps until her parents' death, life had been too easy for Dani. She always had her faith and family and friends to carry her through her struggles. *What struggles?*

She had to laugh as she pondered the ludicrousness of that thought. Why would she be addicted to alcohol or drugs or anything for that matter? Her life had been relatively uneventful, humdrum, worry-free for the most part. Until now, that is. If she hadn't known struggle before, the tragic events of the previous year had served as a rude awakening. "Now would be a good time to take up drinking," she jokingly announced to herself.

"Would that be Patron or caffeine?"

Startled, Dani nearly flipped over the back of her seat as she awkwardly struggled to lug her feet off the desk and onto the floor.

"Travis!" Dani shouted, startled to see him standing at her door. Dani wheeled her chair to the edge of her desk, brushed an invisible crumb from her starched pale blue blouse, and began pecking at her computer keyboard as if Travis had interrupted her work. Leaning back in her chair, she chuckled. "I guess you caught me daydreaming." She smiled coyly at him.

"So what's your pleasure, Patron or caffeine?" he asked again as if it were a serious question, entering her office and quietly closing the door behind him.

Dani instantly was aware that they were alone. She had drawn the blinds to the windows looking out into the main area of the complex so she wouldn't be disturbed by the maintenance workers in the early morning hours. No one could see in, and no one could see out. Her heart began to race. She silently admonished herself for allowing this man to evoke such emotion in her.

"I've never been a fan of either. But don't think the idea of polishing off an entire bottle of Pinot hasn't crossed my mind a time or two lately." Dani could feel herself beginning to blush. She began uncomfortably and needlessly rearranging an already organized desk. She was somehow simultaneously filled with anger and desire. Desire for this extraordinary man who stood only feet away from her, whose musky cologne beckoned her to him, yet anger for the battle he evoked between her heart and her mind.

"How 'bout we share that bottle of Pinot?" Travis began to move closer. "Why don't you let me take you to dinner tomorrow night—strictly as friends," he added. He perched himself on the edge of Dani's desk, one foot secure on the carpeted floor, the other dangling casually, grazing Dani's hand with each sway of his pant leg. His hands boyishly folded in his lap, the pout of his lips made him appear vulnerable.

When her half-angry gaze met his, their eyes held briefly. "I'm pretty sure your wife would have a problem with that," she said sarcastically. It struck her that although her reply was merely a statement of fact, something in her wanted it to be a question that required an answer. In a matter of seconds, her mind created a plethora of scenarios and rational responses: *"Well Dani, it's about time I told you, I've asked Candace for a divorce," "Oh she won't mind, we have an open marriage," "Candace is leaving me for another man, and she wants me to find someone new too," "Candace understands all you've been through and thinks that you need a shoulder to cry on."* Rational? What was she thinking?

"Candace and the kids are going to be on a four-day school field trip in San Francisco. She won't be back until Monday afternoon. Besides, we had the 'divorce' talk again. It looks like it's really going to happen this time," he said, as if he were genuinely saddened by, though resigned to the thought. It made Dani sad too. Not sad that he was getting divorced—obviously that's what needed to happen before Travis would be free to be with her—but sad that he was such a good husband and father and didn't deserve the hell Candace put him through. The affairs, her neglect of the children, which, according to Travis, teetered on abuse, and the way she spent his money. She didn't even have to work, yet she spent money like it grew on trees. And the worst part was that she put on such a great show for everyone. Every time she saw Travis and Candace together, Candace acted as though she adored Travis. Dani assumed that when she'd stop by *The Journal* to see Travis, it was because she'd simply wanted to say "hello" or catch a few rare moments to herself with him. But Travis had told Dani it was just so she could check up on him. She treated the kids like she was interested in their quirky little stories of playground adventures and the new friends they'd made. She acted as though she enjoyed taking them to the park or on picnics at the lake. But Travis had assured Dani it was all for show. Candace's down-to-earth casual dress was also just an act. Travis always said that Candace wanted people to think she was the faithful, submissive, "Joan Clever" kind of wife and mother.

Travis' vulnerability, combined with his need to confide in Dani over the past months, had, in some strange way, created an emotional connection between the two of them. The knowing glances they shared at the office. The "business" lunches that, to the outsider, looked more like intimate dates than two colleagues discussing their upcoming week's itinerary. The anonymous floral arrangements that now arrived on a weekly basis, with simple little endearments attached—"Just thinking about you," "Can't get you off my mind," "You have my heart." Simple perhaps, nonetheless, meaningful.

In an instant, Dani realized the relationship that had begun with Travis' innocent flirtations more than three years ago had evolved into a full-blown love affair of the heart. It hadn't been physical, but the intrinsic emotional tie that had formed between them was irrefutable. It was as though they shared a bond fostered through unimaginable tragedy. Though their respective tragedies, polar opposites on the surface—his of lost love and destroyed dreams, hers of lives vanished and faith abandoned—had become so much a part of who they were and who they had become as individuals; it seemed the heart rendering ties they shared had helped to forge an unbreakable union.

Dani was grateful for having had the rare opportunity of coming to know the real Travis Jakobs. She had grown to admire him for so many reasons. From having the strength to stay in a marriage that had dealt him some difficult blows that no man should have to endure, to helping Stan Montgomery build *The Journal* from the ground up. Travis was a good man. He was wise. He was compassionate. He was loyal. He was, Dani realized, everything she'd ever wanted.

Dani hadn't given him enough credit. She'd always believed the rumors about him; he was a womanizer, a player. That he was always having affairs on his wife. People were so gullible sometimes. Did they not listen? How many times had Travis repeated his personalized mantra? "As reporters, we must always remember that nothing is as it appears. We must always dig deeper to get to the truth." Unfortunately, a lot of people around the office put that mantra to practice only when it came to their reporting, but failed to use the same discretion when it came to forming unsavory opinions about their colleagues. If they only knew! It made Dani so angry to think about what Candace was doing to Travis and to his reputation.

"Dani...are you hearing a word I'm saying?" Travis prodded, intrigued by the curious look in Dani's expression.

When Dani looked back up at Travis, her eyes were filled with compassion, not anger. If anyone knew Travis like Dani had come to know him, they would see that he was anything but the man he'd been made out to be. He was loving, gentle, and loyal. It was his loyalty to his family and his insistence that he would not let his wife's behavior turn into a witch hunt and cause the kids more shame and embarrassment. He risked his own reputation to protect the integrity of his family and even a wife who had treated him so badly. What kind of man does that?

Dani gently cupped her hand over Travis' as she bashfully raised her gaze to meet his. She was awestruck as tears rested on the brim of his blameless eyes. "I'm so sorry for what you're going through." Dani's voice was soothing. "I've been so caught up in my life and my own problems that I wasn't even thinking about how your marriage has been draining you emotionally. I'm sorry I haven't been here for you."

Travis tenderly raised Dani's hands to his lips. He softly kissed the palm of one hand, then the other.

"Dani, my problems are nothing compared to what you've been dealing with." He shook his head as if in disbelief. "Losing your folks in such a horrible way. Your aunt. Then the whole thing with Mason. Not many people could have handled it as well as you have." As usual, whenever someone brought up "the tragedy," Dani felt a knot in her stomach.

"That's one of the things I admire about you the most, Dani, that you're so strong…and independent." Travis forced Dani's chair away from the edge of her desk. He scooted over, positioning himself directly in front of her. He reached down to pull the chair back toward him. His legs straddled hers as Dani demurely reached up and placed her hands on Travis' outer thighs, but she couldn't bring herself to look back into his seductive eyes.

Travis reached down, traced the jawline of Dani's face with the top side of his forefinger, trailing down, eventually cupping her chin in his hand. Tilting her head up to meet his gaze, Travis leaned forward, close enough to taste Dani's sweet breath, though their lips had not yet touched.

Dani's chest rose and fell in unison with Travis', racing at a feverish pace. It was a rapid, silent rhythm that left Dani's head spinning and her knees weak. Dani closed her eyes and inhaled deeply, not only to take in the delicious musky fragrance of Travis' cologne mixed with his natural body aroma, but in anticipation of the inevitable kiss to come.

Eyes still closed, Dani felt Travis' lips graze the sensitive space behind her ear. He used his teeth to lightly nibble the soft, moist skin. Travis brought his other hand to Dani's face, gently sliding both hands around the back of her neck, audaciously entwining his fingers in her long, flowing hair.

Dani could not have resisted even if she had wanted to. Travis brazenly lifted her to her feet, wrenched her tightly against his body and engulfed her mouth with his. Dani's mind wanted to refuse, but her body defied her. She melted in his arms. She returned Travis' consuming kiss with a fervor she didn't know existed within her.

Then, as abruptly as he had consumed her mouth, Travis pried his lips away from hers. Breathing as though he'd just run a marathon, not saying a word, Travis' desire-filled stare penetrated Dani's emerald eyes. He kissed her again. This time, his caresses were gentle and lingering. His supple lips gently trailed over her forehead, the arch above her nose, one cheek, then the other. Every touch sent a chill up Dani's spine. His mouth moved to Dani's neck engulfing every inch of her smooth, fragrant skin. When their lips finally met again, his kiss was warm and inviting, not demanding like the first had been. The first passionate kiss made Dani feel wanted, desired. These gentle caresses made her feel cherished, protected.

Pulling Dani closer, Travis caressed Dani's silky hair as he cradled her to his chest. "Oh, Dani." He kissed the top of her head the same way a father might comfort a hurting child. Dani drew her body even closer. She sighed in the comfort of Travis' arms. "Dani," he continued. "Do you have any idea what you mean to me? You may not believe this, but I think I've loved you since the first moment I met you."

Dani's heart began to race again. Though not from desire this time, rather, from an overwhelming excitement at the words she was hearing. *I've loved you since the first moment I met you.* Why hadn't he told her before now? She'd always thought his attention was merely innocent flirtation. His advances often teetered on the proverbial line, which a married man should not cross, but he always seemed to maintain his integrity— more than most men in a miserable marriage with a cheating, conniving wife would do. In that moment, Dani's admiration for this forgiving, patient man intensified.

Suddenly, Dani felt a sense of panic overwhelm her. Should she tell Travis she loved him too? Did she love him? Were her feelings for him *love*, or merely infatuation? She'd never told a man that she loved him. Her father, yes—her pastor, her friends toward whom she felt affection maybe, but not a man that was expressing his love for her in a romantic way.

Pulling away from his embrace, "I…Travis, I…"

"I know, Dani, you don't know what to say." Travis loosened his hold on her. "You don't have to say anything," he continued. "Believe me, I didn't expect to blurt it out right now…right here." He lowered his face as if ashamed. "I wanted to tell you when the time was right. When my divorce was final. When I was free to love you without betraying Candace, and the kids for that matter."

"I'm so sorry, Dani," he said, shaking his head. "Holding you…kissing you like this…I guess I just got caught up in the moment." Travis continued babbling like a nervous school boy.

"It's just that whenever I see you, it's almost impossible not to sweep you up into my arms and tell you how special you are to me...how much I love you." When his eyes met hers again, a tear gently rolled down Travis' cheek. Dani tenderly wiped it away.

"Don't apologize, Travis. I'm glad you told me how you really feel. I should be the one who's sorry."

"You? Why should *you* be sorry?" Travis was puzzled at her admission.

It was Dani's turn to feel ashamed. "I've been unfair to you, Travis. I've judged you and formed opinions of you based only on rumors. I've been so stupid. I guess I never realized that you were covering for her." Dani could feel the anger build at the mere thought of Candace. "She doesn't deserve you, Travis. You've done nothing but honor your marriage and your commitment to your family."

Travis held her close again for what seemed like an eternity. Then, with a renewed eagerness, Travis' question sounded more like an order. "Have dinner with me. We'll go someplace where no one knows who we are. We'll drive to Sacramento...or over to Reno, find a quaint, romantic restaurant, and just be together." His voice was supplicating,

"Please, Dani. I just want to be alone with you."

Dani's mind was full of jumbled thoughts, her heart— contradicting emotions. Travis could see a mix of uncertainty and compassion in her eyes.

"Just as friends, Dani," he reassured her. "Nothing more. I know it can't be anything more than that until my divorce is final." Travis seemed to be able to read her mind.

"I wish I could, Travis." She smiled up at him. The rugged features of his face were strangely at odds with the vulnerability in his eyes. "Thank you for understanding."

Travis and Dani had once talked about the moral boundaries she had set for herself. He knew she was committed to remain abstinent until she was married. Dani was very clear about her values and commitment to those values. Sometimes, though, she wondered if it was that very challenge that drew Travis to her; as though he thought he could break her. But tonight, Travis had proved her wrong. She could hear the sincerity in his voice when he spoke to her, see the honesty in his eyes. How could she have been so wrong about him?

"I *do* understand how you feel, but please, Dani. I don't think I can bear to be alone this weekend. The house is so empty. So quiet." Dani could tell that Travis was beginning to crack. "I won't cross any lines you don't want me to cross. I promise," he pleaded.

Dani felt sorry for him. He was so vulnerable, almost desperate. "Travis, you know I want to," she hesitated before continuing. "But you and I both know I can't. It wouldn't be right—even only as friends."

"I know," he said, sounding more like a disappointed ten-year-old than a grown man. Dani and Travis stood embracing one another followed by an awkward moment as they heard a knock on her office door.

Startled, they reluctantly parted. Travis hurried around to the opposite side of Dani's desk, while Dani forced herself to look busy at her computer. "Come in," she announced nervously.

"Oh, hey, Travis." It was Jason from production.

"Hey, Jason," Travis responded nonchalantly, as though he had just finished talking to Dani about the news lineup for the next week.

"Dani, you don't happen to have your piece on that new steakhouse done, do ya'?" Jason asked, forgetting that Travis was even in the room.

"Yep. Just finished it this morning. Do you need it already?"

"If you don't mind," he said, peering over her shoulder at the computer monitor. "I'm having space problems with tomorrow's issue. Rich thinks he's the only writer at this damn paper. God forbid he give up a few lines so the rest of you can have something that's not chopped down to nothing!" Jason sounded disgusted. "He's only in it for the 'By Lines'. He'll be out of here as soon as he gets a better offer."

As usual, Travis came to the rescue. "I'll talk to him, Jas. Don't stress."

"Good luck with that!" Jason could not hide his sarcasm.

"I'll email my column to you right now," Dani said as she clicked the *send* tab, still flushed from her encounter with Travis.

Having accomplished what he'd set out to do, Jason bolted out the door, his voice trailing as it closed behind him, "Thanks, Dan…you da man!"

Straightening his tie, Travis walked behind Dani and firmly massaged her shoulders. "Just think about it, Dani. I sure could use some company."

His hands felt so good. "Mmm…," she moaned, resting her chin to her chest. "You're awfully hard to resist."

"Good," he said before leaning down to kiss the back of her neck.

"You know how to reach me, Dani," Travis announced as he turned to leave.

"I'll see you on Monday!" Dani said, acting as though she was exasperated. She was anything but.

CHAPTER SIX

Dani tossed and turned throughout the night. She could not get Travis off her mind. Though she knew she had made the right decision in telling him she could not be with him until he was legally divorced from Candace, she wanted so much to be in his arms right now. She didn't want to wait the six months it would take to complete the divorce proceedings. At that moment, even six hours felt like a lifetime to Dani.

She began to make up excuses in her mind, trying to find something, anything that would justify her seeing him over the weekend. What harm would it do if they spent some innocent time together? After all, they had had countless lunches together brainstorming ideas for the column or talking over new and innovative ideas for the direction of *The Journal*. It was all purely platonic. Maybe if they just went to lunch, then it would feel less like a date and more like a business meeting between colleagues…only without the rest of the colleagues, she reasoned.

Travis had been there for her whenever she needed a shoulder to cry on over the past year. Always respecting her boundaries, even encouraging her. Though she hadn't realized it at the time, thinking he had his own agenda, he had been a good and loyal friend to her. *How could she have been so fooled by rumors and gossip?* She was still beating herself up over it.

Just after midnight, Dani was still wide awake. A half-gallon of cookie dough ice cream was screaming at her from the freezer. More worry-free than she had felt in months, Dani almost skipped as she headed for the kitchen. Ice cream in one hand and spoon in the other, Dani propped herself up on the granite counter. But before the first bite could reach her mouth, Dani nearly fell off the counter startled by the chirping of her cell phone. Sliding the rest of the way off the counter until her feet reached the coolness of the hardwood floor, Dani didn't stop to pick up the container of ice cream that went barreling to the floor in her haste to reach the phone. Looking as though it had been staged, chunks of ice cream splattered the kitchen; all over the walls, the floor, the refrigerator, even landing in Dani's hair.

Finally reaching the desk where she'd left her purse, Dani rummaged past her wallet and sunglasses and all the useless paraphernalia that only delayed her ability to retrieve her phone. "There it is," she exclaimed aloud. Not even stopping to see if she recognized the incoming call, "Hello," she answered, out of breath.

She silently prayed, *Please, God, don't let it be Mason.* In the span of less than twenty seconds, Dani's mind had created a dozen possible scenarios of what could have happened to Mason. David and Tracie had taken all the kids away for the weekend. They were spending two days at Discovery Kingdom in Vallejo. Had Mason had an asthma attack? Had he forgotten his inhaler? How many times had she told him to never leave home without it? Dani was panicked.

"Were you sleeping?" The voice was calm, soothing, almost seductive.

"Wha…who…Travis?"

"I'm sorry to call so late, Dani. I can't stop thinking about you." He sounded sad. "I had to hear your voice."

"Travis. You scared me to death. I thought something had happened to Mason."

"I'm sorry. I didn't mean to scare you."

Dani's heart broke for him. "Don't be sorry, Travis. It's just not very often that I get a call in the middle of the night." She licked a splatter of ice cream that had landed on the corner of her mouth.

Walking back in to the kitchen, Dani slipped on the ice cream that was beginning to melt into the cracks of the wood floor planks. "Whoa…," she shrieked, grabbing on to the counter to stop her fall.

"What's going on there? Are ya' having a party?" Travis sounded amused.

"Hardly." She wiped the ice cream out of her hair with a wet wash rag. "I couldn't sleep either. You called just as I was ready to dive head first into a tub of cookie dough ice cream."

"Ooh…my favorite. Do you have enough to share?"

"Yeah, well there's plenty, but you'd be eating it off the floor"

"That sounds kinky." He laughed.

"No, just sticky." She began cleaning the melting mess off the floor and walls. "It startled me so much when the phone rang that I dropped the whole container! It's all over the kitchen…and me."

"I'd be glad to come over and clean you up." Dani blushed at Travis' directness.

"I think I can manage on my own, thanks."

"So, why couldn't you sleep? Thinking about me?" he said teasingly, yet presumptuously.

Dani was ashamed to admit he was right, but knowing her lie would be unconvincing, "Maybe," she said.

"Me too," he said. He sounded pathetic, desperate. He sounded like she felt.

"*You too* what?" she asked, already knowing the answer.

"I was thinking about you, too," he said in an almost pleading tone. "In fact, I can't stop. You just make me so happy. The way you talk. Your smile. The way you *really* listen to me," he paused. "Candace never listens to me. She really never has. She's always been so self-centered. She acts like she's listening, but she never really hears me. You really listen, Dani. I know I can talk to you about anything."

"You're my friend, Travis. That's what friends do," she said with the kind of sensitivity one would use when counseling a child.

"We're more than that, Dani. And you know it. You can't deny that we're both attracted to each other," he said persuasively.

"I already told you, we can only be friends for now, Travis," she said unconvincingly. "When your divorce is final, we can be together without feeling guilty or as though we're doing something wrong."

"But I'm as good as divorced already. When Candace gets back from the Bay Area, I'm moving out," he argued.

"I know, Travis, but it wouldn't feel right. If we're meant to be together, six months isn't going to change anything," she said absently, wiping up the last remnants of ice cream from the refrigerator door.

"How 'bout this, as soon as the papers are officially filed, we'll start out slow—coffee, or a picnic lunch? Something simple and platonic."

"Travis, I want to be with you too. But we can't. You're an honorable man, please respect my boundaries."

"I do, Dani, I respect you and everything about you," he said. "It's just so difficult not being able to be with you. Seeing you at work just isn't enough for me."

"It's going to have to be for now, Travis," she maintained. "Let's just take things day by day."

"I know you're right, Dani," he moaned. "I'm sorry. I don't want you to compromise your values."

At her end of the phone, Dani smiled. "Thank you for being patient with me, Travis."

"I should let you get back to bed." Travis imagined Dani wearing a short little chenille robe with dried ice cream on her forehead. "Or back to your ice cream," he taunted.

"Okay, smart-aleck, leave me alone!" she said teasingly. Dani was surprised at her own audaciousness. She was comforted by their ability to be at such ease with each other. They just clicked.

"You make me so happy," Travis blurted. "I meant it when I said I love you."

Dani was dumbfounded. "I believe you, Travis. But I don't know what to say."

"Don't say anything. Just know that I love you," he said. "And Dani…"

"Yes?" she asked hesitantly.

"If you change your mind, I'll be home all weekend," he said beseechingly. "You know how to reach me." But they both knew she wouldn't.

Still taken aback by Travis' declaration of love, Dani exclaimed, "I know, but my mind is not going to change, Travis." Though even as she said them, she didn't believe her own words. "Good night, Travis."

"Sweet dreams, Dani."

For a moment, neither of them spoke or breathed. Finally, Dani heard a click, then a dial tone at the other end of the phone.

"Sweet dreams," she said in barely a whisper.

-- -- -- -- --

As she lay awake, restless and confused, the glow of the full moon infiltrated the pale beige sheer curtains that draped her bedroom window. Dani spent the night tossing and turning…1:37…2:24…3:06. Sleep would not come. She tossed and turned until the morning sun replaced the piercing moonlight.

Mason is with David and Tracie and the kids this weekend, she reasoned with herself. I don't have any plans that can't be changed. What would it hurt to grab a burger and fries with him. Maybe go for a drive up to Crystal Peak. Channel 13 News had forecast a beautiful warm sunny day. A hike would do them both good. Travis desperately needed a friend right now. Dani wanted to be there for him just as he had been there for her.

"That's it!" she exclaimed aloud, throwing the covers off her already disheveled bed. "I'm going over there."

Dani decided to surprise Travis. She dressed in a pair of slightly form-fitting faded jeans. They flattered her shapely, but slim figure. The emerald-colored long-sleeved T-shirt complimented her already stunning eyes and accentuated her tiny waist. The casual attire was finished off with a pair of worn leather flip-flops. Dani pulled her hair back in an untidy ponytail, leaving long straggling pieces flowing down her back and framing her face, resulting in a contradicting outward appearance of innocence and sensuality. Dani admired herself in front of the mirror for only a moment.

It was 10:00 a.m. before Dani finished packing a picnic lunch of egg salad sandwiches—Travis' favorite—orange slices, a bag of sun dried tomato crisps, and two water bottles. She threw her hiking boots and an extra sweatshirt in an Eddie Bauer backpack then bolted out the door with the enthusiasm of a child, slamming it behind her.

The fifteen-minute drive up Highway 20 to Travis' house seemed to take forever. She couldn't wait to see him and spend a carefree day talking and laughing and enjoying the beautiful weather. She would make certain that neither of them crossed any lines—just a day of innocent fun. The closer she got, the faster her heart raced.

As her Jeep inched its way down the gravel road that lead to the driveway entrance, Dani paused for a moment to collect her thoughts and emotions. The black marbled granite pillars and wrought iron arch announced the entrance to what could only be described as a storybook manor. Though the home was built less than two years ago, the plush ivy trailing over the rock wall encompassing the delicately landscaped property suggested decades of growth and maturity.

As ludicrous as it sounded, even to Dani's own mind, she could picture herself kneeling among the myriad of flower gardens sprawled over the rolling hills of the park-like domain, planting perennials, positioning them just so to form a perfectly perpendicular design. She envisioned herself in the kitchen cooking dinner for Travis and the kids. Helping Ben with his homework and teaching Kara to tie her shoes, going on adventures with Travis and the kids, discovering new things—all the things a mother—Candace—should have done with her children, but never had. She'd only acted as though she was interested and involved in her children's lives. *Those poor kids*, Dani thought. They deserved so much more than that. Dani couldn't imagine a better father for the kids than Travis, but children need a mother too. Dani looked forward to the opportunity to at least try to be the mother that Candace never was. Of course, she could never take Candace's place as their mother, but she would do her best to give them the life they deserved.

Dani wasn't sure how long she'd been idling at the entrance of the driveway lost in thought when she finally mustered the nerve to drive the final distance of the narrow drive and park under the beautifully columned stylish breezeway. Her heart was pounding again.

Dani stepped out of her Jeep and smoothed the loose tendrils of hair back behind her ears. Not certain whether they would drive her Jeep or Travis' Hummer up to Crystal Peak, Dani decided to bring the insulated picnic bag containing the sandwiches, snacks, and drinks, as well as her backpack into the house. She hurled the Eddie Bauer bag over one shoulder and heaved the lunch bag over the other. Dani wasn't certain if Travis had heard her drive up to the house, but he hadn't come to the door yet.

Dani looked upward at the humongous home. With its half-circle entrance stairs spanning nearly the length of the structure and the marbled beveled pillars, it looked more like the White House than a small-town upper class single family home. Admiring its beauty for only a brief moment, Dani took a deep breath then mustered up the nerve to walk the length of the stairs and approach the brightly stained glass double entry doors.

She knocked, softly at first. When there was no answer, she knocked harder. Should she ring the doorbell? It seemed so formal—as if ringing the bell would elicit a butler, following a formal announcement, *Ah, yes, Mr. Jakobs will see you now.* Knocking was much more intimate. After the third knock and still no answer, Dani finally determined that the doorbell would have to do. After all, it was a large home. If Travis was upstairs or at the back end of the house, he might not hear her knocking.

She pushed the glowing button lightly, as if the result would be a quiet ringing. Instead, even from outside, Dani could hear the ring echo throughout the house. It immediately startled her. Her nerves were already on edge, and the sound pierced her like a knife.

Anxiously waiting for Travis to open the door, Dani heard the faint sound of splashing water coming from around the side of the house. *He must be out back at the pool. He does swim laps every morning.* Setting her bags down on the threshold, Dani headed toward the west side of the house. She was slightly embarrassed, though admittedly enticed at the thought of surprising Travis with nothing on but his swim shorts. She pictured his brown muscular chest and imagined his long, encompassing arms wrapped around her tiny frame, holding her; protecting her.

Nearing the back of the colonial-style house, Dani thought she heard more than splashing water. Was it voices? Suddenly, Dani stopped. Had Candace returned home early? Could it be a colleague? She couldn't let anyone see her at Travis' house. People might get the wrong idea. It would only fuel the gossip about Travis and make Dani look like some kind of home-wrecker. The noise could be the radio, though.

Dani decided to round the corner to the backyard quietly, unnoticed—just in case someone else was with Travis. She didn't want to be seen. She felt a bit like a stalker, but she couldn't risk being spotted. For a brief instant, Dani couldn't help but think how ludicrous this was. Showing up unannounced, fantasizing about a relationship that was, at best far-fetched, sneaking around like a prowler—what was she thinking? Even with those thoughts, the spontaneity of it all excited her. She'd never done anything like this in her life.

Continuing her way to the corner of the house, Dani could hear the vivid sound of music. The reverberation confirmed that it was merely the radio she'd heard, putting her at ease. Nervously, she tidied her hair again, less out of concern for its disarray, more out of anxiety for the impending moment.

Confidently, Dani stepped over the patch of Vinca, which in its invasiveness had overtaken much of the cascading walkway, and headed around the bend leading toward the backyard.

As she rounded the curve, Dani stopped dead in her tracks. Travis was there, but he wasn't alone. The color drained from Dani's face as a combination of shame and humiliation overcame her. Sarah James was there too. Travis' intern at *The Journal*, Sarah was a high school senior who had been working at *The Journal* for less than a year.

Travis stood in the shallow end of the pool, balancing Sarah as she lay with her back resting in Travis' arms as though he were giving her an informal swimming lesson. Sarah giggled coyly as Travis pretended to throw her into the air. The two embraced and began kissing passionately.

To her right, Dani noticed a patio table covered with clutter. Pale pink roses stemming from a clear crystal vase, empty champagne glasses, a pitcher of orange juice, and plates with strawberries and half-eaten waffles were strewn over the table.

Dani felt sick. Had Sarah come over this morning? Or had Travis called her last night after Dani had refused to come? Was Dani merely one of a long line of potential candidates on Travis' "to-do" list? How could she have been so stupid? How could she have let herself fall for him? He told her he loved her! She had been enamored with him! During the sleepless hours of the previous night, she had even allowed herself to believe she was falling in love with him!

As a myriad of thoughts and emotions invaded her, it all of the sudden occurred to Dani that she had thus far gone unnoticed. She was already humiliated enough, the last thing she wanted was to be seen by Travis or Sarah. Slowly, quietly, she back-stepped, not taking her eyes off the embarrassing display of affection that was taking place in the pool. Nearing the corner of the house, Dani turned and started back toward the front yard. She wasn't sure if her legs would collapse from the heaviness she felt. Her heart was racing again, this time though, it wasn't from excitement and anticipation, but rather, from shock.

By the time she reached her Jeep, Dani was having an anxiety attack. She began to panic, feeling as though she could not get breath into her lungs. *Focus…slow, deep breaths…focus…*Dani had only two anxiety attacks in her life; both were during life-altering experiences. The first was when she learned of her parents' death and the second, when her attorney told her that Mason's father wanted custody. Though this didn't compare to either of the previous situations, it was certainly life changing.

She closed her eyes and concentrated on her breathing. Dani was feeling flushed, but her breathing gradually slowed. As her lungs cleared, so did her mind. *I've got to get out of here*, she thought, fumbling for her keys that she'd left lying on the passenger seat. She barely managed to fit the key into the ignition. She had to steady her right hand with her left to finally get the vehicle started. Giving it more gas than she expected, she sped off, leaving skid marks on the pavers under the breezeway. She hurled down the driveway, wanting to get as far away as she could.

Tears streaming down her face, Dani drove like a maniac, taking the twists and turns of the highway dangerously fast. She didn't care. At that moment, she didn't care about anything. *How could I have been so stupid!* She slammed her fist on the steering wheel. The clear, sunny morning had turned to overcast, yet there wasn't a cloud in the sky.

"I can't do this anymore!" Dani screamed, to no one, to the whole world, to God. But only One of them heard her cry. She swerved around a sharp curve, tires screeching beneath her. Traveling southwest on the two-lane highway, Dani's Jeep drifted off the left side of the road, causing her to lose control. Dani overcorrected, sending the vehicle tumbling down a steep embankment.

Dani had heard accident victims describe their ordeal as though it happened in slow motion, in their mind's eye seeing the faces of family and friends, memories flash before them, and contemplations of a life lived, good and bad. Only now could she empathize with their tragic experiences. Randy… Britta… Mason… David… Tracie… Amanda… Travis. There were others, so many others.

Randy on a playground, Dani's pink and lavender calico dress blowing in the breeze as her daddy pushed her toward a cloudless oblivion until her tiny toes nearly reached the sky, *"Higher, daddy, higher!"*

Britta in the kitchen, pasta cooking on the stove, sauce simmering. A thousand Sunday "spaghetti" nights flashed before Dani's eyes. *"Who wants to say grace?"* Britta's voice familiar, welcoming.

"I love you to heaven and back." Over and over, Mason's words echoed in her mind. His dimples. His laughter. His cry.

"It's out of our hands, Dani. God's in control." David's voice reverberating in her ears.

"You're like the sister I never had." Tracie's tone calm, loving.

"I'll get the help I need this time. I won't run from the program. I promise." Amanda's desperate, futile pledges.

"I think I'm falling in love with you, Dani." Travis' empty, intangible assurances.

She saw them all—heard them all, as if for the first time, or perhaps the last.

As the Jeep came to a crashing halt teetering precariously against a billowing pine tree, raining debris momentarily turned the day into night. The warmth of her own blood trailing from her forehead blinded Dani's eyes.

The last image Dani saw was the silhouette of a man. Behind him was a penetrating glow. The dark, faceless figure turned away from Dani and began walking toward the light. Then the man stopped, stood in silence for only a moment staring straight into the radiant brightness, and turned back toward Dani. His masculine figure was illuminated in the glow that now shown behind him. Dani could see herself, as if in a dream, standing at the end of a long corridor wearing the same pink and lavender calico dress she had worn as a child while her father pushed her higher and higher on the park swing. Dani watched herself raise one arm to her brow, as if shading her eyes from the intense light and trying to make out the person in front of the illumination. But all she could see was a faceless being, somehow familiar, yet unrecognizable. The figure lifted his arms as if beckoning her to him. Dani didn't hesitate. She took one weightless step forward, then another, and another.

CHAPTER SEVEN

When Dani came to, the room seemed to dance around her as she tried to bring her vision into focus. The bright overhead lights, beeping monitors, and distant muffled voices were all foreign to Dani. She was clearly in some type of medical facility. *Probably a hospital*, she thought. *But why?* Her head was throbbing. As the room began to spin faster and faster, Dani felt like she was going to vomit. She squeezed her eyes closed trying to ward off the bile that was threatening to erupt from her stomach.

She rolled to her side willing the nausea to subside. When it finally did, Dani moaned in agony as the memories of the accident and the events that led up to it began to flood her mind—Travis' big, beautiful home; the picnic basket; the swimming pool; the champagne; Sarah in Travis' arms. The thoughts caused Dani to wince more out of humiliation than pain. Then she remembered her frantic getaway. She'd sped down the long driveway and onto the highway paying no attention to anyone or anything around her. She remembered the curves of the road and the shadow of the trees. She remembered the sound of the tires screeching. She remembered the tumbling…over and over and over.

She remembered her body thrashing from one side of the Jeep to the other. She remembered a loud, crashing thud. She remembered the blinding blood pouring from her head. She remembered the silence. She remembered the faces, the voices, the light, then the darkness.

As she began putting it all together in her mind, Dani felt a gentle hand caress her forehead. She turned her head, and for a brief instant, expected to see her mother's loving face, hear her soothing voice. Instead, Dani saw Tracie. The two women locked eyes for a moment. Tracie was the first to speak. "Dani, we've been so worried about you." She leaned forward to give Dani a careful but warm embrace. As the two women hugged, it occurred to Dani that she had no one left. No mother to care for her when she is sick, no daddy to visit her at the hospital, no children to come home to. David and Tracie had become her new family—Uncle Buck, Samuel, and Kylie. Dani embraced Tracie even harder as she thought about the love Tracie and David had shown her. She was momentarily ashamed for the way she had tried to push them away. She was grateful that they had not let her. They'd been determined to help make life as normal as possible for Dani and Mason. Tracie was only nine years older than Dani, but she had become like a mother to her. No, Dani thought, she had become more than that. Tracie was her best friend, the sister she never had, her mother and confidant all wrapped up in one. Then there was David. Dani had grown to trust him completely. He had become her mentor, her advisor, her brother. Strangely, though, Dani had not felt a fatherly connection with him. Nonetheless, she had grown to love them all. How could she have ever questioned their love for her. Her heart ached.

Maybe it was the physical trauma her body had undergone, or perhaps it was simply the strain of all she had been through in such a short period of time, but Dani could not contain her emotions. As she and Tracie clung to one another, Dani began sobbing uncontrollably. Tracie didn't ask any questions, she simply held Dani until her cries subsided.

When the women finally loosened their embrace, Tracie asked with genuine concern, "How do you feel?"

The throbbing in Dani's head had become slightly more tolerable. "I feel okay, except for a terrible headache."

"Do you remember what happened?" Tracie asked.

"Some of it," Dani said. "I think I was unconscious part of the time."

"You were. Apparently, when the paramedics arrived, you were out cold. But as soon as they wheeled you into the ambulance, you started to come to," Tracie offered. "They said you were in and out of consciousness for the first hour."

Dani was remembering bits and pieces of the traumatic experience; the sirens, the voices, the oxygen mask covering her face.

"You're fine, Dani," Tracie assured her. "They're going to keep you for a couple nights because they think you have a slight concussion. As soon as you arrived in the emergency room, the doctors conducted a thorough cerebral evaluation. You have some cuts and bruises, but otherwise, you're all right."

Dani wasn't worried. Though her body ached and her head pounded, she instinctively knew there was nothing seriously wrong.

"God was protecting you, Dani. You shouldn't have walked away from that accident," Tracie's voice cracked as she said it. "A witness said your Jeep rolled over five or six times. It's completely totaled."

Horrified at the possibility, Dani asked, "Was anyone else hurt?"

"No. It looks like you took a corner too fast and lost control," Tracie said. "Don't you remember"?

"Like I said, I remember pieces of it," Dani said. "It's all a little blurry."

"Where were you coming from Dani…before the accident I mean?"

Dani cringed as she thought about the humiliation of seeing Travis with Sarah. "It's a long story," she said. "I'm not sure I want to talk about it." Then, remembering the picnic basket she'd left on Travis' front porch, Dani panicked. As Tracie searched Dani's face, she could see a look of terror.

"What, Dani? What is it?" Tracie was apprehensive as she watched Dani's complexion turn to a pale shade of ivory.

"I'm so embarrassed," Dani admitted. "And so ashamed," she said dejectedly.

Over the next half hour, Dani told Tracie the whole story, from the innocent flirtations to the scene at Travis' house. Somehow, she knew Tracie would not judge her. And she was right. Tracie listened to Dani with compassion.

When Dani was finally finished telling Tracie all that had led up to the accident, she said, "The thing is, no one would even know about it, except that I left the picnic basket setting on Travis' front porch." She looked disparaged. "He had to have found it."

"Well," Tracie said, feeling protective of Dani, full of anger for Travis, "if Travis Jakobs has any decency in him at all, he'll use a little discretion and keep it to himself!" Tracie's voice softened, "Besides that, Dani, it really doesn't matter who knows what. What matters is that you're all right," she said supportively.

"It's just so humiliating." Dani hid her face in her hands. "I was so stupid."

"You weren't stupid, Dani. You were vulnerable. He took advantage of that." Sensing Dani's need to absorb all that she had already known in her own mind, but had verbalized aloud for the first time, Tracie allowed Dani her privacy.

"Oh," Tracie jumped up, "I better call David and the kids. They've all been so worried about you." She smiled. "Mason and Sam painted you pictures and can't wait to give them to you."

Heading for the door, Tracie shouted over her shoulder, "I'll be right back. I need to call and let them know you're awake." Tracie's voice faded as she scurried off. "They'll be so excited to see you."

As Dani sat in silence, she realized she had half expected Tracie to pull a verse out of the Bible, reminding her that it was Dani's lack of faith and failure to seek God's direction that had led her down the terrible path she had chosen with Travis. But Tracie hadn't done that—that wasn't her way. Tracie never judged. She never put herself above anyone. She was wise, offering Godly advice when Dani needed it, but humble, inherently knowing when words were not needed.

Dani knew how she had wound up in that hospital bed. She had tried to take control of her own life, when all along, she knew she had to trust in God and in His plans. She had grown so far from Him since her parents' death. She was angry at Him. She felt as though He was punishing her. She had questioned Him over and over, "What have I done to deserve all of this pain?" She had screamed to God more times than she could remember. But even in her pain, Dani knew that God had not abandoned *her*, rather, *she* had abandoned God.

At that very moment, Dani recommitted herself to God.

Today was the start of a whole new life.

-- -- -- -- --

The following week, with her head held high, Dani marched into Travis Jakobs' office.

Startled, Travis bolted from his black leather swivel chair. "Dani," he said, half surprise, half trepidation masking his face, "you're back."

Awkwardly making his way to Dani from behind his desk, he leaned forward offering her a welcoming peck on the cheek.

Dani recoiled as he moved closer. She turned her face to one side and put her hand to his chest preventing Travis from following through with his intentions.

Heeding Dani's implied warning, Travis nervously confessed, "I'm glad you're alright, Dani. I was so worr.."

But before Travis could finish his sentence, Dani interrupted, "You were worried about what, Travis? That your wife might discover what you've been up to? That Sarah might find out what a slug you are?" She paused, making a conscious effort to avoid letting her emotions get the best of her. She didn't want Travis to know just how much he had hurt her.

As if he was an eight-year-old schoolboy who just got caught cheating on his math exam, Travis lowered his head and looked down at the floor. With his hands in his pockets, he rocked back and forth from his heels to the ball of his feet, "I'm sorry, Dani," he confessed. "I am so in love with you. And when you turned me down that night, I was just so lonely."

Travis' seemingly innocent manipulation may have worked on Dani before, but never again. "Stop, Travis!" she demanded. "No more of your lies. No more of your self-pity. In fact, no more of any of this!"

Now perched on the edge of his desk, Travis looked as though he was going to laugh. His arrogant demeanor infuriated Dani even more.

"What's that supposed to mean, Dani?" Flinging his arms around as if mimicking Dani, he sarcastically repeated what Dani had said, "No more of any of this? No more of what?"

"It means, Travis," Dani said confidently, "I quit!"

"You quit? You can't quit," Travis argued. "What will you do for work? It takes a lot more than three years as a *food critic* to make it as a writer. You have no real experience, Dani. Be serious."

"I couldn't be more serious, Travis," Dani said without hesitation.

"C'mon, Dani, you know you don't really want to quit. Besides, who will cover your piece for tomorrow's issue?" he asked, half joking.

"I don't know and I don't care." Then smugly, "Maybe Sarah can do it. She seems to be able to fill my shoes pretty easily, don't you think?"

Not waiting for a response, "Ya' know, the only thing I regret is leaving *Stan* high and dry. Unlike you, he's always treated me with respect and dignity."

Without another word, Dani opened the door to Travis' office and was gone.

As the automatic sliding doors to the entry of *The Journal* building closed behind her, Dani felt only a tinge of pain. In every sense of the word, Dani truly was leaving her old life behind.

Strangely, the uncertainty of what her future held didn't frightened Dani, instead it excited her. Dani's heart skipped an extra beat at the thought of what God might have in store for her.

-- -- -- -- --

It was after a warm Sunday dinner at David and Tracie's that Uncle Buck approached Dani, "You're perfect for the job," he argued. "Your background, your degree, your inherent need to help others are all exactly the things someone in this position needs to be successful. And you told me yourself that you've dabbled in photojournalism—that's just icing on the cake. You have a knack for communicating, in your writing, and the way you interact with people. These people need you."

Uncle Buck talked. Dani listened.

"I know Uganda seems like a world away, but it's no different than helping serve food down at the soup kitchen or recycling bikes for the homeless, only, it's on a grander scale. Dani, this is the opportunity of a lifetime," Buck was determined.

"While you're there, you'll have the freedom to write about virtually anything. It's time *The Humanitarian* expand its horizons, jump out of the box, and force not just change among the American culture, but open hearts and minds to the idea of improving the lives of people a world away. The disease, the famine, the residual effects of war—all are daily obstacles for these people. They have to fight day-by-day just to survive." Uncle Buck was nothing if not persistent.

"The words you write, the pictures you capture will tell their story, Dani. Someone has to bring the lives of the exploited Ugandan people to the front doors of America." The wheels were spinning in Dani's head.

"You'll work independently, visiting the war-torn communities where missionaries from all over the world are helping to rebuild—not just homes and economies, but hearts. But for the most part, you'll be on your own. You'll have unlimited creativity in writing your article. You can't tell me that doesn't spark some interest in you, Dani. I know you too well."

"Buck, we met four months ago. You hardly know me *at all*." Dani protested, even though she felt like she'd known him all her life.

"I know you, Dani. Better than you think." He shook his head from side to side, slowly, deliberately, thoughtfully."

He looked her directly in the eyes, "You're me thirty-five years ago. You have the same spirit. The same drive. The same desire to single-handedly change the world, you've said that yourself. Yes," he chuckled, "we even have the same *stubborn nature*. I'm willing to bet you've got plenty of hard lessons to learn ahead of you, Dani. Just like I did."

"Stubborn nature!" she exclaimed, almost amused. "And I've learned enough lessons already, thank you."

"That's just like you, Dani. Dwell on the only not-so flattering aspect I mentioned." Then, as an afterthought, he said, "Although, even your stubbornness can work for you at times. It's worked for me." He smiled warmly.

With a sense of seriousness, Buck took Dani by the shoulders. "Of all the wonderful things about you, Dani, the thing that still worries me is the part where you want to 'single-handedly change the world.'" He drew her toward him and held her tightly, just as her father might have done. She felt protected in his fatherly arms.

"What do you mean?" she asked, almost knowing what his answer would be.

"You know what I mean, Dani." He pulled free from her embrace and cupped his hands around her face, leveling his eyes to hers. "You can't do this one single-handedly. But of course, you already know that. You've known it all your life. Just like me and everyone else in this world, you are powerless without Him."

Dani tensed, "I know that, Buck." She gently placed her hands over his and removed them from her face, cupping them tenderly with her own delicate hands beneath her chin.

With a ferocious passion in his voice, Buck continued, "I know you know it, Dani. But there's a difference between *knowing* it and truly *believing* it...*living* it...*surrendering* to it." His voice became gentle again. "Dani, you've spent your entire life living for Him. Maybe this last year was a test - perhaps a cruel one - but in a sense, a test of your faith."

Buck continued, "Until last year, Dani, your trials had been relatively simple. You really never had a need to question or challenge Him. Anyone can be faithful to a God who allows them a life full of joy and very little struggle. What could be easier?" He looked at her without condemnation. "But the true test of faith lies in our struggles—what we make of them—how we overcome them."

Dani was feeling defensive. She thought for a moment about the validity of what Buck was saying. Was he right? She had been blessed with incredible parents who loved the Lord and loved her and gave her everything she ever needed. But they didn't hand her things on a silver platter. They had taught her the value of hard work. She *had* experienced struggle. She *had* seen sorrow. She *had* felt loss. Maybe not on a level comparable to that which she'd experienced over the last year, but she *had* had trials in her life. Buck was wrong, she assured herself. After all, how many eighteen-year-old women find out they will never have children of their own?

Dani's faith had not faltered back then. Or had it? She vividly remembered being angry with God. But had she turned away from Him? At the time, she had thought to herself that no man would ever want to marry her if she couldn't have his children. She recalled a day, following the haunting news, when she was alone in her room and screamed out to God. "You know that all I've ever wanted is to have a family...to be a wife and mother!" She had shouted, "Why have I spent my life living for You if *this* is what I get in return?" Of course, it was an emblematic question, but she'd wanted an answer. It never came. She'd simply learned to accept it, or rather, ignore it. But on those occasions when she relived the haunting memory of that life-changing revelation, she still felt bitter. Who wouldn't? She had rationalized, unsuccessfully.

If it had been a test of her faith, then she certainly hadn't passed. If this past year was another test, she had failed it terribly. And she'd been on a downward spiral ever since that fateful day last spring. She'd isolated herself from the very people who had been there for her all her life— her church family. She'd nearly allowed herself to have a relationship with a married man. She'd given up the things in her life that had made her who she was; the Word, her commitment to prayer, her faith. She no longer recognized the sad, hopeless person she saw each morning in the mirror. But, as hard as she tried, she didn't know just how to come back. Or maybe she just wasn't ready to try quite yet.

With tears in her eyes, she said, "It's true, Buck. I haven't stepped up to the plate. So, if I've failed so miserably, why do you want me? What do I have to offer?"

"You have *you* to offer, Dani. Your education, your life experiences, your kindness, your compassion, your time, your love." His enthusiasm growing, "Deep down inside, Dani, you have hope. It illuminates from you even through these rough times. It's there, just dying to be shared with others. The way you used to, not so long ago."

Buck continued, "I know, I know. You're wondering how *I* know what you *used* to be like? I know because I see it in Mason. I see it in the way he looks at you. I see it in this situation with David and Tracie. You hurt so badly, yet you're always encouraging everyone – everyone except yourself. You're strong, Dani. You may not think so, but you are."

He went on, "Dani, it wasn't just coincidence that you walked out on your job at *The Journal*."

Dani interrupted, "No, it was just *stupid!*"

"No. It may not have been the way you would have liked to do it, but it opened up an incredible opportunity for you." Buck's excitement was becoming contagious. "Let's talk about tests, Dani. That situation with Travis Jakobs… that was one test you passed with flying colors. Things could have gone completely different had you allowed it to. But you didn't."

"How did you know about Travis?" Dani asked, horrified

"I've lived in this town a long time, Dani. Very few things get past me."

"I'm so humiliated. And if *you* know, then *other* people know too." She put her face in her hands and rested her elbows on her knees as she sighed in unwelcome resolution.

"Don't worry. Everyone doesn't know," Buck assured. "Besides that, Stan Montgomery said he's been waiting a long time for someone to put Jakobs in his place."

"Stan knows?" It was an agonized allegorical question.

"He said he always knew you had a lot of character. He's proud of you, Dani." Then with an expression of admiration, "So am I."

Dani was never so grateful to have Buck as a friend.

"It's time to move on, Dani. To take what you've learned through a year full of heartache and disappointment, and grow from it. Use it. Let it ignite a fire inside of you." He began pacing the floor like a caged lion waiting to be set free. "Forget whatever plans you had, Dani. You know as well as I do, plans are useless. God has your every step already planned.

"I don't want to preach to you, Dani. I'm not telling you anything you don't already know. I'm just asking you to let it happen. Just put your trust in Him. He knows what He's doing." Again, he looked at her, gently tilting his head to one side. "He has incredible things planned for you, Dani. "Just wait and see." He smiled.

"Buck, it all sounds incredible. The thought of doing something that might actually make a difference is tempting. And I'm grateful you have that level of confidence in me. But, you know I can't leave Mason. He's just been through too much."

"I knew you were going to say that," he said. "And I understand your concerns. But, Dani, he's doing great with David and Tracie. He's adjusting well to all the changes." Buck saw the look of terror in Dani's face. "You'll be gone only five weeks, Dani. It might do you both some good."

"How could it possibly be good for either of us to be separated for five weeks? He depends on me," she argued.

"I know he does. And you depend on him. It's understandable." Buck chose his next words carefully. "Have you considered that maybe you depend on each other a little too much? That maybe it's preventing both of you from moving forward?"

The expression on Dani's face changed from fear to that of worried confusion. But before she could respond to his charge, Buck jumped in.

"All I mean, Dani, is as difficult as it is to accept, I think you know in your heart that Mason is right where he belongs. It doesn't make you any less significant in his life—the two of you have an especially unique bond that can never be replaced—but it means that you now play a different, but equally important role in his life than you did before."

Comprehending the truth of what Buck was telling her, Dani's heart ached. A myriad of jumbled thoughts invaded her mind as she pondered the reality of the direction their lives had taken. She thought about the progress Mason had made, particularly over the past few months. He had meshed well with the Fowlers. He clearly loved David and Tracie. His brother had become his best friend, and he had taken to his baby sister as though it was his sole responsibility to look out for her and protect her from the bumps and bruises of her miniature life. He fit in as though he'd always been a part of their lives. He was thriving at school. Even his speech impairment had all but vanished, except for those moments when his excitement took over. He was content. He was happy. The thoughts evoked contrasting feelings of joy mixed with sadness for Dani. She was pleased that Mason had adjusted so well, but she was also resentful, in a sense.

Of course, Mason's happiness was most important. But on some level, she was ashamed to admit even to herself, Dani had hoped things would not have worked out so smoothly with the Fowlers. In the end, it would be easiest for everyone involved if they all returned to their old lives—Dani and Mason one family and David, Tracie, Samuel, and Kylie another. But it hadn't worked out as Dani had imagined. It had all come together so seamlessly.

Buck sat in silence, allowing Dani time to process, what her face told him, was an unwelcome revelation.

Though it pained her to admit it, Dani knew in her heart Buck was right. She *had* been clinging to an illusory fantasy that she and Mason could not survive without one another. When, in fact, Mason was not only surviving, he was flourishing. Dani questioned herself silently, *Have I prevented Mason from moving forward? Has my dependency on him, in some way, made him more dependent on me?* The thought of her own selfishness triggered an instantaneous nausea deep in Dani's gut.

But five weeks was a long time. Even if Mason was happy with his new life, he and Dani had never been apart for more than a week at a time. She wasn't sure he could do it—or rather, that *she* could do it. Though the war continued in her mind, Dani knew she was fighting a losing battle.

"I didn't mean to hurt you by saying those things, Dani," Buck offered. "I just want what's best for you and Mason both. And I truly believe that even with all the pain you've been through, there's a light at the end of the tunnel. You have a talent that few writers possess. You have passion. You have integrity. You're tenacious. There's a reason God gave you those qualities. You're young with the entire world at your disposal. You can't ignore the opportunity that He's put right in front of you."

Resolutely, Dani sighed, "I hear what you're saying, Buck. I've always known that God would not have given me such a passion for writing if He wasn't going to use it for His glory. I guess I've just been waiting for Him to tell me what to do, where to go.

"And the thing that you said about Mason...the two of us depending on each other so much...you're right about that too. It's just so hard to let go." She struggled to fight back the tears. "I try to imagine our lives a year from now, even five years from now, and I can't. A year ago, I could have drawn a storyboard—in perfect little blocks—of what my future looked like. Now, it's hard to form a picture in my mind of how even tomorrow looks. When I try, it always includes Mason. So, now, how do I create an image of a future without him?" Dani's voice was pleading. She needed Buck's wisdom now more than ever.

"That's just it, Dani, you don't have to imagine your life without Mason. He'll always be a part it. Maybe not like he used to be, or like you imagined a year ago or even six months ago, but you'll always have each other. You and Mason, David and Tracie, Samuel and Kylie; you're all a family now. It's crazy, it's unconventional, it's bazaar, but it's also wonderful and precious. I know you still have doubts about David's motives—that's natural, but you know in your heart he loves Mason. He would give his life for his son. And whether you're willing to admit it or not, Mason's happiness is the very thing that makes *you* happy." Buck's words emanated a perfect mix of compassion and reality.

As Buck spoke, an overwhelming feeling of peace engulfed Dani. She instinctively knew it was time to open her heart and mind to Buck's offer. Perhaps Africa would bring her some sense of closure and provide the new beginning for which Dani had been longing. "Tell me more about Uganda, Buck. What exactly can I do for you?" Though even as she spoke the words, Dani knew that Buck's offer had less to do with what she could do for him and more to do with what Buck was trying to do for her.

-- -- -- -- --

Dani and Buck talked late into the night. "Though the violence has decreased, the past few years have left the country in shambles, physically and spiritually. The people of Uganda have been traumatized by the violence they not only witnessed, but experienced on a personal level. Very few families have been spared the pain of losing a loved one. It isn't something that happened to someone else—it happened to all of them. The war left thousands homeless, parentless, hopeless, and in poor health. Now they're struggling to rebuild their lives."

Dani listened intently. She wasn't immune from the tragedies and aftermath of war. In fact, after her senior year of high school, she had spent an entire summer in Africa working as a missionary. She remembered how she felt when she first stepped foot on the unfamiliar land. She felt like a dubious intruder who had happened upon a secret society. The pungent, even rancid smells overwhelmed her senses. She remembered feeling as though she might faint, but that if she did, no one would help her, but for the frightened, uneasy flight mates who de-boarded the plane alongside her. Dani knew, though, that she had gone there for a purpose. She was there to serve Christ—to share with the people His love and sacrifice and the hope that only He could offer. She knew God would protect her. And he had.

As her thoughts drifted, the seriousness of Uncle Buck's tone quickly brought Dani back to the moment. "Dani, this place is like no other you've experienced or probably ever will again. Though the war is technically over, there exist pockets of terrorists and rebels who are committed to one cause or another. They commit suicide bombings nearly every day, taking dozens—even hundreds—of others with them all in the name of their God and the theologies on which their mission is founded. They particularly don't welcome the American presence. There's confirmed stories of missionaries being kidnapped, tortured, and killed."

Buck looked at Dani with a seriousness she was seeing for the first time. "Everything you say and do, Dani, could put your life in danger." But Dani wasn't afraid. "You'll basically be the eyes and ears for

America. You'll be taking photos and conducting interviews with the citizens of Gulu, the doctors at the hospitals and clinics, and the various missionary groups. I want you to *become* one of them…to immerse yourself in the everyday lives of these people. I don't necessarily want you there as a missionary. Of course, I want you to share Christ any time the opportunity presents itself and God opens a door for you, but you're going to be there with the goal of bringing a part of Uganda back to America, the good and the bad. Americans need to know the reality of what is taking place over there. They need to step up to the plate and do something about it. We are going to help open their eyes and ultimately their hearts to the Ugandan people.

"I know I'm beginning to sound like a televangelist," Buck continued. "But, Dani, this is something that God has been calling me to do for a very long time. He's given me—given *you*—the avenue through which to do it. *The Humanitarian* is the perfect outlet for the story. I have no excuse for not listening to Him now. This is our chance to truly make a difference and let God use us both."

Dani felt honored and at the same time strangely humbled.

As clearly as Dani knew at the age of fifteen after writing her first article for her high school newspaper that she was destined to become a writer, she was certain that God was now calling her to Africa. But somehow she knew that *this* was so much bigger. Perhaps, she considered for a brief moment, because it was *His* plan, not *hers*. "When do I leave?"

Uncle Buck smiled.

CHAPTER EIGHT

The week before Dani's departure to Uganda was spent running around doing last minute errands. Her arm was sore from the IG vaccine, the last of the Hepatitis B series, the typhoid shot, and an updated tetanus.

She had finally received her official passport and visa just two days before she was to leave; nothing like starting the trip out on a stressful note. Dani discovered that her health insurance did not provide coverage for members traveling outside the United States, but Buck assured her that the *Humanitarian* worked with an organization that could provide her adequate temporary coverage while she was on assignment.

On assignment. That sounded good to Dani.

She spent nearly a week just packing her bags for the trip. The summer had started out with unusually high temperatures in Gulu, the area in Uganda she would be spending a majority of her time. Though the average June and July temperatures were in the mid to upper seventies, the first week of June had already hit four record high days of 90 and above. Dani, who tended to prefer cool temperatures, still wasn't certain what type of weather to expect and unclear of the type of accommodations Uncle Buck had arranged for her, didn't want to find herself scarce of appropriate clothing. *I'll pack for the unexpected*, she determined. A dozen T-shirts, three pair of shorts, two sweatshirts, a pair of jeans, a pair of khakis, and a dozen or so undergarments later, Dani's bags were packed and ready to go.

-- -- -- -- --

The more than twenty-two combined hour flight from Sacramento to New York, New York to London, then London to Uganda—not to mention the five hours of total layover time in between—was grueling, but to Dani's surprise, she hardly slept a wink on the plane. Dani spent her time reading an African-based publication translated into the English language that Uncle Buck had given her before leaving the United States. She wanted to do whatever she could to lessen the culture shock inevitably awaiting her. She watched a newly released movie on the flight from Sacramento to New York, but it seemed to make her more fatigued. She slept relatively sound on the flight from New York to Heathrow, waking only to the overhead announcements from the pilot. Dani was sure she would get plenty of sleep during the last leg of her flight to Entebbe. But with the combination of the anticipation and the unknowing, sleep was hard to come by.

Now, as the plane descended toward the landing strip, it all became so surreal. The view of the rugged landscape seemed to stretch for miles. Dani had flown into airports all over the United States—Seattle, Denver, Dallas, Chicago—but as the plane prepared to land, she felt like she was entering an entirely new world altogether. It was nothing like she had imagined—like it was years before—it was worse. She mused at the thought of what Buck had said to her, "I want you to *become* one of them; to immerse yourself in the everyday lives of these people." She wondered silently if Buck knew, as she suspected, that he was throwing her to the lions.

-- -- -- -- --

Dani was pleasantly surprised at her accommodations. Buck had arranged a driver to pick her up at the Entebbe airport and transport her to her humble temporary shelter in Gulu that would serve as her office-slash-bedroom for the next five weeks. The two-hundred-mile drive had been arduous and Dani couldn't wait to lie down. Scanning the compact room, she saw that it encompassed a small twin sized iron bed with a single thin cloth for a bed covering. Even the lumpy pillow looked fluffy and inviting. But Dani had a lot to do before she could settle in for the night.

The room contained a small window on each of the north and south walls. The windows were the crank type which one had to wind in order to open and close them. Next to the bed was a small wooden table with a vacant open shelf. On top of the table sat a lamp stand with a brightly lit bulb. Dani assumed that, at one point, the lamp had been covered with some sort of shade, softening the glow of the light. In the left back corner of the room, an opening led to a bathroom, or rather, a room with a copper pipe protruding from one wall, which served as a shower. The makeshift toilet appeared to drain into the same receptacle as the shower water. A small hole in the floor reeked of what smelled like sulfur. In the opposite corner sat a shabby metal table with an extension cord duct-taped to the side and running to an electrical outlet behind the small bed. As far as Dani could tell, the plug was the only source of electricity to be found. Even in their simplicity, though, the meager furnishings would suffice. Dani didn't need much.

After settling in and spending the remainder of the evening unpacking her belongings, Dani opened her Bible and began reading. The words were familiar, comforting her in what should have been an anxious and overwhelming time. It wasn't long before the arduous trip took its toll on Dani, and she was dead to the world.

-- -- -- -- --

When Dani awoke the next morning, she felt reenergized. She decided to meander into town to get her first glimpse of the world that would be hers over the next several weeks.

The skepticism toward the Americans was evident as Dani roamed the dusty streets of Gulu. Her first few days in Gulu had offered Dani the realization that while many Ugandans welcomed the missionaries and media teams' presence and the help they brought with them, others despised their unsolicited interference.

Dani's fair complexion, not to mention the camera strapped over her shoulder, made it evident to onlookers that she was not native to this land. And anyone who wasn't a local was inherently considered an outsider.

The children were blatant about their curiosity in Dani and the other outsiders. Some stared inquisitively, others walked up to Dani questioning her anomalous attire, sometimes rubbing her ivory skin. It wasn't the first time they'd experienced the peculiarities of the Americans, but even now, they remained intrigued by the strangers' diverse customs.

Dani's research had helped prepare her for what she knew would be somewhat of a culture shock. But Dani knew from experience that until one is immersed within a culture and actually living and seeing the day-to-day goings-on, can one truly begin to understand the level of poverty at which these people live. The last few days had brought Dani that kind of understanding.

The street children—parentless, homeless, residual victims of a war-torn, impoverished land—ran rampant through the dusty streets of the city. Though the war had officially ceased, a degree of civil conflict remained, and the community did not have the subsequent means necessary to provide for the well-being of the children left behind. The community simply adopted them as a whole. But even those families that remained intact barely survived. It was an endless day-by-day effort for most to simply keep their families fed; little remained for the street children.

Researching the plight of the street kids before leaving the States for Africa, Dani discovered that the children are, in essence, residual victims of the God's Chosen People terrorist group.

Formed in the early 1990s by two brothers and self-described prophets Nthanda and Uzuma Ohakim, the GCP's original mission was to overthrow the Ugandan government and replace it with a regime that would implement the group's slanted interpretation of Christianity. Many Africans viewed the GCP as a type of cult whose ultimate goal, at the peak of their existence, was to uphold the Ten Commandments. The GCP's collective interpretation of the commandments, however, arguably warped and skewed in a way that serves, in their own view, to justify and legitimize their unscrupulous agenda. As the group's regime grows, so does the increase in violent attacks.

By means of convenience, children have become the main target of the GCP. The group members' mode of operation includes abducting children and young adults, transporting them to surreptitious bases, and terrorizing them by repeated rapes and beatings. Most of the kidnapped girls eventually become sex slaves to the GCP members.

More often than not, the children are forced into slavery as guards, concubines, and soldiers. As compulsory participants, the children— many as young as four years old—are forced to march strife in the north. Some are even required to kill members of their own families to protect their own lives and the lives of their brothers and sisters being held captive alongside them. At last count, more than twenty thousand children from across northern Uganda had fallen victim to the atrocities of the GCP.

Reportedly, Dani learned, the GCP eventually expanded it's terror to include the violation of human rights of the Acholi tribe in northern Uganda. Confidential intelligence have identified and implicated GCP members in the killing, maiming and kidnapping of a number of Acholi tribe members. Countless numbers of people have been mutilated and killed in unprovoked random attacks.

While the government as a whole claims to despise the actions of the GCP, rumors that the Sudanese government supplies arms and other forms of assistance to the GCP run rampant.

Though the GCP attacks have been unpredictable over the past decade, the atrocities they perform remain relatively unchallenged, in part due to their sheer numbers and partly due to fear of retaliation. During their decade long operations, numerous American missionary organizations have infiltrated Uganda and surrounding communities and helped to rehabilitate thousands of displaced children left homeless, parentless, and ultimately shattered by the GCP and it's horrific end.

Unfortunately, the GCP still exists, and it is widely believed that the group continues to function primarily on the doctrine of its founding fathers. The direct impact of their cruel and torturous operations is evident around every street corner and darkened alleyway of the Guluan culture. But resilience has served the Ugandan children well.

As Dani continued her meander through the dusty streets, she saw the positive results of a culture rich in agriculture and renewable resources. Today, many of the young adults have, with the aid of human rights groups, defeated their captors and forged a relatively bright future.

Though still children by American standards, many victims of the GCP have been forced to grow up quickly. They work in the agriculture industry to help provide for themselves and their extended family members. Comprising the most important sector of the Ugandan economy, the agriculture industry employs over 80 percent of the workforce in Uganda and the surrounding communities. The warm, moist environment serves to produce good grazing land for cattle, sheep, and goats. However, as if the residual effects of the GCP's terror weren't enough, a recent multi-year drought ravished the land, leaving acute food shortages, in part, making it difficult for the people to exist strictly off the land as they had once done.

As a result, most street children resorted to stealing their food and huddling together on makeshift cardboard beds during the night for warmth. Their feet have become so calloused from running bare, the soles now served as a leathery barrier against the sharp pebbles and debris through which they trudge. Their feet, their faces, and everything in between were stained by the red earth that seemed to obscure all that stood in its way. The children drank and cleansed from the same water that served as the laundry washing pool for the community. They seemed to migrate in groups, creating their own little families.

As her thoughts and camera lens returned to the moment, Dani raised her Nikon, snapping photos of a nearly nude child - save a makeshift pair of shorts - dig through one of a myriad of trash piles strewn throughout the streets and alleyways of the city. Whether the child was a boy or girl, Dani could not tell. Though thin and drawn, the infantile facial features told Dani that the child could not be more than five years old.

She watched as the grubby child could not contain his excitement when he retrieved what appeared to be a minute piece of discarded millet bread. He immediately began gnawing at the stale, provisional meal.

A commotion across the road caught Dani's attention. In front of what looked to be some sort of medical clinic was a man with disheveled light brown curly hair wearing a pair of khaki-colored pants with various size pockets stitched up and down the legs. He had on an unkempt buttoned down denim blue dress shirt hanging loosely over the waist of his pants. The sleeves were rolled up to his elbows, and there was a visible ring of perspiration under each arm. He wore a pair of brown leather flip-flops revealing, even from a distance, dust-caked feet. Around his neck was a dangling stethoscope with the chest piece hanging from its stem and tucked into his shirt pocket.

Dani moved closer to get a better look at what was causing all the hubbub. Camouflaging herself, she moved from tree to tree, tucking behind structures and hiding behind her camera while taking candid shots of the intriguing chaos from a distance.

As she moved closer, so did the details of the photos. The children's faces all donned gleeful smiles. There was laughter and an easy playfulness emanating from them that Dani had not seen before in the faces of the children.

Many shoeless and shirtless, the children gathered around the oddly out-of-place-looking man. Approaching from the man's right side, Dani observed him handing one of the children a red rubber ball. The other children clapped and jumped up and down enthusiastically.

Slipping some sort of metal box into one of a plethora of pockets on his pants, the man reached into another cubby and pulled out a bag of dried fruit. The children swarmed him like a flock of vultures.

"Whoa ya', little rascals," the man said in a playful tone. Dani could tell by his voice he was an American. The smallest child in the group reached her hands toward the man, wanting him to pick her up. The man bent down, gently picked her up under her arms, and rested her on his lap. The small child was enamored with him, staring up at him as if in wonder.

"Dr. Jacks...Dr. Jacks...you have more fruit?" a boy asked in some sort of broken dialect.

"Not today, Bolade. Tomorrow," he promised.

Just then, a humid breeze picked up sending Dani's flimsy wide-brimmed mesh fishing hat flying toward the jubilant little group. Dani let out a little squeal as she scurried to retrieve it, capturing the children's attention.

"I get it," cried a barefoot little boy with nothing covering him but the torn remnants of a cloth which served as shorts. The hat landed on the ground just outside the circle of tykes. The boy ran toward it, but the wind picked up again, sending the hat twirling through the air.

"I've got it!" the man herald as he fumbled to get hold of the hat, which landed directly at the feet of the little girl who had been sitting on his knee.

For an instant, the man's eyes locked with Dani's. He stood and robotically walked toward Dani, the child on his hip and the hat in his hand.

"This must be yours," he said, handing the hat to Dani.

"Thanks," Dani said bashfully. But when she stretched out her arm to take the hat from him, the man teasingly pulled it away.

"Hold on...not so fast. You can't very well accept a gift from a man whose name you don't even know, now can you?" he hoaxed. His voice was soothing, almost inviting. Dani liked it. But she wasn't sure she liked *him*!

"A gift?" she screeched, grabbing for the hat. The man held the hat even further from her reach. The little girl on his hip covered her mouth and giggled at Dani's obvious annoyance.

Infuriated, Dani was determined not to give into this man's childish conduct. "That's okay," she said. "I have another one just like it." She didn't really, but she wasn't about to let this strange man win at his own game. Dani turned around as if to leave; the man gently clutched Dani's shoulder, spinning her back around.

Furious, "Who do you think you are?" she shouted. The man laughed, angering Dani even more.

"You don't get a lot of dates, do you?" he continued to egg her on.

Ready to explode, Dani barked, "You are *the* most—"

Before she could finish her scolding, the harebrained man reached up, placed the hat on Dani's head, and yanked it snuggly down, covering her eyes.

Before she could react, the man extended his arm toward her. "I'm Jacks," he offered.

"I don't really care who you are," she said defiantly. She lied. Dani was intrigued by him.

Engrossed by Dani's entertaining behavior, the girl on Jacks' hip cupped his ear and whispered something indecipherable to Dani's ears.

"Yes, she is," Jacks said, capturing Dani's glance again. Dani wondered how she could be so intrigued by this man, and at the same time, want to pummel him.

"What did she say?" Dani demanded curiously.

"She said that you're funny."

"Huh, uh…did not!" the girl exclaimed lightheartedly. "I said that you're prett…" Jacks playfully muffled the girl's mouth as if to prevent her from speaking.

Dani couldn't help but find the exchange endearing. Her boiling blood began to cool. Following Jacks' mischievous lead, Dani teased, "So you think I'm pretty, do you?

"I suppose you're not too bad yourself," Dani joked. In reality, up close Jacks was even more attractive than from a distance. He had piercing blue eyes and a chiseled jawline. The curve below his brow sloped just right to form a perfectly shaped nose. His skin had a sunbaked glow to it with a hint of stubble just beginning to form on his chin. His lips had a sultry pout to them; his smile warm and welcoming.

Dani couldn't resist her feisty nature. "Good thing your looks make up for your lack of personality," she added.

"I get that a lot," he teased back, "usually, though, when people insult me, I at least know their name."

Ignoring Jacks' prompting, Dani turned her attention to the children, whose fleeting interest in Jacks just moments before, were now chasing down a flock of baby chicks running rampant through the busy street. Raising her camera, Dani began snapping candid shots of the children. "Who are they?" she asked motioning toward them.

Anxious to join her cohorts, the little girl wriggled free from Jacks' arms, kissing him tenderly on the cheek before planting her feet on the ground. Jacks patted her head lovingly. "Be safe, my little mzao."

Directing his attention back to Dani, he said, "They're all street kids. They've all lost their parents to either disease or war." He began walking in the direction of the medical building. Dani instinctively followed.

"The country is so poor it's not able to do much for them." Jacks looked sad when he said it. "They manage to get by though. They scavenge and beg and sometimes steal if necessary. Many of them are brothers and sisters—the older ones look out for the little ones."

As they entered the building, a mixture of ammonia and antiseptics invaded Dani's senses. For a brief moment, it took her back to her accident. She heard the sirens, felt the chaos. It was a time she wanted to forget.

"Are you okay?" Jacks asked, looking at her with intrigue.

"Sorry," Dani said. "Walking in here brought back some strange memories." Jacks was curious, but didn't press her.

Jacks opened the door for Dani to a small room with two shabby couches setting face-to-face separated by an old metal buffet-style table whose legs had been cut down to the height of a living room coffee table. On the table sat three coffee mugs, one with the handle missing and another with a large chip out of the rim. Papers were sprawled across the scratched metal and a plump woman with red hair intermingled with strands of grey, who looked to be in her early sixties, was intently examining the papers' content.

As Dani and Jacks entered the room, the woman peered up at them from behind a pair of wire-rimmed glasses. "Jacks, how are you this morning, lad?"

"I'm good. Started early so I'm finished with my rounds for the day."

"How's that little Midyan faring this morning?"

"He seems to be improving a bit. He was able to take fluid orally today," Jacks reported. "I even got a smile out of him."

"You have a way of doing that, young lad. You could get a smile out of a leprechaun with an empty pot at the end of his rainbow!" Her laugh was loud and boisterous.

Dani couldn't help but smile.

"Who's the pretty young thing alongside ya' there?"

"I'm sorry, Maddie. This is my new friend..." Jacks hesitated.

Reaching forward to offer her hand to the kind woman, Dani said, "Danielle. Danielle Shaw. It's nice meeting you."

"You an American too?" the woman asked.

"Yes, ma'am. I'm from California. I'm here writing an article on the conditions of the Ugandan people following the war," she offered. "Although, I'm considering changing my angle after seeing the children and the struggles they've had to overcome in the face of such devastation." Dani could not hide the pain she felt for all the innocent victims she'd encountered during her brief time there.

"That they have"—Maddie offered in agreement shaking her head as if in disgust—"that they have." Rising from the lumpy couch, Maddie tried to disguise the wrenching ache in her knee, but the pain was evident on her face.

"How about I stay and help you with your rounds today, Maddie?" Jacks offered.

"No thanks, lad. Taking care of these little ones is what keeps me young," she said, limping toward a rusty, but functional coffee maker which held a half-empty pot of black coffee. "Well…them little ones, this here coffee, and the good Word." She chuckled.

Concerned about Maddie's unsteady stride, Jacks asked, "You sure?" Secretly hoping she would decline his proposal but prepared to follow through with his offer, he added, "I'm not doing anything this afternoon."

"You go enjoy yourself. It's not every day you get free time around here." Then eyeing Dani, the elderly woman roguishly offered. "Or get to spend it with a lovely young thing like that." Jacks only smiled, though he silently agreed.

Jacks didn't need to be told twice. He hoped Dani's afternoon was free as well. He reached for a faded orange Giants baseball cap with a frayed bill that hung from a nail protruding from the wall. Thrusting it firmly on his head, the bill facing backward, Jacks looked like a teenager headed for the high school homecoming game. To Dani, the unpretentious, casualness of his actions overpowered the presumptive, arrogance of their initial encounter. Dani grew more intrigued with Jacks by the minute.

As the two exited the clinic, Jacks stopped just outside the entrance door. As if inspecting her, Jacks looked Dani up and down. "You look like a Danielle," he said. "I like it."

For some reason, Jacks' outward scrutinizing of Dani infuriated her. *How could a man she barely knew send her on this strange sort of emotional roller coaster?* One minute, he appalled her; the next, she was enraptured by him. Before Dani could voice her displeasure, Jacks proceeded, "Well, Danielle, what are your plans for the rest of the day?"

Caught off guard, Dani stuttered, "I…uh…I have to work."

"If your work involves that camera, consider me your personal tour guide for the afternoon," he said. "I can show you an Africa you've never seen before."

Dani wanted to refuse, but her fascination with Jacks combined with the practicality of his offer forced her to submit. "All right, I guess. I am kind of lost. My maps are more confusing than helpful," she admitted.

Jacks was right. Over the next several hours, he led Dani down the dark alleyways of the village and across the busy streets of what was otherwise, the business district of Gulu. He pointed out the makeshift homes and the myriad of parentless children who fought for their very survival. He shared about the brutality of the war-impoverished culture and the history of its people. He spoke of the years of viciousness that had been loosed upon an otherwise blameless society. The stories he told of disease and famine that he witnessed were heartbreaking. Dani realized that the atrocities the African people had endured over recent years could never be adequately described in the words of a book or magazine. It was the photos, candid snapshots of these people's everyday lives that would serve to tell their story to a world thousands of miles away.

It was dark before Dani finally returned to her provisional shelter. She lay restless in bed that night thinking of the children she'd encountered. For a brief moment, she even allowed herself to think of Jacks.

-- -- -- -- --

The next day, Dani and Jacks' time was occupied with their respective responsibilities. Dani spent hours writing about the things she saw the previous day; the things she learned. She and Mason had promised to email each other every other day. She hadn't sent him a message since her layover in London, so in her first email after arriving in Gulu, Dani described the city and what her living arrangements were like, but she told Mason mostly about the children she had observed the previous day. Dani knew Mason would like hearing about the street kids. She asked him how school was going and if his little sister was still going through her "biting" stage. As would become their custom over the next five weeks, Dani ended her message with ISDLY.

Jacks spent his day the usual way—making rounds, telling stories to the children, administering medications, treating the treatable, helplessly standing by while others took their last breath. All the while, Jacks' thoughts inevitably returning to Danielle, and hers to him. He had spent a restless night thinking; foolishly daydreaming of what could be.

-- -- -- -- --

The following day, Dani and Jacks were able to spend the afternoon together. After hours of roaming the streets and photographing the people, Dani and Jacks found a wooden makeshift bench to sit and rest their aching feet. Dani looked at Jacks. "What is it exactly that you do here?" Dani asked.

Jacks readily offered the information as if rehearsed. "Our hospital serves as the primary provider of inpatient healthcare for the Gulu District and functions as a referral hospital for all of northern Uganda. In addition to inpatient care, we provide outpatient care and some of the team operates an additional outlying health center. While not as extensive, HIV research is also part of the work we do. Despite the difficult circumstances, there are those who are fighting back against disease in Uganda. That's where we fit in."

Dani listened intently, absorbing the tragedy of it all. "Why are there so many children though? It seems like everywhere I look, there are far more indigent and diseased children than there are adults."

"Primarily because of the GCP." Jacks' voice resonated a mixture of anger and, perhaps, fear.

It hadn't taken Dani long to discover that the primary dissension in the area was caused by the ongoing yet less prevalent war between the rebel GCP and the Ugandan government.

His jaw clenched, Jacks' passion was evident as he spoke, "The war and displacement have profoundly disrupted the provision of healthcare in the region. Malaria, TB, and AIDS are rampant in settings where medication and access to clinics and hospitals is inaccessible. The lack of sanitation, crowded conditions and diminished access to medicines and medical facilities lead to poor health outcomes."

Dani had read that many people, both within Uganda, and those on the outside believe that the Ugandan government, as well as the world, have failed in their responsibility to protect the people of northern Uganda from the violence, economic insecurity, and ravages of infectious diseases that are prevalent in the region. And even more than that, they've failed to protect the children. Jacks was merely reiterating what Dani already knew.

Late in the afternoon on their third "outing" together, Dani and Jacks walked along the outskirts of town sharing a piece of fresh green mealie bread they'd bought at the market earlier in the day. Dani looked at Jacks. "So why are you here, anyway? I mean, I understand what you do, but why Uganda? Why Gulu? Why the children?" The questions were simple. The answers, she knew inherently, were wrought with a depth she had yet to understand.

Jacks hesitated as if carefully considering his response. He looked intently into Dani's eyes. "The same reason you're here—to make a difference. We're both part of the solution to a tragic situation, we just play different roles." Jacks moved closer to Dani. She could see the conviction in his eye—the passion. She felt tingles run up her spine, though she wasn't certain if it was because of what he was saying, or because of the close proximity. Maybe both.

He twisted his body in an attempt to face her directly. He leaned in. "You report to the world the devastation that's going on here. People like me read about that entire family with AIDS in Africa or the malnourished babies in Bangladesh. We read it in the *New York Times* or the *Humanitarian*," gesturing to Dani as if in mutual understanding. "Or we get a glimpse of it on the morning news. That's how it starts." He leaned in even closer. "Before you know it, you're a part of it. You're drawn to it. It pulls at your heart." He leaned back in his chair.

Buck continued, "Then you put your own problems aside and replace your self-pity and selfish goals with a desire to use the gifts and skills that God has blessed you with. And you pray that in some small way, you can help make someone's life a little better."

He touched her; not with his hands, but with his words. Dani sat silently for a moment. "But how do you know where you're being called to go…what you're being called to do?" she asked.

Jacks reached up and cupped Dani's face in his gentle hand. He grazed his thumb over her silky smooth cheek. "You just know, Dani." Then, as if returning to consciousness after a long dream, Jacks dropped his hand from Dani's face and clasped them together before leaning forward and dangling them between his knees.

Jacks lowered his head, almost in a bow. "You pray about it. You trust. You have faith. You wait for His voice. You pray more. Then you go."

"But I thought we're not supposed to 'make plans'," Dani recounted with a touch of sarcasm. "That God has everything already planned out for us."

"We start making plans only when God sets them in motion. I believe He gives us the guidance and direction, but we have to do the legwork." Jacks smiled affectionately at Dani. "Look at it this way, have you ever wanted something so much and planned so hard to make it happen, only to discover the end results weren't what you had hoped for or how you had pictured? That's because that dream, that goal was all about *you* and what *you* wanted. We've all done it. Sure, it's great to have dreams and goals and plans, as long as you make sure that's what God has planned for you."

Jacks looked as though he were about to burst with passion. "The only way to be certain is by asking Him, by praying for His wisdom and discernment. And not stopping." He stood up and began pacing, not nervously, but with anticipation. "You may have no idea what the outcome will be, but you know it doesn't matter, because it's in His hands!"

Dani spoke quietly, "I used to have that kind of faith."

-- -- -- -- --

Over the next week, Jacks and Dani managed to see each other every day. Each moment she spent with Jacks, Dani learned something new about the Ugandan society...about him. She knew from that first day that Jacks was good with children. Everywhere they went, the children knew Jacks and would swarm around him like bees to honey. While Dani had a difficult time understanding what the children were saying most of the time, Jacks understood their broken dialect as if the kids were speaking English as clear as day. The way he interacted with the kids impressed Dani. He was gentle and playful and compassionate. He always had special treats hidden in his pocket or an exciting story to tell them. The kids loved Jacks, and it was evident to Dani that he loved them too.

CHAPTER NINE

It had been a week since they'd first laid eyes on one another. After a long, exhausting day spent touring an outlying clinic, Dani was walking alongside Jacks, replacing the film in her camera when he declared enthusiastically, "Spend the day with me tomorrow. I want to show you something." He sounded like a child anticipating his next adventure to the zoo.

Though she wanted nothing more than to spend the day with Jacks, Dani hesitated. "I have too much to do. I can't afford to take an entire day off."

"Sure you can, Danielle," Jacks pleaded. "Besides, it will be a day of research. You can't effectively write about the Ugandan people without understanding their culture." Dani loved the way Jacks said her name, *Danielle*. She hadn't told him that most people called her Dani. Then again, Jacks wasn't most people.

"I could use some more photographs. Something beyond Gulu; something outside the confines of the city," she contemplated aloud.

Jacks grinned from ear to ear. "I won't disappoint you. I promise!" He looked like a mischievous little boy with his wide eyes and dimpled cheeks. *He's adorable.* Dani smiled at Jacks' excitement.

"Be ready at daylight!" he said. "I'll be by to pick you up then."

"Pick me up?" Dani had only seen Jacks take the matatus—which was sort of a minibus—taxi, or walk to home, to work, to the market. Available vehicles were few and far between. Where did he suppose he would find one?

"Yes, pick you up. You didn't think I was going to piggyback you eighty miles, did you?"

"Eighty miles?" she said curiously. "Where exactly are you taking me?" Dani had become comfortable with her surroundings; the relative close proximity of her areas of research kept her securely confined to within walking distance of anywhere she needed to go. She liked it that way. She wasn't certain she wanted to roam the uncharted plains of Africa!

"Trust me, Dani. You won't regret it."

What was funny is that Dani *did* trust Jacks. She barely knew him, but something told her that she could trust her safety to him, even her life. "Does it have to be that early?" she whined like a child.

Jacks laughed. Dani was an incredibly beautiful woman who possessed wisdom beyond her years, but sometimes, the little girl in her would come out. He cherished both. "Yes, miss night owl. We'll want to get an early start." Before he left, Jacks wrapped his arms around Dani. She felt an odd mix of attraction and security, like she used to feel when her daddy would comfort her as a child when she'd fallen and scuffed her knee. But the attraction wasn't so much physical, as it was emotional. Yes, the physical attraction was undeniable, but the emotional connection was overpowering. Inexplicably, she felt linked to Jacks, and he to her.

Jacks reluctantly loosened his embrace and forced himself away from Dani's arms. Their eyes locked. Jacks cupped Dani's face in his hands without breaking their gaze, and he stared into her eyes intently—invading her mind, as if reading her thoughts. His warm, sweet breath intermingled with Dani's, though their lips hadn't touched. Dani's heart began to race. She was sure Jacks could hear its deafening rhythm. The upward tilt of her head met perfectly with the downward tilt of his. She closed her eyes, anticipating his soft, supple kiss.

For a brief instant, Dani imagined Travis' face and the way his mouth had engulfed hers. She retreated, repulsed at the thought. How could she be thinking of Travis while standing in the arms of a man like Jacks? The two men were polar opposites. Travis could never—never had— come close to evoking the feelings that were brewing in Dani at that moment with Jacks. As if repelled back to reality, Dani instantly realized that Jacks' lips had not yet touched hers. Confused, she slowly opened her eyes, only to find herself looking squarely into his. What she saw was kindness, passion, sadness, joy all in one. Then, a single tear fell from Jacks' eye. Dani instinctively reached for his face and gently wiped away the tiny droplet. For a moment, Dani felt like Jacks' protector. She wanted to shield him from whatever, whoever was the source of his pain. She wanted to hold him like he had just held her. Comfort him. Safeguard him from the hurt that had invaded his face. She slowly lowered her hands from his face, over his shoulders, and down his spine. As she began to move closer to him, Jacks pulled Dani's face toward his and kissed her gently on her forehead. His lips lingered there for what seemed like forever. Then, in a husky voice, "Good-bye, Danielle. Sweet dreams." And he was gone.

-- -- -- -- --

The sun was just beginning to peek over the weathered mountains as Dani sat on the front stoop of her bungalow relishing a cup of fresh steeped tea. She'd made enough for Jacks too, though, by his own admission, he wasn't much of a tea drinker. *Jacks…mmmm.* She inadvertently closed her eyes as she remembered the gentleness of Jacks' touch only hours before. The sweet smell of his breath. The vulnerability in his eyes. Who was this man invading her every waking thought? He was a stranger, yet so familiar. He was rugged, yet gentle. There was a hardness about him, yet his heart was soft. He was an open book, yet there was something mysterious about him. He was innocent, yet wise. He confused Dani, yet left her feeling content. He scared her, yet she felt protected by him. He reached deep in to her very core, yet seemed to hold her at a distance. He was every man she'd ever know, yet every man she'd never known. *She wanted to know him.*

The sound of a vehicle horn broke the morning's relative silence. Dani had become so accustomed to the rooster's daybreak crow and the chickens' incessant clucking that she was now oblivious to their intrusive annoyance. She squinted her eyes as a trail of dust followed an approaching beat-up old four-wheel-drive faded green Chevy truck. Dani stood up, shielding her eyes from the rising sun with her free hand.

The driver's side door flew open even before the truck came to a complete stop. "Let's go, Danielle!" Jacks was dressed in a pair of khaki shorts that hung below his knees and a form-fitting faded gray T-shirt that read "PBR 2002" with the silhouette of a bucking bull in the background on the left upper portion of his chest. His comfortable looking beige work boots reached halfway up his calves with dingy white socks stretching just beyond. Dani had to laugh as Jacks jumped from the rickety old truck and headed toward her.

"Ready?" Jacks asked, leaping on to the porch, scooping Dani up in his arms and twirling her around as though she were a little girl. Dani's tea went splashing out of her mug and on to her cut-off denim shorts. Taken aback, Dani squealed, more in delight from Jacks' playfulness than withdrawal from the scalding tea.

"Ouch! That couldn't have felt good. Sorry, Dan." Jacks was caught off guard by his own casualness. *Dan? What, was she, his college buddy?* He was embarrassed, yet at the same time, bewildered by his natural presumptive familiarity with her. *How could he feel so comfortable with a woman he barely knew?* Jacks' slight blush made Dani giggle.

Dabbing a paper napkin to the tea stain on her shorts, Dani assured, "That's okay, Jacks. I actually think it's kinda cute that you called me Dan. Danielle is so pretentious anyway, don't you think?" she said teasingly.

"No," Jacks replied. "Danielle suits you better. It's elegant." He looked away coyly, "just like you."

It was Dani's turn to blush. Awkwardly flattered by his comment, Dani retorted clumsily, "Oh yeah, the cut-off shorts and raggedy T-shirt scream elegance." Sarcasm was right up her alley.

Jacks glanced over Dani approvingly. "The look suits you." Noticing the half-dried tea stain on her cut-offs, Jacks countered, "Sorry about that."

"No, biggie," she said nonchalantly. "I better go change though."

"Don't bother. You're going to be filthy before the day's over anyway." Jacks smiled. "But you might want to grab a sweatshirt."

"I've never been on a date that was prefaced by 'you're going to be filthy' when it's over," she said, feeling slightly humiliated at the realization that she used the term date. Trying to avoid Jacks' glance, Dani busied herself by reaching for a sweatshirt that was sprawled over the back of the front porch chair and shoved it into her backpack.

Jacks smiled to himself then tried to ease Dani's embarrassment. "Well, I guess that makes us even then, because I've never been on a *date* through the African wilderness!" he said, emphasizing the word date.

Jacks' attempt at making Dani feel comfortable worked. She returned an appreciative smile. But her smile faded as she quickly realized Jacks had used the words African Wilderness! "What?" she shouted. "You're scaring me, Jacks!"

With a mischievous laugh, Jacks grabbed for Dani's hand and hurled her off the porch, draping her tiny frame over his shoulder. With an unsteady grip, Dani's backpack crashed to the ground. Jacks reached down and retrieved it without missing a step. Fighting to be let down, Dani demanded, "Put me down. You're going to break your back!"

"You're as light as a feather. My stethoscope weighs more than you!" he countered. When they reached the truck, Jacks theatrically tossed Dani onto the passenger seat. He slammed the door and headed around to the other side in a pretend limp, holding his lower back. "I think I pulled a muscle," he groaned. Dani acted agitated, but she wasn't.

When Jacks pulled himself up onto the driver's side seat, Dani playfully, but forcefully slugged Jacks in the arm. "Ouch," he said, wincing. "My back *and* my arm." He wrinkled up his nose as if in agony. "I think I need a doctor."

"You're going to need a doctor if you keep it up," she said in a teasing manner.

Buckling herself in, Dani noticed the floor board beneath her feet was so worn she could see the dusty road below. "Where did you find such a fine specimen?" she teased, wiping dirt from her cut-off jeans.

"I bought it!" Jacks proudly exclaimed. "This beauty is *all* mine." He put the truck in gear and began a slow chug heading toward the outskirts of town.

Dani couldn't help but laugh at Jacks' juvenile enthusiasm.

"You paid *money* for it?" she returned rhetorically, wriggling to dislodge the lump protruding from the back of the bench seat and in to her spine.

"Did you say we're driving eighty miles—through the African wilderness no less—to get to your mysterious destination?" As she asked the question, it occurred to her. "Eighty miles each way...or round trip?"

Jacks laughed at the look of panic on Dani's face. "Ah, give her a chance. Eloise grows on ya'." He patted Dani's knee in a playful motion.

"Eloise?" she asked. "You named your truck?"

"Of course, I named her. She looks like an Eloise, don't you think?"

"*Eloise* looks like she's seen better days," Dani confirmed.

"Nah, she's got a lot of life left in her," Jacks assured. Teasingly, he said, "Well, hopefully, she has at least one hundred sixty miles left in her," he continued.

"Eighty each way?" Dani screeched, as the rickety old truck tossed her from side to side.

Heaving his head back in laughter, Jacks taunted playfully, "I thought you were tougher than that Danielle."

Danielle. She briefly lost her train of thought. Then, she exclaimed, "Okay, tough guy, pull over. I'll do the driving."

Jacks complied with Dani's lighthearted demand. He pulled the truck to the side of the road and vaulted to the dusty ground below. A cloud of dirt followed him as he walked around to the passenger side.

Dani had already slid across the scratchy, torn seat and planted herself at the wheel. Putting Eloise in gear, she was off even before Jacks could close the door.

"Whoa there!" he shouted in amusement, reaching for the dash to steady himself. Jacks liked Dani's feistiness. It gave spunk to her otherwise gentle, sweet nature.

Dani was enjoying being behind the wheel. She hadn't driven a vehicle since she was in the United States. As they drove, Dani was enthralled by the beauty of the land. What started out as desert-like terrain, gradually turned into the semblance of the African wilderness about which Jacks had so casually teased that morning before setting off on their adventure.

Dani was in awe of the wildlife they encountered along the way. The buffalo and antelope were abundant along the route. Continuing down the rugged road, the terrain began to change from the dry desert like atmosphere to a lush tropical green milieu. Dani and Jacks spotted a number of giraffe and elephants feeding and grazing among the rich vegetation.

Though Jacks still had not told Dani where they were going, the beauty of the expansive land was a vision that she would not soon forget. While Jacks had experienced the scenic drive before, it always left him speechless.

Lost in the beauty of their surroundings, Dani and Jacks sat silently absorbing the splendor before them for what seemed like an eternity as the rickety truck plugged along.

Jacks' voice broke the silence. "I never get tired of this," he said, scanning the approaching horizon. Menacing clouds were visible in the distance, threatening rain over the untamed African savanna.

"Ready to tell me where we're going?" Dani asked, still scrutinizing the details of her surroundings. "Or are you going to keep me in suspense?"

Jacks loved Dani's ornery, playful side—almost as much as he loved her kind, passionate side. "Have you ever heard of Murchison Falls?" he asked.

"Uh, huh," she said. "It's in the Murchison National Park, isn't it? In fact, the park was named after the falls, I think."

"Yep. It's actually one of Africa's largest national parks," Jacks said. "The Nile River runs through what's called the Rift Valley. The falls are at the end of a narrow fissure, that even from a distance, are breathtaking. I've never seen anything like it.

"The first time I saw the falls, it was by accident." Jacks' face looked as though he were in a distant place.

"I'd been hiking through this incredible terrain surrounded by chimps and water birds and all kinds of other wildlife, taking photos like the ones you see on the cover of *National Geographic*. Then—it was almost like in a dream—I came to the end of an overgrown trail and in to this clearing. I looked up and saw this one-hundred-forty-foot waterfall cascading into the river below." Jacks nodded his head back and forth as if in disbelief.

"I can't even begin to describe it, Danielle. It's something you have to see to believe."

Dani tried to imagine the falls. Just hearing Jacks describe it reminded her of her childhood days on the Yuba River. She could almost hear the shallow rapids flowing across the granite boulders into the pristine swimming holes below. The memories gave Dani a sense of calm.

Jacks continued, "This is going to sound corny, but I've never felt closer to God than that day when I was standing beneath that cascading water, showered by a foggy mist."

"It doesn't sound corny at all," Dani said. "There's something about water—especially the river—it has a sort of cleansing effect."

Timidly, she continued, "Almost like being…"

"Baptized," they said in unison.

Dani turned and looked at Jacks; their eyes connected. "Yes," Dani reiterated, "baptized."

As she forced her gaze away from Jacks, Dani jerked the steering wheel trying to avert a humongous lion crossing the road just feet in front of them. Eloise nearly tumbled off the shoulder as Dani swerved back and forth trying to gain control of the vehicle.

Over the next hour, Jacks and Dani talked about everything from politics and economics, to Jacks' work at the hospital and Dani's research. Dani learned that Jacks' favorite food was beef—New Yorks, Fillets, Prime Rib, but nothing topped a thick, juicy Ribeye. Dani had to agree, though tacos took a close second. They talked about music and movies. They talked about favorite restaurants, favorite cities, and favorite actors. They discovered that they both loved Rocky Road ice cream and Captain Crunch cereal. Jacks was a morning person, Dani a night owl; though Jacks already knew that about her. They talked about their faith, though neither of them revealed what had lead them to Christ. Dani wasn't sure why, but she was hesitant to share her past with Jacks and, clearly, he wasn't willing to reveal anything about his. It occurred to Dani that each time their conversation began to get personal, in fact, one of them managed to change the subject. Once again, only the creaking and cracking of the ancient truck could be heard as they both grew lost in their private thoughts.

It all seemed so curious to Dani. Though Jacks was more than vague about his life until now, she still felt as though he was somehow revealing himself to her in way he had seldom done before. Dani was content with that for now. She hoped to spend the next few weeks getting to know Jacks. She didn't want to think beyond that.

After a long, comfortable stretch of silence, Dani looked toward Jacks. His head was casually rested against the passenger side window. Adrift in a dream-filled sleep, Jacks' breath was steady and shallow. He was a beautiful man.

-- -- -- -- --

"Turn here," Jacks bolted from a death-like sleep, scaring Dani senseless.

"Jacks!" she yelled, grabbing at her heart. "You scared me to death!"

"I see that. You nearly jumped through the front windshield," he teased good-heartedly.

"Very funny." She pretended to be angry.

A two-mile narrow road overgrown with a myriad of large-leaved fig, River Bushwillow, Wisteria and

Baobab trees lead them to a small makeshift dirt parking lot overgrown with shrubs and vegetation.

"Are you sure we're in the right place?" Dani asked Jacks curiously. "It doesn't look like anyone has been here in years."

"We're in the right place," Jacks assured. "It's my secret shortcut." He smiled mischievously.

After parking Eloise under a billowing Waterberry tree, Dani and Jacks jumped down from the rusty metal door frame onto the moist foliage-covered ground. Jacks unstrapped a khaki-colored canvas day pack from the back end of the truck. Dani pulled a red baseball cap from her bag and reached for a pair of knock-off Dolce and Gabbana sunglasses.

Looking up, Jacks playfully laughed out loud at the oversize spectacles taking up half of Dani's face.

"Ready?" he asked as if preparing to engage upon an undiscovered land.

The hike to Murchison Falls was spectacular. Dani saw more wildlife in one day than, it seemed, in her entire lifetime. Jacks was familiar with every species of bird—cormorants, kingfishers, fish eagles, herons, ducks, bee eaters—he knew their origin, what they ate, their approximate population. Dani was impressed with his knowledge.

Halfway into the hike, Dani and Jacks rounded a corner only to be confronted by a towering grayish-white bird with a bill the size of a clown's shoe.

Jacks grabbed Dani's arm and pulled her back into the shadows of the surrounding Cape Cycad trees.

"Shhh…," he whispered trying not to disturb the magnificent creature. "You know what that is?" he asked.

Following Jacks' lead, in a hushed voice, Dani offered, "It looks like a stork."

"It's a shoebill, also known as a whalehead. They're very rare. In fact, I've never seen one except in magazines and books."

"It almost looks prehistoric," Dani observed.

"Well, it sort of is. Its scientific name is the Balaeniceps rex," Jacks recounted. The dinosaur-like name made Dani think of Mason. *Mason would love this,* she thought. A tinge of pain pierced her heart. She missed him so very much.

Noticing a look of sorrow on Dani's face, Jacks' hesitated for a moment, but he didn't ask any questions.

"The species get its name from its gigantic shoe-shaped bill. Go figure," he said, followed by a hushed laugh. "Look!" Jacks whispered, pointing to two miniature versions of the massive bird emerging from the shadows.

"Those are her babies. They're more of a light brown color." Jacks was entranced by the unique beings.

Dani was in awe too—more of Jacks than of the unusual animal.

Dani listened intently as Jacks told Dani everything she could have ever wanted to know about the shoebill.

"The population is estimated at between five thousand and eight thousand. Most of them are found in Sudan.

They're listed as a vulnerable species under Bird Life International." Jacks was like a walking encyclopedia.

"What does that mean? Is it like being threatened or endangered like the American bald eagle used to be?" Dani asked

"Exactly," Jacks confirmed. "They haven't reached the threatened or endangered level yet, but because they are constantly being disturbed by hunting and increasing tourism, they could make the threatened list sooner than later."

Attempting to clear up any confusion about the plight of the shoebill, Jacks continued, "Don't get me wrong. Just like with most cultures, tourism is necessary for the African economy. Even hunting is all right—it goes on in every faction of the world—like everything, though, it just needs to be done in moderation."

Jacks was not only an intelligent man, he was practical as well. Dani admired that quality in a person. As he continued with his history of the shoebill, Dani slowly raised her camera and snapped several compelling shots of the birds in their natural habitat.

"What's really interesting is their existence is recorded as far back as the Egyptian times. The Arabs referred to the bird as *abu markub*, which means 'one with a shoe'," Jacks offered as if reading from a thesaurus.

"Let me guess, they know that the shoebill is as old as the Egyptians because some archeologist found hieroglyphics or some type of Egyptian writings on a cave wall," Dani said, almost in jest.

Impressed, Jacks teased, "Okay, Miss Brainiac. Since you're so smart, what do they eat?"

That was easy. Everyone knows birds eat insects and small reptiles among other things. "They eat bugs and fish and frogs," she announced playfully pretentious, placing her hands on her hips.

"Yeah," Jacks corroborated. Then, eyes bulging as if he were terrified he said, "But their favorite thing to eat is baby crocodiles." As he was saying the words, Jacks reached over and pinched Dani's arm.

Dani screamed, sending the shoebills skittering into the protective foliage. "You scared me to death!" Dani scolded. She reached over and, for the second time that day, slugged Jacks in the arm.

"Ouch," he winced. "That hurt. My arm's still sore from where you punched me this morning!"

Dani rolled her eyes in feigned annoyance. But in truth, Dani loved Jacks' good-natured mischief.

Jacks and Dani continued their trek through the jungle-like terrain. Sometimes they talked. Other times they trudged along lost in their private thoughts; sometimes commenting on the beauty of the terrain, other times admiring its exquisiteness in silence.

In the distance, Jacks and Dani could hear the sound of streaming water. Stopping in his tracks, Dani nearly ran into the back of Jacks. "Listen," Jacks said. "We're almost there." He began jogging, as though being beckoned by the cascading lull of the river.

Picking up the pace, Dani hurried to catch up with Jacks.

Out of breath, Dani finally reached Jacks. "Slow down," she said, instinctively reaching for his hand.

Without thought, Jacks engulfed Dani's petite hand with his own consuming one and firmly led her toward the approaching sound. The simple touch of his hand sent a bolt of lightning through Dani's body. It terrified her to realize that she was falling for Jacks. *No,* she thought, *I've already fallen.*

-- -- -- -- --

Brushing spider webs and twigs from their bodies, Dani and Jacks ascended from the footpath mostly hidden by plush jungle vegetation and into a spacious field of vibrant yellow African daisies. Simultaneously, their feet stopped moving as they stood face-to-face with the most brilliant sight either of them had ever seen.

Though Jacks had visited the falls before, it's indescribable wonder made it feel like the first time.

Looking up at the cascading water, Jacks imagined it was what Heaven would look like. With a crack in his voice Jacks stated the obvious, "It's breathtaking, isn't it?"

Dani was speechless; she only nodded her head in agreement. Jacks forced his gaze away from the splendor of the falls and looked toward Dani. But this time, it wasn't the falls that took his breath away; it was Dani. Jacks swallowed hard trying to hold back the emotions this place...these falls...Dani collectively evoked in him. He had never seen a more picturesque place in his life; never known a more beautiful person.

Aware of Jacks' piercing gaze, Dani bashfully turned away then attempted to change the subject. "I'm starving! Got anything good to eat in there?" she asked, motioning toward Jacks' worn day pack.

Gaining his composure, Jacks boasted, "You probably don't know this, but you are in the presence of the best chef from here to Singapore...and everywhere in between." They both laughed. He sat down next to Dani on the thin patchwork blanket she had packed and, crossing his outstretched legs, rested back on one elbow. Unzipping his day pack with his free hand, he began retrieving the lunch items from his pack one by one. As he removed the items, Jacks described each delicacy with precise detail, setting one after the other on the sprawled out blanket.

"First," he said, pulling out a plastic container, "we have chilled spiced carrots." Dani took the package from Jacks, held it at a distance, and looked at it as if it contained a poisonous insect. She inspected the contents of the container curiously. Jacks was amused by Dani's childlike behavior.

"Give me that," he ordered playfully, grabbing the container out of her hands and tossing it on to the blanket.

Unwrapping a thin cloth napkin folded in the shape of a knapsack, Jacks revealed a crumbly cake-looking sort of bread. "Next, is my famous green mealie bread, otherwise known as corn bread." To Dani, it looked delectable.

"You'll like this," Jacks promised. Displaying a container identical to the first, Jacks offered, "This is dried fruit chutney with apricots, peaches, dates, and raisins. It has all kinds of pungent spices added to it. That's what makes it taste so good." Jacks pulled out a piece of the dried fruit and directed it toward Dani's lips. Bashfully, she opened her mouth and received the appetizing little treat. Savoring its sweet, yet tangy flavor, Dani closed her eyes. "Mmmm…" Jacks had to force his eyes away from her.

Distracting himself, Jacks continued, "Now for the main course." He held out another container, similar to the others, only larger. He popped open the lid and sniffed its contents as if it were an expensive bottle of wine. Tossed among the fresh salad greens were the heartiest portions of rock lobster Dani had ever seen. The lobster was mixed with a variety of fresh crunchy vegetables and tossed with a light herbed lemon dressing.

Retrieving the last of his hidden treasures, Jacks flaunted a foil-wrapped clay bowl. Loosening the surrounding cover from the terracotta dish, Jack revealed an unidentifiable yellow colored blob.

"What's that?" Dani shrieked. Jacks loved the way Dani could transform herself from a wise, sophisticated woman in one instant to an innocent, giddy schoolgirl the next.

Jacks could not disguise his disappointment as he peered at the tousled dish. "Well, it was supposed to be dessert. Fresh baked Klappertert to be exact," he bragged proudly.

"And, what, may I ask, is Klappertert?" Dani asked with disgust, maintaining her childlike manner.

Thrusting his head back, Jacks laughed. "Klappertert is the African name for coconut pie."

"Oooh…that sounds good." Dani rubbed her hands together in anticipation. "What are we waiting for?"

"Dig in!" Jacks handed Dani a fork and a half-frozen water bottle. The icy water felt good streaming down the back of Dani's throat.

Dani and Jacks took turns eating from the various containers. Experiencing the delectable concoctions was an adventure in itself. They ate until their stomachs could hold no more.

They talked and laughed until their cheeks hurt. They sat in silence taking in all the wonder that surrounded them. They talked reservedly about childhood memories. Each could tell the other was hiding behind something, neither not quite knowing what it could be.

Dani told of her carefree summer days on the river and her "secret" waterfall. She described her childhood paradise in detail, reliving her days there like it was yesterday. "Hardly anyone knows where it is…well, if they do, nobody wants to hike all the away out there anyway."

She closed her eyes as she reminisced. "When I was really little, my mom and dad and I would go out there and swim and jump from the rocks. I never got out of the water." She giggled. "By the end of the day, I looked like a shriveled up prune."

Then, with a melancholic air, she said, "Now, it's where I go to think, to clear my mind, to feel close to God." Jacks quietly absorbed Dani's tales. Closing his eyes, he tried to imagine himself there—at Dani's secret falls. In his mind, she was right there beside him. He envisioned her face, her eyes, her lips, her ebony hair, the curve of her waist, her long, slender fingers.

"What were you like as a little boy?" Dani wondered.

Fearful of opening himself up to unnecessary pain, Jacks didn't answer at first. But as he lay there next to Dani, listening to the harmonic sounds of the untamed African jungle, a sense of peace overwhelmed him.

Jacks voice finally broke the silence. "When I was a boy…"

Jacks talked about waking up at sunrise the first day of summer break each year and riding his bike until the sun set behind the mountains. He would ride for miles and miles, exploring, learning, living. To Jacks, there was nothing more freeing than riding down a secluded country road, breeze blowing through his hair, arms outstretched toward the sky.

It was Dani's turn to imagine herself in Jacks' dreamland. As her mind visualized a rambunctious little boy courageously venturing out into the world, Dani smiled to herself. Her mind drifted to Mason.

Lying back on the soft blanket, staring up at the sky, Dani and Jacks' palates were full and their eyes grew heavy. They fell asleep to the sound of gushing water spilling into the glistening river.

An hour later, Dani and Jacks were startled awake by what sounded to Dani like a band of trumpets. They both sprang to their feet, hearts pumping. Dani grabbed Jacks' arm, pulled him to her, and held on for dear life. "What was that?"

Jacks pulled Dani closer, as if he were her protector, though Dani didn't need his protection. "Loxodonta Africana," Jacks replied very deliberately. "African elephants."

Then Dani saw them. Across the river was a herd of massive grey elephants. Two of the bravadoes animals stood at the river's edge drinking the brisk waters of the Nile. One was knee deep beneath the falls, irrigating itself with the refreshing liquid. Three others stood in relative close proximity feasting on the abundant vegetation lining the tributary walls. Noticing the two strangers invading their privacy from across the water, the largest of the herd released a thunderous cry. Warned by their triumphant leader, the submissive group began a slow but watchful retreat back to the safety of the jungle from which they came.

For the umpteenth time that day, Dani and Jacks marveled at the sheer magnificence of all this feral land had to offer.

The last swaying tail a blur, Jacks glanced at his watch.

"We better start heading back too," Jacks said, comparing their impending hike back to the truck to that of the elephant's journey.

"Already?" Dani whined. "I don't want to leave."

"Me either," Jacks assured her. "But travel times through African National Parks are limited to between 6:30 a.m. and 6:30 p.m." Dani and Jacks would have to hurry to make it out of the park in time.

CHAPTER TEN

Dani awoke the next morning full of anticipation and a newfound hope that hadn't existed in a long time. Her mission today—capture the inner workings of the medical clinic and ensnare images of the doctors and nurses who gave so generously and selflessly their hearts and lives to an otherwise forgotten facet of a society.

So not to interfere with the natural goings-on of the medical staff's everyday functions, Dani quietly roamed the hospital, unintentionally scrutinizing the intricate details of the sterile compact rooms and hollow corridors. She found the hygienic and subdued atmosphere of the hospital's internal workings to be eerily at odds with the filth and chaos of the outside environment.

Though technologically deprived by American standards—from the rusted oxygen tanks and defibrillators to the creaky iron beds and wheelchairs—the hospital staff and patients alike treated each piece of equipment as though it were a prized gift. And to them, it was. The oxygen tank meant one more day a mother with AIDS could spend with her newborn child. The defibrillator offered life to a dying heart. The hospital bed provided rest for a weary body. The wheelchair—a passport to freedom for an otherwise bedridden man. Some served to save lives, other served to give life. Each piece cherished, treasured. Even an austere wooden crutch with tattered rubber hand grips served to bestow independence to the dependent; so simple to some, a life source to others.

Dani observed the faces of the confined patients and their visitors as she quietly eased her way down halls and past open doors. As she snapped photos of the people—their hands rugged from a lifetime of farming, their feet scarred by the brutality of their land, their faces etched by an existence of pain and sorrow— she couldn't help but think through each scar and wrinkle told a story of hardship, for many, their eyes told something different.

Dani could see a peacefulness in their eyes. She could feel it in the intimate and gentle way they spoke to one another. Some were on their deathbeds, others returning from the brink, yet they were happy. Truly happy, as though they had accomplished what they were brought into the world to do, and now they were readily anticipating their next journey. But Dani knew life hadn't always been this peaceful for them. She knew that their very existence was founded on a heritage of adversity and forged with devastation.

What happened to the people she'd met as a know-it-all teenager just coming out of high school? Nearly a decade ago, she had integrated herself into an economically deprived culture barely existing in a war-torn land. She had forced herself on people who had little or no hope. Their ears had been closed to the truth she had so desired to share with them back then. Their eyes had told only of grief and pain. She had left this land those many years ago feeling as though she had failed. Her only solace was in the hope that she had planted seeds in a land that was otherwise desolate. How those seeds were cultivated was up to God.

Over the past several weeks after returning to the same streets on which she had walked and from where she had witnessed with her mission team, Dani gradually began to notice a subtle change. The living conditions these people had to endure appeared relatively similar to that of the Uganda with which she'd become familiar almost ten years ago. Most remained impoverished. Many were struggling with disease and hunger. To Dani, very little had changed. Yet, the more time she spent with these mysterious people, it occurred to Dani that while the external elements remained the same, something had changed internally. In their hearts. In their minds. In their spirits.

As she listened to the laughter of gathering visitors in one room, the harmonic voices coming from another, and victorious prayers of thanksgiving filled with peace and hope coming from others, Dani realized at that moment what it was that gave these people such an immovable peace of mind. Yes, their hearts still hurt, but unlike the past, the pain was fleeting, eventually to be replaced with peace and contentment. In many of their faces, Dani somehow saw an indispensable peace that could have only come from Christ.

Room by room, Dani took notes and captured glimpses of a foreign world—a world that required no words to tell its story, no narratives to evoke the innermost emotions within its observer. She took photos of the extraordinary, as well as the seemingly insignificant that served to define a society light years away from that which she had known throughout her life.

As she roamed the empty halls, the silence surrounding Dani was occasionally interrupted by the beep of a monitor, the distant squeak of cart wheels rolling along the uneven concrete floor, and whispered conversations between medical staff and their patients. There existed no hustle and bustle of visitors, doctors and nurses, and maintenance workers that seemed to be ever present within the hospitals and clinics in America.

As Dani approached a small isolated room at the end of a long corridor, she could hear the faint sound of a man's muffled sobs. Moving closer, she heard the angelic hymns of a woman singing softly in a tongue that had become vaguely familiar to Dani over the past several weeks.

Without a sound, she inched her way to the opened door of the compact room. Except for the conflicting sounds of the man's cry and the gentle harmonic voice intermingling, the room revealed nothing about its contents.

Camera raised, Dani peeked around the door frame ready to capture what she hoped would be a memorable moment frozen in time; one she could use to help tell the story of a distant culture, of a people so far from the minds of those she knew. But as she silently stepped through the doorway, she instantly felt like a trespasser. No one saw her. No one heard her. Yet, she knew she was intruding on something private. Something personal. Something that should be shared between a select few. Not with a stranger. Not with a prowler attempting to steal away permanent evidence of a family's most intimate moments. Not with her. Dani felt ashamed as she lowered her camera.

The hushed silence that saturated the room seemed contradictory to what she saw. There was half a dozen medical staff—doctors and nurses alike—tending to one infant or another. Each child was isolated in his private incubation tomb. Some had monitors and tubes attached to various body parts. Others, simply surviving on their own.

Dani could only watch helplessly as a nurse gently stroked the cheek of a voiceless yet strangely mobile baby. A doctor placed a rugged, encompassing hand on the miniature back of a chocolate-colored bundle. The child appeared to be resting peacefully, though the pain in the doctor's eyes told Dani differently.

A movement caught her eye. Dani's gaze was drawn to the far corner of the room. A man sat in a blue paint-chipped metal chair, gently cradling a newborn baby to his chest. His face was buried deep into the white cotton blanket that secured a lifeless child. At the man's feet sat a seemingly emotionless woman. Arms wrapped tightly around the man's legs, her tear-stained face showed an indescribable sorrow, yet was peaceful all at once; her eyes, looking upward, yet fixed on nothing. Her angelic voice permeated the room with words that seemed to flow without forethought—as if they were words permanently etched in the woman's mind—as though she had sung them before.

Lost in her own thoughts, Dani wasn't certain how long she had lingered in the open doorway, but now, though the scene remained relatively unchanged, the sobs had quieted.

Dani silently backed away from the intimate little room and continued her one-woman tour of the hospital. Journeying down each corridor, peeking into rooms; some strangely secluded, others busy with a calm cadence of staff and patients alike tending to their business, Dani snapped photos and took mental notes of what she saw—of what she felt. What may have seemed mundane to most, left Dani in awe. The way these people communicated with one another—the compassion in the eyes of each and every staff member amazed Dani. The gentle tone of their voices as they spoke to patients and their family members struck Dani to the core. These people weren't merely doctors and nurses, they were people. People who truly cared. People who felt pain and sorrow just like the patients for which they were caring. These were remarkable individuals who chose to leave the familiar comforts of the relatively simple American way of life and volunteer their services to help perfect strangers. Dani was overwhelmed by the realization that these doctors and nurses offered so much, yet received so little in return.

In one room stood a blonde-haired, blue-eyed nurse who appeared to be no more than fifteen years old. She was situated in front of a fragile-looking girl sitting in a rusty wheelchair holding a cracked mirror with a plastic pink handle. "They look just like yours!" the little girl joyfully exclaimed in broken English. "Will you braid my hair like this every morning?" she asked in anticipation.

Tugging on one of the perfectly braided ropes that rested over the little girls' shoulder, the helpful nurse enthusiastically offered, "Yep. I might even be able to find some ribbon to make them look even more beautiful than they already are!"

The wheelchair-bound girl grinned from ear to ear and, scrunching her shoulders in excitement, silently clapped her hands together wanting not to disturb the other two children who were resting peacefully in adjoining beds.

The caring nurse bent down and affectionately embraced the girl. "I will see you tomorrow, Nsia." The nurse kissed the girl's cheek and smiled warmly at Dani as she exited the room.

Each room that Dani approached brought with it more than mere photo ops. Each scene told a different story—brought its characters to life. One room filled with laughter, another filled with silence, yet another filled with the hollow beeps of monitors and otherwise sterile lifesaving equipment.

As she approached the last door at the end of the west corridor, Dani could hear the soothing sound of Jacks' distinct voice and the rallying rhetoric of a young child.

The day she met Jacks, Dani had noticed the rectangular shaped object that he sometimes carried in the right hand lower pocket of his doctor's coat. Though, on that first day, surrounded by the rambunctious group of children, he seemed to be using it for some sort of game. She wondered why he would keep it in his pocket while conducting his rounds.

Now, as Dani stood by quietly taking in the scene, she watched as Jacks completed his exam of the submissive little patient then retrieved the peculiar object from his pocket. Dani strained her eyes to get a better glimpse of what appeared to be a vintage tin box whose colors were faded by years of either neglect or use—one could not be certain.

Her curiosity rose as Jacks pried the tightly secured lid from the unique box. He reached in and pulled out a small red ball and a half-dozen metallic jacks pieces. Jacks held the ball, then the metal pieces in front of the boy's small tanned face and curiosity-filled chocolate eyes. With each item he introduced, Jacks appeared to be explaining to the boy the object's relative importance.

Dani was fascinated by Jacks' ability to speak the native language so fluently. Though she understood very little of the conversation between Jacks and the small boy, the passion behind Jacks' words was evident.

Again and again, Jacks proceeded to bounce the red ball of rubber on the unsteady table that rested in front of the young boy, and gracefully, effortlessly scoop up one of the shiny jacks pieces, simultaneously engulfing the conflicting materials of the soft rubber and taut metal in his smooth hand.

When there was only one jacks piece left, Jacks, once again bounced the rubbery ball off the table and scooped up the red ball along with the last remaining piece of metal. He grasped the game pieces in his hand and cradled them to his chest as if protecting the inanimate objects from whatever outside elements might threaten to separate the interdependent pieces.

He continued his tender conversation completely captivating the curious little boy's attention. As Jacks spoke, he appeared to be asking the boy questions. With each question, the boy slowly but deliberately nodded his head. Eyes wide open, as if hearing an adventurous story for the first time, the small boy's face was consumed by a smile that reached from ear to ear.

Jacks handed the boy the small metal jack before gently kissing his forehead. "Good-bye, my little friend," he offered in the boy's erudite Bantu language. Jacks ruffled the boy's hair before turning to exit the room.

"Good-bye, Dr. Jacks! Come see me tomorrow," the boy hollered back. Dani understood the audible language far better than she could speak it.

Unaware that Dani had been watching him, Jacks headed toward the door, nearly plowing over Dani as he bounced the small red ball on the floor's hard surface and attempted to place it back in his pocket.

"Whoa there!" Dani exclaimed as she instinctively grabbed for Jacks' arm, trying to keep from cascading to the floor. Jacks reached around Dani's waist helping to steady her. Dani's body twirled around and her hand rested on Jacks' broad chest. Startled by the physical predicament in which she found herself, Dani mechanically tried to pull away from Jacks' embrace. But he pulled her even closer. Dani didn't resist.

Dani was physically attracted to Jacks, but there was something more than that. As their eyes met, Dani wanted to turn away from Jacks, but she couldn't. At that moment, she felt protected. She imagined herself resting her head on his chest and feeling the pulsating beat of his heart. His breath was warm and sweet. His eyes piercing hers, Jacks reached up and gently entwined his fingers through the tendrils of hair that trailed over Dani's shoulder.

Jacks was holding Dani so tightly, she could hardly breathe. Dani wasn't certain if it was her own heart she heard beating, or Jacks'. If not for a muffled giggle coming from the compact room jolting them back to reality, Dani and Jacks could have spent an eternity in each other's arms. They reluctantly peeled their bodies and their gaze away from one another.

They looked toward the brown little boy sitting coyly in his bed, covering his eyes, pretending as though he couldn't watch the silly display before him. He giggled again, pulling the white cotton sheet over his head in a childish attempt to shield his face.

Dani reached for the rubber ball that had fallen from Jacks' pocket and came to rest between a corridor wall and the wheel of a vacant metal gurney. Holding the ball toward Jacks as if displaying it and examining it at the same time, Dani said aloud, "So *that's* why they call you *Jacks*?" It was more of a statement of understanding than a question.

Dani and Jacks began a slow pace down the corridor as Jacks began to explain how he uses the jacks pieces to tell the children about Jesus.

"I explain to the children that God is kinda' like the red rubber ball and that 'we' are like the jacks pieces. Every time the ball bounces down to the ground, it swoops a jack up with it. Just like God—Every time He looks down on earth, He finds someone to bring back to heaven with Him. I explain to them that sometimes He takes *someone* with him, and other times, He takes someone's *heart* with Him." Dani found Jacks' trivial explanation very endearing.

Jacks continued, "I try to help them understand that in order for our bodies to go to heaven, we have to first give our hearts to Him. I tell them that when we give our hearts to God, He takes it immediately...right now. And then later, when He's ready, He comes to get our bodies too."

Jacks looked at Dani without a hint of humiliation for his juvenile reasoning. "I know it sounds silly, but somehow they seem to understand what I'm telling them."

"It doesn't sound silly at all," Dani said. "It's great when you can find a way to connect with someone, and they're open to hearing the truth." She sighed. "And kids are like sponges, they soak it all up."

"And they can't get enough," Jacks chortled. "That little guy in there asks me to play my version of jacks with him every morning. He names all the jacks pieces. The names are mostly the same—the names of his mother and father, sisters and brothers, and his closest friends. But once in a while, he'll add another name—someone he's met in the cafeteria or another patient strolling down the corridors."

Jacks continued, "He has no fear. Everyone he meets immediately becomes his friend. And whether they want to hear it or not, he tells them about Jesus. He shows them his jacks piece and repeats the story he's heard me tell to the other children a hundred times before."

Dani thought, *If only I could be that kind of witness.* She thought of the pain and tragedy that had created the cynicism in her and her subsequent lack of faith. She mused over her own self-centeredness as she and Jacks turned a corner to find a tiny sterile room, damp with humidity where three sick or wounded children lay silent in their private pain.

"I just need to check on a couple more of these little guys," Jacks said.

Jacks hesitated for a moment before turning toward the opened door and pulled something from his pants pocket.

"I made something for you, Danielle."

Displaying a hand-carved cross made out of two miniature pieces of driftwood attached to a macramé chain, Jacks offered, "I found the wood on the banks of the river yesterday." He sounded more like a nervous schoolboy than the confident, sophisticatedly handsome man that he was. "I made it for you last night."

Dani reached for the dangling cross, running her fingers over the smooth, weathered wood. Lifting her eyes from the necklace to Jacks' face, Dani found

Jacks' penetrating gaze. In his eyes, Dani could see the same love that she felt in her heart.

Grasping the necklace in trembling hands, Jacks lowered it over Dani's head; the cross pulsating with the rise and fall of her erratic heartbeat. Neither of them spoke, their eyes told what the other was feeling. Dani comprehended at that moment what Jacks had realized the day before at the falls. In the few days they'd spent together, Jacks and Dani had come to share a love formed not on time and familiarity, but on an unspoken bond which could have been created only through God's divine intervention to fulfill His purpose. What that purpose was remained a mystery to both of them. But, instinctively, they knew; God's plan was unfolding before their eyes.

Jacks caressed Dani's silky cheek. The warmth of her skin sent a welcoming chill up his spine. Dani's hand encased his; their fingers intertwining in a symbolic union.

Neither of them knew how long they'd been standing there lost in each other's eyes—in each other hearts, when the rattle of a rickety wheelchair broke the contented silence. Maddie appeared from a room two doors down the hall. Impervious to her obvious interruption, she offered jovially, "Good morning, Doctor." Then with raised brows and a mischievous grin, she turned to Dani. "Good morning, Danielle."

As if caught with their hands in the cookie jar, Jacks and Dani released their grasp. "Hello, Maddie," Jacks replied.

"Good morning," Dani followed.

Maddie wheeled the chair past them without another word, giving Jacks a knowing wink. Her footsteps fading down the hall—the epiphany-induced connection between Jacks and Dani momentarily broken—Jacks spoke softly. "I'll be just a minute," he said, before quietly tiptoeing into the small room.

Dani stood at the door as Jacks approached a young child, no more than five years old, who appeared to be sleeping soundly. Sitting on the edge of the boy's bed, Jacks whispered, "Good morning, Yachleel." Though barely audible, the boy's eyes fluttered open to the sound of Jacks' voice. A welcoming, though forced smile consumed his face.

"How are you feeling this morning?" Jacks questioned, with obvious concern in his voice.

"Better," the boy said, unconvincingly. Then, noticing Dani across the room, temporarily forgetting his pain, the boy's grin widened.

Dani watched as the small boy with the pencil thin arms leaned toward Jacks and whispered something in a hushed voice. The question was barely audible to Dani as she leaned against the doorframe from across the small, disinfected room.

Cupping his hands around his mouth in a futile attempt to be discrete, the little boy shyly inquired, "Who is the pretty lady?" Dani smiled affectionately.

Jacks' eyes turned from the boy, and slowly, deliberately drifted to Dani. Their eyes locked instantly. It felt so natural; no awkwardness, no self-consciousness. Dani felt an unprecedented sense of intimacy with Jacks. In that moment, she knew she had never seen a more beautiful smile.

Without taking his eyes off Dani's, Jacks unconsciously reached for the boy's hand and cupped it in his own, then in a low, almost guttural Ugandan tongue, unfamiliar to Dani, he said, "My miracle from heaven."

Then it came. The cursing sound of thunder as breaking glass sprayed across the tiny room, with a force that sent furniture and bodies plummeting through the air.

Dani couldn't see through the glass in her eyes, the flames, and the smoke. But she could hear—screams, cries, then in the distance, sirens. "Danielle, get out of here!" came Jacks' muffled plea. The noise, the pain, the smells began to fade. Then came the darkness.

CHAPTER ELEVEN

Drifting in and out of consciousness, she remembered the sound of the ear-piercing explosion. The instant pain. The instant fear. She remembered being pulled from the room as remnants of the demolished building weighed heavy on her legs. She remembered the boy's white-toothed smile against the velvety chocolate skin. She remembered Jacks. She remembered.

Dani tried to open her eyes, but it was useless. The throbbing pain seemed to begin in her toes and trail all the way up her spine to her frontal lobes.

She could feel the sterility of her surroundings and instinctively knew she was in some type of hospital, reminiscent of the days following her accident. The smell of antiseptics and cleaning agents mixed to form a pungent, but sterile type of odor. Though she wasn't sure why, the smell had a sort of soothing effect on Dani.

Remembering the rubble and the cloud of dust settling over her following the horrific thundering explosion, Dani became momentarily perplexed. Was it yesterday? A week ago? A month ago? She had no concept of how long she'd been here...in this bed...in this hospital. She was sure she was in a hospital, but what hospital? Was she back in the United States or still in Uganda? Her mind was reeling with confusion and pain.

*Beep...beep...beep...*the rhythmic sound permeated the room. Though she was groggy, she was slowly becoming conscious of the excruciating pain in her right leg. But as the physical pain began to take shape, so did the memories of those last moments.

"Jacks...Jacks...Where are you?" She'd called his name over and over. She remembered cries coming from the hospital corridors. She remembered screams coming from the streets. But coming from the small room, she remembered only silence.

"Don't leave me, Jacks." She couldn't remember if she had spoken those last words aloud, or simply heard them in her mind's subconscious.

Again, she tried opening her eyes. They refused to do what her mind was telling them to do. Then she realized it wasn't for lack of trying. Her eyes were covered. She reached up slowly and lifted her hand to the bulky bandages that encased her head. Though the tears had no place to run, Dani could feel their burn.

"Dani, can you hear me?" Buck's soothing tone allowed her a momentary sense of peace.

"Buck, is that you?" In her sedated state, Dani couldn't be certain.

Buck breathed a sigh of relief at the sound of her voice. "Yeah, kiddo. I'm here, Dani. You're going to be fine."

"Where am I?" Dani asked, turning her head toward the direction of Buck's voice.

"You're at a hospital in Kapala. You were rushed here in an ambulance with a fracture to your leg and your face full of charred glass following the bombing." He squeezed Dani's hand gently, yet reassuringly.

"How long have I been here?"

"Four days. You've been unconscious all this time. You had me worried, young lady." Buck spoke in a joking manner, yet Dani couldn't mistake the compassion embedded in his words.

"When did you get here?" She managed to ask through the incessant throbbing in her head.

"About thirty-six hours after it happened. I received a call when you were on your way to the hospital. Per Buck's instructions, since arriving in Africa, Dani had worn a lanyard around her neck containing her photo and other identifying information to be used in the event of an emergency. "I had a minor issue with my passport, but I made it here by the time you came out of surgery. They had to repair your fractured leg." Buck continued, "You have a metal plate infusing your fibula and tibia bones together and a couple of pins holding them in place, but the doctors say it should heal without any problems. You'll have to have the plate removed at some point, but it sounds like it's a relatively simple procedure." He didn't mention to Dani that she would have to undergo months of physical therapy. All in due time, he thought.

"Then there's your eyes. They had to remove a dozen minute pieces of glass, but there doesn't appear to be any permanent damage." Still holding her hand with one of his own, he patted it with his other. "They'll know more when they remove the bandages," he promised, as much for his own reassurance as for Dani's.

"When will that be?" she wondered.

"They've just been waiting for you to come to." Buck kissed Dani's hand, rested it to her side and stood. "I'll let them know you're awake."

As Dani listened to Buck's fleeing footsteps, the affection she felt for this man whom she'd known for less than a year overwhelmed her. "Buck, thank you for everything. Not just for being here, but for everything you've done for me."

Buck turned, paused for a moment, and spoke with complete humility, "Dani, it's I who should be thanking you. You've added so much to my life. You're like the daughter I never had." Holding back tears, Buck cleared his throat.

For the first time, Dani heard Buck's voice tremble with emotion. "Losing you would be like losing a part of my heart." Before disappearing into the corridor, he said in an even gentler tone, "My cup runneth over, Dani. My cup runneth over."

-- -- -- -- --

Buck waited outside Dani's room while the doctor carried out his examination. Before removing Dani's bandages, he turned off all the lights in the room and opened the window shades slightly. With his flashlight, the doctor performed a cursory examination before instructing Dani to carefully and slowly open her eyes. He warned that even a small amount of light would likely be painful and that exposing her eyes to the light would have to be a gradual process.

Buck was getting antsy. The examination was taking too long. He prayed.

He prayed some more.

After what seemed like an hour, the doctor exited Dani's room with good news to report. A thorough examination showed that a majority of the damage to Dani's eyes had, in fact, been surface injuries. The sutures to her lids and surrounding area were healing nicely, and the cuts caused by the glass fragments had not left permanent damage.

When Buck returned following the doctor's examination, he and Dani sat in silence for what seemed like hours. But a question was weighing on Dani's mind. She had to know.

In a whisper, she asked, "It was the GCP, wasn't it?" She knew the answer before she asked it.

Buck hesitated, "Yes, Dani. I'm afraid so." He continued with an air of disgust, "Because they resent the rising presence of the missionaries and the government interfering with their agenda, they're becoming much more specific in their attacks and far less concerned with the 'collateral damage' as they refer to it."

Dani knew that collateral damage meant the loss of lives.

"The GCP hasn't officially taken credit for the bombings yet, but government officials are releasing reports that indicate the planning of the bombing may have been in the works for weeks, even months beforehand. They just didn't have enough information as to when and where it would happen." Buck began pacing back and forth in the tile-floored room.

"The initial investigation indicates that the bombing was, in part, a result of the GCP's resentment of the influx of medical professionals and healthcare workers in the region, who speak openly about the role the GCP has played in the spread of HIV among the Ugandan women," Buck told Dani. "They claim that they are being blamed for an epidemic that subsisted long before their own existence."

Dani heard what Buck was saying, yet she could only think of one thing. "Buck, there was a man. I know him only by the name of Dr. Jacks," Dani's voice quivered. "I have to know if he's alive—and a boy. I was with them when the explosion happened."

"Dani…" Buck hesitated. "Dani, most of the entire west wing of the hospital was destroyed. You and a few others were protected by some structural walls that stood in that particular corridor." His voice softened, "Very few got out alive."

A lump caught in her throat. "The entire west wing?" It was a rhetorical question, barely audible even to herself.

"Most were killed." Buck, too, could barely contain his sorrow. "Those who weren't, suffered devastating injuries." Buck was trying to be strong for Dani. Though Dani could not see his tears, she could hear them in his voice.

"Many are still missing. It will likely be months before they have a true account of the number of deaths." Buck choked over his next words, "Some remains are so small, Dani, that it's impossible to identify them." He knew his account of what happened was brutal, but he also knew Dani would want the truth. She would need the truth.

Dani sat voiceless. As her eyes began to adjust to the filtered light, she could see the otherwise invisible particles of dust as they danced through the air between the alternating rays of light and shadow.

As her mind began to absorb the brutality and senselessness of what had happened—the lives that were lost, the innocent children, Jacks—she no longer wanted to see. She simply wanted to close her eyes; to drift off to sleep, never to awake again.

CHAPTER TWELVE

The morning after returning home from Uganda, with lingering pain in her leg, Dani rushed to see Mason. She stood, unnoticed, leaning against the doorjamb of Samuel and Mason's bedroom relishing the easiness of Mason's movements, as he played contentedly with his new little brother. The two boys were playing "pirates," both with patches over their eyes and matching red bandanas covering their heads. Mason had a plastic silver sword and Samuel had a fake plastic hook attached to his right hand.

"Let's hide the gold in the treasure chest," Samuel said to Mason.

"Yeah, then we'll hide it under our bunk beds. Then nobody can find it. It'll be our secret hiding place!" Mason said with excitement. Both boys looked around as if to make sure no one was there to see their new hiding spot.

At once, the boys saw Dani.

"Dani!" Mason dropped the plastic sword and raced toward Dani. "You're back!" He exclaimed. "I missed you."

"Oh, little man, I missed you too." She kneeled to the floor on one knee then hugged him and caressed his supple cheek. "You look like you've grown a foot since I left." David smiled at the joyful reunion as he entered the room and sat on the bottom bunk.

"Maybe I have," Mason said with wide eyes. "Have I, Daddy?" He looked toward David.

David saw Dani's look of surprise as their eyes connected. "Maybe not a foot, kiddo. But you've grown a lot," he said.

"Do I look like I've grown a foot too, Dani?" Samuel said with as much anticipation as Mason.

"I think you've grown two feet," Dani teased as she gave Samuel a big squeeze.

"Uh uh." He giggled. "Then I'd be taller than you, Dani!" He kissed her on the cheek and returned to his treasure chest. Dani was touched by his affection toward her.

"Dani, I was sad when you left. But I taught Daddy and Tracie our special prayers, and they said them with me every night." He squeezed her. "That made it sort of feel like you were here."

"I'm so glad, Mason. My prayers made me not miss you so much either. But I thought about you every day." Dani said with a strange sense of mixed emotion.

"Know what else, Dani?" he questioned with anticipation.

"What?" she said in amusement at his obvious joy.

"Daddy told me that he loves me to heaven and back just like you do." Mason leaned toward Dani and whispered in her ear, "Does it make you sad that I told daddy about how we love each other to heaven and back?" he said with a hint of worry in his voice. Dani's eyes welled up. He was always thinking of everyone else. He was so sweet and sensitive... so innocent.

-- -- -- -- --

The months since she'd been home flew by like a whirlwind. Buck busied Dani with short assignments here and there, but it was more than enough work to make ends meet with a little extra to toss into savings each month. Besides, though the physical therapy had helped, Dani's leg hadn't completely healed, and she sometimes had difficulty getting around. After absentmindedly making the usual monthly deposit into Mason's college fund that she had started for him more than two years ago, Dani rested her pen on the antique cherry roll-top desk that sat in the tiny room which served as both a breakfast nook and an office. She leaned back in the black leather roller chair and reached around for the soft chenille pale yellow throw that had been draped over the chair's back and wrapped it around her shoulders.

She gazed out at the maple trees blowing in the gentle breeze and smiled to herself at the sight of an elderly couple who appeared to be in their mid-eighties strolling hand in hand along the pathway through the adjoining park. They looked so happy, so content—as though they hadn't a care in the world. Dani wondered to herself what fates life had brought them. Had they survived heartache? Had they lost loved ones? Surely they had. They had probably been through wars, the Great Depression. Yet, they appeared joyful, at peace with one another, with life. Dani wondered if she would ever feel that way again.

The events of the past few years, always in the forefront of her mind, began replaying over and over in her head. Her parent's death. Her and Mason's difficult adjustment to losing the people they cared most about in the world. A father Mason didn't even know he had, appearing out of nowhere. The ensuing struggle to find balance in their lives. The almost-affair with Travis— what had she been thinking? Her trip to Uganda. The explosion. The hospital. Jacks. It was all so surreal. A lifetime of experiences wrapped up in less than two-and-a-half years.

Today, the pain was all too vivid, all-consuming. Today, she longed to have Mason sitting on her lap cuddled up with her in the silky layers of the chenille throw just like he'd done so many times before. Today she longed to have her family back. She knew it could never be the way it was when her parents were alive, but she wanted desperately for it to be just her and Mason.

Deep inside, Dani still hoped that somehow, someway, she and Mason would be together again—just like it was during those months following her parents' death. She had grown to not only respect the Fowlers, but to love them as well. They were good to Dani and Mason. They treated her like family. Dani was grateful for that. But the pain of Mason being torn from her life when the two of them needed each other so badly still stung. Though recently, Dani wondered if she hurt more for herself than for Mason. The loss of Jacks only served to foster even deeper feelings of loneliness.

It was clear that Mason was happy—maybe even as happy as he had been when Britta and Randy were alive. He fit in with his new family as though he had been with them forever. So did Dani. Nonetheless, she often fought the inherent meshing that was taking place with such ease between the Fowler family and her. She felt a strange sense of betrayal. It was as though if she were to allow herself to be accepted by the Fowlers—to become a part of their family—she would be betraying her own family. She feared that the closer she became to David and Tracie and the children, the hazier the memories of her family would become.

Sometimes, perhaps after a long enjoyable day spent with Mason and the Fowlers, Dani would wake in the night in a panic. Her parents' faces blurred. Their voices muffled. She would take a long deep breath trying to remember the fragrance of the lilac body lotion her mother used to wear. She would caress her own cheek yearning to feel the tiny prickles of whiskers as her daddy kissed her forehead each night before bed when she was a little girl. Was she beginning to forget them? Was her love for them so fleeting that it was so easily replaced with the love of another family who she'd known for such a short time—the very people who threatened to destroy the bit of semblance she had left of the only family she had ever know? Was she really that callous, that shallow to allow her love for her own family—or the memory of them—be overshadowed by the love she was beginning to feel for the Fowlers?

Inexplicably, since returning from Africa, just as Dani would allow herself to feel connected with the Fowlers, to love and be loved by them, she would pull back, become distant. She would sometimes see Mason do it too. Every once in a while, he would have a far-off look on his face—as though he were in a different time, a different place. His eyes were sad. But even when the sadness was there, Dani thought she could still glimpse a tiny spark. As though Mason were remembering times, places, people that made him simultaneously happy, yet sad. Dani supposed that was the way it worked when people lost loved ones. Hadn't Mason's therapist told her as much? But it lightened Dani's heart to realize that those times when Mason was in his own little world were becoming less and less frequent. Dani even noticed that on those occasions when Mason retreated to that other place in the far reaches of his mind, he would often come back to reality reenergized in a sense; smiling, happy. If Dani could only be like Mason—have the faith of a child—then her memories of her family, and of Jacks, would make her smile, rather than cause her to cry. Someday, maybe. Someday.

Dani leaped to her feet as the telephone brought her back to the present. "Hello," she answered in a hurried voice.

"Did I wake you, Dani? I'm so sorry, I thought you'd be up by now," came Tracie's voice on the other end.

"No, Tracie, you didn't wake me. I've been up for hours," Dani replied, watching the sweet elderly couple disappear beyond a grassy knoll at the far end of the park. "What's up?"

"I was hoping you wouldn't mind an extra guest at dinner on Sunday."

Dani envisioned Tracie running around the house with Kylie on her hip, picking up toys and clothes, tripping over Tonka trucks and dinosaurs, hands full, with only her shoulder left to clutch the telephone receiver to her ear. "Of course, I don't mind. Have I ever minded before?" Dani questioned with a hint of irritation.

"Well, it's David's brother. And you know how I'm always talking about finding you a nice man and trying to fix you up with one of David's friends or one of his coworkers? Well," she continued, "I didn't want you to think that that was what I was doing." Dani heard the dryer buzzer go off in the distance as Tracie feverishly rambled on. "We didn't even know he was coming. He just called last night and asked if he could come see us and maybe stay a few days. He was hoping to—"

Dani interrupted, "Tracie, don't be silly, it's not a problem. But since when does David have a brother? I've never heard of him."

"To make it short, until this morning, David hadn't spoken to Tim—that's his name—in almost seven years. It was right after Tim's wife, Christina, was killed in a car crash. They'd only been married a little over a year when it happened. David went out to Chicago for the funeral. Tim was pretty distraught. David wasn't much help either. He had just finished drug rehab and was still trying to get his life back together. He wasn't sure what to say or do for Tim; he just sort of felt like he was in the way.

"Anyway, David had to get back to work, so a few days after the funeral, he came back to California. After that, David called Tim every day, but Tim wouldn't answer his calls. Tim didn't want anything to do with David…or anyone else for that matter. He tried to contact some of Tim's friends that he'd met at the funeral, but no one knew where Tim was—at least that's what they said. David would send him letters, but they would be returned unopened and *undeliverable*."

"And David hasn't spoken to him since?" Dani prodded, not waiting for an answer before continuing. "Do you even know where he's been all these years? Or where he lives?"

"Well, yes and no," Tracie admitted. "I think he's still living in Chicago. A year or so after Christina's death, David was at a pastoral school in Denver when he ran into a mutual friend that he and Tim had gone to high school with. They ended up going to lunch together. This guy, Phil something-or-other, told David he had heard that shortly after Christina's death, Tim had gotten caught up in the drug scene pretty heavily again and that he was eventually discharged from the Navy.

"I've never met him." Tracie's voice was solemn. "David only has a few pictures of Tim, and he was so young. Back then, he and David looked so much alike.

"All this time, he didn't know if Tim was even alive."

"So he just called up out of the blue?" It was more of a statement than a question.

"Uh-huh. I think David was still in shock when he left for work this morning," Tracie said, followed by a nervous chuckle.

"Well, what did Tim say? Where has he been? What has he been doing? Did he sound angry?" Dani's curiosity was getting the best of her.

"I'm not exactly sure. David answered the phone, and I don't think I heard him say more than a half-dozen words." Apparently, Tracie was as in the dark about what Tim had said as Dani was.

"David just hung up the phone, said that Tim had called, would be here on Friday and would be spending a few days," Tracie offered with another nervous chuckle. "He was in sort of a daze all morning. Didn't say much of anything. Even the kids asked what was wrong with him."

Tracie continued, "The only thing we really talked about is if we should change our plans over the next week. Ya' know, cancel Monday's Bible study, our trip to the City on Saturday, those kinds of things."

"Of course," Dani replied. "We'll skip Sunday dinner this week too. In fact, if you want me to take the kids so the three of you can have some time alone to catch up—I'm sure you'll have a lot to talk about—I'd be glad to have them."

"Thanks, Dani. But David and I agreed that it's best we keep things as normal as possible," Tracie said. "Besides, Tim might want to get to know his nephews and niece," Tracie's voice trailed off slightly. There was an awkward silence between them.

"I'm so sorry, Dani. I didn't mean—"

Dani butted in, "You didn't say anything wrong, Tracie. And you're right. Tim should have a chance to meet the kids. He'll love them. How could he not?" Even with her own words of encouragement, Dani's heart felt heavy. Just one more person to pull Mason away from her. One more person to add to the perfect little family that the Fowlers had created. *Stop!* Dani told herself. *You're just being selfish.* How could she deny Mason all the love that he deserved?

Why was it so hard for her to accept that they could all love Mason? That the Fowler's love for Mason didn't diminish the love that Dani had for him? Or maybe, just maybe, Dani thought, she was afraid that Mason's love for her would fade. Maybe, she thought, if Mason's life with the Fowlers was too good, too fun, he would no longer need Dani. Then where would she be? Her family would be literally nonexistent. And one day, after she was gone, the Shaws would be merely a memory, if that. Even memories fade after time. The footprints would be all but washed away. "Hel-lo. Dani, are you still there?"

"I'm sorry. What did you say?" Dani tried to focus her attention back on the conversation.

"I was just saying that dinner is still at six on Sunday. The usual spaghetti and salad with ranch dressing."

"Are you sure? I don't want to intrude," Dani said with an unconscious slight of sarcasm.

"Of course, Dani. It wouldn't be the same without you. And I promise I won't try to do any matchmaking. Besides, he could be married for all I know." In an instant, Tracie's voice turned to panic. "What if he's still using? He used when he was in high school and supposedly he started using again after Christina died…What'll we do?"

Dani could understand how a person might resort to drugs to drown out their problems, to push away the bad memories. "You'll welcome him anyway. You'll be gracious and loving like you are to everyone," Dani directed with an air of authority.

"Just treat him as though he were one of the people from Celebrate Recovery. You treat them and love them like they're your brothers and sisters. Well, this will be even easier—he *is* David's brother. And whatever baggage he brings with him, you'll show love to him anyway." Dani continued, "And if he is still using and needs help, maybe you and David are an answer to prayer. Maybe that's why he's coming here—to get clean and reconcile with his brother." Dani was merely trying to ease Tracie's anxiety. She was making assumptions. She had no idea why David's brother would come back into their lives after so much time. She also knew that God works in mysterious and incredible ways. Who knew what He had in store.

In a calm, gingerly voice, Tracie conceded, "You're right, Dani. I don't know what I'm worried about. I think I'm just nervous about meeting him. And I'm afraid that David might get hurt again."

"*He's* reaching out to David. *He's* making the efforts this time. That says something, doesn't it?" Dani encouraged.

"I suppose," Tracie conceded.

Dani could hear Tracie's voice return to its hurried pace as though she had changed TV channels. "I've got so much to do before he gets here. This house is a mess. I've got dirty laundry piled to the ceiling. I'm going nuts!" Tracie exclaimed.

"Relax," Dani said soothingly. "I just need to throw my hair back in a pony, and I'll be there in a half-hour."

"You're the best, Dani!" She could hear the smile in Tracie's voice. "What's that you and Mason always say to each other? ISDLY?" Tracie giggled like a little schoolgirl. "That goes for me too Dani, ISDLY! See you in twenty-eight minutes!" Click.

Dani stood in front of the window with the receiver still plastered to her ear. She had been on an emotional rollercoaster ride all morning. And Tracie's last statement set her off. *ISDLY* was a Shaw expression. Her family coined it and only her family had the right to use it. Who did Tracie think she was, taking something so precious and intimate and tossing it at her as though it was something you say to any old stranger? Like "have a nice day" or "can I offer you something to drink?"

Dani's blood was boiling. Really, who did Tracie think she was? Was she trying to take *everything* from her that Dani held dear? Was her sweet, loving way just a facade? The perfect pastor's wife, the perfect mother who never angered, never raised her voice, never judged, who smiled and laughed more in one day than most people do in a lifetime. *That goes for me too Dani, ISDLY!* Was it simply Tracie's way of not just thrusting the knife in Dani's heart, but twisting it as it plunged deeper and deeper into her chest? Did Tracie really think that acting kind to Dani now, would make it easier when they decided that Dani was too much of an intrusion on their perfect little family and she'd be sent packing? She was on to Tracie now. Dani wasn't going to be a part of whatever game she was playing. She would march right over there and give Tracie a piece of her mind.

-- -- -- -- --

Dani pulled into the driveway with a screech. The entire drive over to the Fowler house, she planned what she was going to say. She would tell Tracie exactly what she thought about her sweet little supportive-pastor's-wife show. She would give her a long spiel about hypocrisy. Something about how God knows who she truly is and that even if everyone else could be fooled by her little facade, God knew what was really in her heart. She would end it with a warning: *Mason is my family, he belongs with me, and I'll fight you to the ends of the earth to get him back!* At that moment, Dani decided she was done with her passive, walk-all-over-me ways.

Dani marched up the walkway and through the front door, not stopping to knock. Though, what was intended to be a show of aggression failed to have its intended effect. Dani couldn't remember the last time she knocked before entering the Fowler's home. It had been only weeks after they had started their Sunday night dinners that Tracie said to Dani as she stood in the foyer of the tidy little house, "You don't have to knock, Dani. You're family, and family doesn't knock before they come in." Hugging Dani, she'd said, "Besides that, if I leave David to tend to dinner for more than eight seconds, we'll have to order take-out!" Dani remembered that day with a faint smile. Tracie had thrust the baby into Dani's arms and ran off toward the kitchen ranting something about overcooked pasta.

The memory lightened Dani's mood, if only slightly. Her pace slowed as she first searched the living room for Tracie, then the kitchen, before she heard a catchy little tune come drifting out from the laundry room, which sat adjacent to the sun-filled kitchen.

What began as a quiet rhythm in Dani's ears seemed, in an instant, to permeate the entire house. Dani stopped before reaching the door to the laundry room.

> *Jesus, keeper of this life,*
> *You are my refuge, my savior my guide.*
> *Watch over this little one tonight,*
> *Guard her every footstep as she travels this life.*
> *And in some quiet moment, draw her to Your side,*
> *That she may come to know You As I have come to know*
> *You, As the keeper of this life.*

Amidst the soothing melody of Tracie's voice, the churning of the washing machine, and the tumbling of the dryer, Dani heard a soft contented 'Jesus' escape little Kylie. It sounded to Dani as though she was attempting to sing along with her mother.

Dani stood in the middle of the kitchen for what seemed like an eternity trying to regain her nerve to barge in there and say all the things to Tracie that she had planned to say on her drive over. She took the final three steps toward the door and effortlessly, soundlessly pushed the halfway closed door all the way open.

Sitting crossed-legged on the dryer, surrounded by a pile of dirty clothes, Tracie sat, eyes closed, cradling her nearly-three-year-old baby girl to her chest, gently rocking the precious bundle back and forth as she continued the mesmerizing melody.

That she may come to know You, As I have come to know You, Jesus As the keeper of this life.

Dani stood for a moment longer taking in the picturesque scene. So as not to intrude upon the intimacy of mother and child, she slowly backed out of the doorway of the compact room and pulled the door closed to its original place. Dani turned and robotically made her way to the front of the house and out the entryway. She lowered herself to the wood-planked single porch step and sat with her elbows resting on her knees, her face in her hands.

Dani was ashamed. How could she have ever believed that this precious woman who had become her friend and confidant was anything other than what she appeared? Tracie had not been acting, putting on a facade. She truly was the perfect pastor's wife, the mother who never angered, never raised her voice, never judged, who smiled and laughed more in one day than most people do in a lifetime. Of course, Dani knew that Tracie was *not* perfect, that she was fallible and sinful just like the rest of us. But she also knew that Tracie's love was genuine, authentic. "She is the ultimate example of how God wants each of us to love one another," Dani whispered to herself.

Dani hadn't heard the footsteps approaching from behind. "Oh, Dani, I didn't know you were here. I was in the laundry room, then I went to lie Kylie down for her nap," she explained. "Why are you sitting out here? I told you, you never have to knock, silly. You know you can just come in."

Voiceless, Dani raised her head from her tear-drenched hand and looked up at Tracie.

Tracie's face paled, "Are you alright, Dani? Why are you crying? What happened?"

Dani was speechless. She couldn't find her words.

"You're upset about what I said on the phone." It was more of a statement of fact than a question. "I'm so sorry, Dani. I can be so insensitive sometimes." Her voice began to quiver. "I've just always heard you and Mason say ISDLY to each other and thought it was so sweet, so I asked Mason what it meant."

Tracie continued with her apologies, "After I hung up the phone, I started thinking that maybe I shouldn't have said it. That maybe it was something that should be left between you and Mason. Dani, please forgive me," she begged.

Dani let Tracie go on. "I only said it, Dani, because I truly *do* love you. You're like a sister to me...more than that...you're like a sister, a mother, a daughter, and a best friend all wrapped up in one person." Tracie was crying uncontrollably now.

"Please, Dani, please forgive me," Tracie pleaded as tears rolled down her cheeks. "You must know that I would never intentionally hurt you." She paused, "You *do* know that don't you, Dani?"

Dani moved her mouth in response, but no words would come. The emotions that had built up had consumed her entire being; they lodged in her throat.

"I...you..."

Tracie threw her arms around Dani's neck. "Oh, Dani, I'm so sorry...I'm so sorry...I'm so sorry..."

Dani slowly, methodically returned Tracie's embrace. She swallowed hard. "You have nothing to be sorry for. I'm the one who should be asking for your forgiveness," she said in humbled resolution.

Tracie pulled away from Dani's embrace and rested her hands on Dani's shoulders. "What do you mean?" she asked through her sobs.

"You have been nothing but kind and loving to me since the day I met you. You and David both. You've invited me into your home, into your family. You've treated me with respect even though you didn't have to. We both know that I would never have had a shot at getting custody of Mason. I was fooling myself into thinking that it was all in my control and that *I* was allowing you and David to become a part of Mason's life. When all along, I think I knew I had lost him from that first day at the courthouse."

Tracie interrupted, "We would never—"

Dani stopped her before Tracie could finish her thought. "I know. I've always known. You would never keep me from Mason, even though you had every right to. From the moment I met you, I've tried to find reasons, just *one* reason, to dislike the two of you, justify my feelings of resentment toward you. But I never could." Dani began to cry again.

"And I gave you every reason to hate me. I was mean. I was ungrateful. Even when I could see that Mason was happy and content. I think I was jealous that he loved you so much." Dani shook her head in disgust at her own words.

"Mason does love us. I don't think Mason has ever met a person he didn't love. He has a precious heart." Tracie continued, "But the love he shares with you is irreplaceable. It's founded on years of commitment and trust. He has that kind of love in his heart because of you…you and your family. You taught him that. You demonstrate it every day in the way you live, the way you treat others, the godly example you set." Tracie wiped away a tear that had teetered on the brim of Dani's chin.

"But the way I was feeling about you, the things I was accusing you of in my mind…" Dani buried her face in her hands again. "I'm so sorry."

"Whatever it was, it doesn't matter, and I forgive you." She stroked Dani's hair as a mother might do.

The two women sat in silence for several moments, both sniffling away their remaining tears. Dani raised her head. "Thank you for loving me."

Tracie gently cupped Dani's face in her hands. "Thank you for being so lovable." They both laughed—less out of humor, more out of an emotional release.

Tracie threw her arms around Dani and gave her a tight squeeze. "Now let's get off our fannies and get moving. This house isn't going to clean itself!" she exclaimed.

Tracie looked at her watch. "Oh lordy, the boys are out of school in less than three hours!"

Dani jumped up. "I'll start on the bathroom!" she exclaimed with one last hug.

Tracie was right on her heels. "I've got the kitchen."

CHAPTER THIRTEEN

Dani and Tracie spent the next day getting the guest room ready for Tim. The Fowlers had been using it as an office/sewing room/storage space/library, and it wasn't habitable for the creepy-crawly spiders that sometimes showed up on David's computer screen, let alone a brother he hadn't seen in over five years. The two women spent most of Thursday organizing and moving everything that wasn't going to be used in the near future to the garage. They wasted nearly an hour going through a box of clothes the children had outgrown. Each piece of clothing brought back memories for both Tracie and Dani. Most were happy memories, but for Dani, some were sad.

The box included the dark navy suit Mason had worn that first day at the courthouse—the day Mason was to officially become Dani's adopted son. But then the phone call had come. Dani tried to shake the memory as she ruffled through the clothes to find a tiny pink sleeper that Kylie had worn home from the hospital and a white islet gown Tracie had sewn for the baby's dedication at church. There was a pair of blue jeans and a race car t-shirt that Samuel had worn on his first day of kindergarten. Tracie found a blue and red pair of Spiderman socks that he'd worn for twenty-one days straight, refusing to take them off except to bathe—he even wore them to bed. Tracie chuckled as she explained to Dani that she would wait for Sam to fall asleep, sneak into his room, gently take the socks off of him and throw them in the washing machine. She would make sure they were back on his feet before he woke in the morning.

It was all so surreal to Dani that a simple piece of clothing could evoke such vivid memories and elicit so much emotion. But then, Dani was emotional about a lot of things these days.

An hour and a half later, the women were filling one entire corner of the garage with bins of fabric packed with a dozen unfinished projects Tracie had begun but hadn't had time to complete. They were going through books, getting rid of the older, less utilized ones to make room on the library shelves for newer ones that had been piling up on the floor next to David's desk.

David was a book hound. Most of what he read was biblically based. But he also read a lot of non-Christian books so he could acquire an understanding of the different beliefs and cults and other nontraditional theologies. If nothing else, he'd read them so he was better able to dispute claims that were not consistent with the Bible. He had found that among the participants in his Celebrate Recovery group, there were a lot of questions regarding different philosophies participants had learned over the years, teachings on which their lives had been founded, and simple questions about what was right and wrong in the eyes of God.

David would always explain to the group that the Bible had all the answers and would conduct Bible studies with them, but he would suggest they read additional books that might help them to better understand the passages in the Bible. He would often suggest books that might help them better relate to 'real-life' situations as they often put it. But in truth, the books and the Bible studies and the Friday night meetings all helped in David's own recovery as well.

He learned something new every day about himself and his ever-changing relationship with Christ. He sometimes even felt guilty because many of the participants of his Celebrate Recovery group saw him as a mentor. They often looked up to him and viewed him as a person who had been where they had been or still were, who had overcome his addictions, and now faced a struggle-free life with none of the temptations of drugs or alcohol or the hundreds of other addictions that the rest of them faced every day. He had to remind them continually that the temptations were still there, and he was no better than them. That, though he had overcome his own addictions, it was only because of his faith in God that he was able to find the strength and will to not fall back into his old way of life.

His own life experience was why David was so good as the new assistant pastor at his church and as the leader of the Celebrate Recovery program. He had lived the same kind of life as many of them had. He could relate and he didn't judge. He could emphasize with their daily struggles, the temptations they faced, the stereotypes that others placed on them, and the residual effects of abusive behaviors on family and friends. He understood. But he was also the perfect example of how amazing God's grace is. He was a testimony to God's incredible forgiveness. People were able to look at David and think, "If *he* can be forgiven, then maybe *I* can too."

As Dani continued to rearrange books on the shelf and place them in alphabetical order by the author's name, she couldn't help but think of David and the incredible husband and father he was. Everything he did, he did full force. He did it with conviction and as though he was created to do just that very thing at that very moment. He was always humbled by his mistakes and would never take credit for his successes. He would say that his successes weren't his own. That he couldn't accomplish *anything* good without God's hand in *everything*. He was right, of course. But Dani had not met many people in her lifetime who were so completely humble the way David was. He was a good, honorable man. Dani had known it from the beginning. Although, at first, she had tried to deny it. She wanted to despise the man who had come into her life in one instant and threatened to take away the only thing that still mattered. But Dani knew in her heart she was wrong. David's intentions were good. She knew that David truly believed that what he was doing was the best thing for all of them, especially Mason. He believed that Mason had the right to know his father. He believed that Mason deserved to have the love of as many people who were willing to give their heart to him. He had no intention of taking Mason away from Dani. All he wanted was to surround him with more love than any boy could have ever dreamed possible. That's what David desired for Mason—joy and peace and happiness, and of course, for him to always walk in God's truth and live his life in a way that would glorify and honor to Jesus. A tear streamed down Dani's face as she silently embraced the journey that God had taken her through over the past two years and where it had lead Mason and her. She marveled that, at barely seven years old, that's exactly what Mason did—honor and glorify God in all he said and did. Dani held a book to her chest, closed her eyes, and whispered quietly, "Thank you, Jesus, for your incredible blessings."

"Are you all right, Dani?" Dani hadn't heard Tracie come into the room.

Dani looked at Tracie, with a tear dripping from her chin and a smile on her face, she said, "I couldn't be better. I'm happy, I'm peaceful, and I feel incredibly content right now for some reason." She shook her head with a look of confusion, "I don't know what it is. It's as though in an instant, this warmth came over me and, and all of a sudden, all the pain and worries that have been lingering in the back of my mind were erased!" Dani walked toward Tracie. "You know all those little things I worry about like where is my work going to take me, or am I going to have enough money to pay my bills, or will I ever find a man to marry me—you know, that's a big one." They both laughed. "But even the big worries—you know, like Mason—what's going to happen with him? What kind of man is he going to grow to be with all he's seen and experienced in his short little life? You know, all the things we talk about. The stress of it all just seems to have gone away!"

Tracie wrapped her arms around her sweet friend. "That's all I've ever wanted for you, Dani. For you to be happy in whatever situations God puts you. And for you to be able to accept that as long as you constantly seek Him and His guidance and direction, that wherever you are and whatever you're doing, you would *know*, I mean truly *know* that it is His will for your life." Tracie pulled herself away from Dani's embrace. "And that with that knowledge, He would fill you completely with His peace and contentment."

Dani caressed Tracie's face affectionately with the back of her palm as a sister might do, "Thank you for never giving up on me and for always praying for me.

You know," Dani said as the tears dissipated, "I could always feel your prayers, even when I was in Uganda. Sometimes, I would be walking lost in my own thoughts and prayers, then suddenly stop. I would turn around because I was sure I heard your voice…or David's voice. I would even hear Mason's voice. Of course, you weren't there. But it felt so real." She smiled. "I remember wondering to myself, 'I wonder if they're praying for me right now. Or maybe they're just talking about me.' But it always made me feel good, as though I was still near you."

"You *were* near us. We were praying for you, Dani— all the time. We prayed for you in the morning and at night. We prayed when we sat down to eat. I would pick the boys up from school, and Mason would say that he had been thinking about you and wanted to pray for you. Sometimes, I would be doing dishes or folding laundry, and you would just be so heavy on my heart that I just had to stop what I was doing and say a quick prayer." Tracie continued, "Sometimes, it would be a prayer for something specific, and other times, it would be just that God would protect you. But we never stopped praying for you, Dani. We never will."

Once again, Dani had to fight the tears. She never felt so loved. When she finally found her voice, all she could say was, "Thank you."

-- -- -- -- --

The two women worked all day to get the room in perfect order for Tim. Tracie wanted to make sure he felt welcomed and comfortable. And if Tim wanted to stay longer to connect with his brother again, Tracie wanted him to have a space of his own.

"Tim should be here sometime on Sunday." Tracie continued, "We're going to have dinner around five thirty. It's earlier than usual, but I'd like to get the kids to bed a little early so we can have time to visit with Tim in the evening.

"You can come for dinner, can't you?" Tracie asked with only a slight hesitancy. Tracie knew what tomorrow was, but she wanted to do whatever she could to make it bearable for Dani. She thought that Dani might want to be surrounded by people who loved her while she faced the two-year anniversary of her parent's death.

"Thanks, Tracie, but I think I need to do this on my own," Dani said, attempting to be brave. "I was thinking that it might be good for me to go out to the gravesite. I haven't been able to go since the funeral. It's just been too difficult."

"I know. We make it a point to bring Mason out there on the first Sunday of every month. He used to be sad whenever we'd go, but believe it or not, he looks forward to going now." She continued, "We always get flowers, lilies for your mom, because Mason says he thinks they would be her favorite. We also bring a chocolate ice cream cone for your dad every time."

Her eyes glistening with tears, Dani looked at Tracie. "Chocolate was always dad's favorite."

"Mason said that every night, he and Randy used to sit out on the deck and see who could spot the most shooting stars." With a gentle voice, Tracie continued, "He said they would have a contest to see who could eat his ice cream cone the fastest. Did they really do it every night, Dani?"

"Yep. Well, every night when he was living with my folks. But of course, Amanda had him some of the time." Dani remembered as sadness swept over her.

"But without fail, whenever Mason was with mom and dad, there was always chocolate ice cream in the freezer, even in the winter time when the temperature was below zero." Dani chuckled. "I think it was mostly dad's way of justifying his ice cream addiction. Mom was always watching dad's diet and making sure he ate healthy. But I think he knew she wouldn't be able to resist the nightly chocolate ice cream eating tradition to which dad and Mason had become so accustomed.

"But dad loved his 'special' time with Mason. Just the two 'men' all alone, talking about the stars, and how clouds form, and what heaven might be like, and a thousand other thoughts." Dani smiled with the memory of her father and Mason.

"I miss them so much," Dani whispered, barely audible.

Tracie set her coffee down and reached across the counter to gently caress Dani's hand. "I know you do, Dani. I'm sorry things have been so hard for you. You and Mason have been through more in the past two years than anyone should have to experience in an entire lifetime.

"I know you probably don't want to hear this, but you're a stronger person because all that has happened to you. None of it makes sense, and it all seems so tragic and unfair, but it's all part of a bigger—maybe even better— plan." Tracie's words mimicked those that Jacks had spoken to Dani that day in Gulu.

Tracie squeezed Dani's hand. "It's almost like we become so complacent with our lives and the people in them. We take them for granted and expect that they'll always be here. We begin to make plans for our future, it's only natural. We come to depend on them for our security, our happiness, our well-being." Tracie stood and walked toward the kitchen window that faced the children's swing set in the grass-covered backyard.

"Then, it's as though God says, 'Look at *Me*! Put your faith in *Me*. I am the *One*. I am the *only One* who can meet your needs and fulfill the desires of your heart." Tracie turned to face Dani. "I'm not saying that that's what you did, Dani—become complacent or take your family for granted. I'm just saying that we all make plans for our lives, our futures. There's nothing wrong with that. But the hardest thing to do is say, 'I know my plans may not be yours, God, so help me to accept your will for my life'." Tracie reached for her coffee mug and cupped it with both hands as if to warm them. "I learned that lesson a little too late."

Dani watched as Tracie's face turned an ashen tone. "What do you mean?"

In a shaky voice, Tracie began, "You know that I was raised in a godly home. I went to Christian schools all my life. My family and my church were my life. I was always very outspoken about abstinence until marriage and spearheaded big events that included well-known speakers and entertainers as a way to spread a positive message to teenagers about abstinence.

"I knew I was going to be a virgin until I got married. I wanted to save myself for my future husband." Tracie began to pace nervously.

"I had my whole life planned out. I would go to a Christian college right out of high school. I would meet my future husband right around my sophomore year. He would be on his way to a successful career. We would date the next few years and get married the summer after graduation… of course, he would have saved himself for me too. I would be the elementary school teacher that I was so certain I was meant to be. We would have the typical 2.5 kids, a dog named Fluffy, and the white picket fence." Tracie chuckled cynically. "It was a perfect plan."

There was a moment of silence before either of them spoke. Dani wasn't sure she was prepared to hear what Tracie was going to say next. Finally, Dani asked, "Then what happened? Something changed all of that?" It was more of a statement than a question.

Tracie's hands began to tremble. Dani grabbed for Tracie's cup just before it went tumbling to the ground.

Dani reached for a paper towel and wiped away the small amount of spilled coffee that had fallen to the floor. "You don't have to talk about it if you don't want to," Dani assured Tracie.

Tracie pulled a bar stool from under the counter and strategically positioned herself with her hands folded and resting on the counter in front of her. "No. I need to tell you. I've wanted to tell you for a long time. I just never found the right time." Tracie took a long, deep breath. "It happened when I was a senior in high school. Our youth group had gone to pizza and bowling on a Friday night. There was a whole group of us. We'd bowled until almost midnight when we all decided to head home. We had done the same thing a hundred times before—Pizza at Antonio's, then we'd walk the three blocks to Discovery Lanes to bowl and just hang out.

"This particular night was no different. After bowling, we all walked back to Antonio's and headed for our cars. I had driven alone because I had a student government meeting that went until five thirty, and I knew I was going to be late to pizza," Tracie hesitated.

"Anyway, we all said our goodbyes. I was the last to get into my car. By this time of the night, Antonio's was closed, and there wasn't anyone else around. I started to back up as everyone else was pulling out of the parking lot in front of me. I heard a loud bang and thought I had backed into one of the brick planter boxes that lined the parking lot. I put my car in park and got out to see if it had been damaged. I didn't think anything about it until I walked around the back end of the car, and there was nothing there—no planter box, nothing. All of a sudden, a chill ran up the back of my neck, and even though I couldn't *see* anyone, I could *feel* that someone was there." Tracie looked down at her nervous hands as if she was ashamed.

Before I knew what was happening, a man pushed me onto the backseat of my own car. He never said a word. He just held a knife to my throat the whole time. It was all over in a matter of minutes, but it seemed like hours." Tracie pressed her palms to her eyes trying to stop the tears from coming. Dani just listened, trying to be strong for Tracie, but barely able to contain her own emotions.

Tracie reached for a tissue. "The next thing I knew, I was sitting in the driver's seat of the car and my dad was pounding on the window and shouting my name. He kept yelling, 'Open the door, Tracie. Open the door.' I remember that I couldn't look at him. I was so ashamed."

Now, it was Dani who felt ashamed. She didn't know what to say; didn't know how to comfort her dear friend.

She walked toward Tracie and put her arms around her and simply held her. "It wasn't your fault,

Tracie. It wasn't your fault. You had nothing to be ashamed of."

Tracie sniffed, "I know that *now*. But at the time, all I could think of was what a disgrace it would be to my family. I felt like everyone would look at me differently. I was scared and humiliated and so terribly ashamed."

Tracie stood and nervously smoothed the creases from her pants. "There's more," she said.

Dani sat in silence, her heart aching for Tracie as she listened to how her life unfolded in the aftermath of her assault.

"I sort of withdrew from everyone and everything. I stopped seeing my friends, missed a lot of school. I wouldn't even open up to my mom. I started going to counseling, but nothing helped. I even stopped praying. I didn't care about anything. Then I missed my period. But even before that, I knew. I didn't tell anyone until I was almost six months pregnant. I think I was in denial. Like…if I didn't say the words, it wasn't real." Dani noticed an odd sense of calm wash over Tracie's face. "But it *was* real."

Tracie went on, "By the time I told my folks about the pregnancy, I had already decided that I was going to place the baby for adoption." She shook her head as she remembered back. "They were a mess. They didn't know what to do or even how to support me with my decision. I could see that they felt helpless. I think I hurt more for them than for myself. But in the end, it was the best thing for everyone."

Dani was speechless. She poured herself another cup of coffee absently spooning heaps of sugar into the steaming liquid.

By now, Tracie had gathered herself and had regained the color back in her face. She took hold of Dani's hand, removed the spoon and placed it on the counter. Tracie could tell by the look on her face that Dani was dumbfounded. "Ask me anything, Dani. It sometimes feels better just to talk about it."

"But…so…you have another child out there somewhere?" Dani asked, not really expecting an answer.

"Yes." Tracie smiled in obvious sentiment. "A fifteen-year-old daughter. Her name is Emily. She lives in Ohio with her parents and four brothers."

"Do you ever see her?" Dani had so many questions.

"I receive photos of her about once a year, usually around her birthday." Almost as an afterthought. "She looks like my mom, big green eyes and strawberry-blonde hair." Then, as if returning from a dream, Tracie continued, "It was an open adoption, which meant that I could have contact with her. I saw her three times that first year. But every time I would have to say goodbye, it tore my heart out. Back then, California had a reclaim period of one year. That meant I could change my mind about letting her go up until Emily was a year old—no questions asked. They never said it, but I think her adoptive parents were worried that I *would* change my mind."

Dani was in awe. "What an incredibly unselfish thing to do."

"I didn't feel selfless. I felt like I was a horrible person. How could a mother give up her own child? But I realized that my baby girl deserved more than I could give her. She deserved to have a mother and a father who loved her. To be part of a family who could provide for her, where she could be spoiled by her daddy, cuddled by her mama, and protected by her brothers. Besides that, every time I looked at her, I thought of that horrible night. That one night ruined my life. I wasn't going to let it ruin hers too."

Dani was still trying to take it all in. "What a dreadful memory to have to live with. How did you get through that and still turn out so...normal?"

Tracie chuckled. "'Normal' is a relative term." She could see by the look on Dani's face, that it was her turn to comfort Dani. "I lived through it, Dani. It took a lot of years of trying to do it on my own. And even more years learning to trust in God again and grow from it and even learn from it. How do you think I met David?" Tracie asked redundantly.

"Celebrate Recovery? I always wondered, but didn't want to pry."

Tracie affectionately ruffled Dani's hair. "How many times have I told you, you're my family, you can talk to me about anything.

"David helped me through some really tough times. At the time, he didn't lead the group. He was still recovering, at the same time I was trying to deal with my own addictions. But he was a lot further along in his recovery than I was," Tracie explained matter-of-factly.

"What do you mean your 'own addictions'?"

"I mean that I found my own way of coping. I started eating...a lot. Every time I'd get stressed out or face something sad or uncertain in my life, I would eat. Food made me feel better. My weight eventually began to spiral until the doctors were seriously worried about my health. My parents really encouraged me to try

Celebrate Recovery. I finally did. And I haven't stopped going since."

Tracie began busying herself by emptying the dishwasher. "So that's what I meant when I said, 'it's all part of a bigger, better plan'. What happened to me was tragic, not as tragic as what happened to you, but it was certainly life-changing. Through it all, I met an incredible man who loves Jesus first and would give his life for me and the kids. I'm constantly amazed at how God works. I know this, Dani, everything that happens has a purpose. I believe that God doesn't necessarily *make* things happen, but He does *allow* things to happen. We may never know why certain things happen, but one day, we will. He'll reveal it all to us in his perfect timing. It may not be until we get to heaven, but it's all a part of His plan. And the thing is, it's not in our control." The two women were silent lost in their own thoughts.

In almost a whisper, Tracie said, "I'm sorry, Dani. I didn't mean to preach."

"I didn't feel like you were preaching. It felt more like God was speaking directly to me, but using your body and your voice," Dani confessed. "Although I know those things theoretically, I think He needed me to hear it from you."

It was as though in those intimate moments that the two shared, Tracie revealing her most sacred, personal experience with Dani, that a dam had broken. They felt closer and more connected than ever before. Dani wanted to know more, but she knew that Tracie would open up in her own time. She was content in knowing that Tracie was truly her best friend and most trusted confident.

For the quadrillionth time that day, Tracie and Dani shared an affectionate embrace. This time, though, there was an inexplicable bond that passed between them. One that Dani knew could never be broken.

By the end of the day, Dani and Tracie were both emotionally and physically drained. The strain of what Tracie had revealed and the anxiety of seeing Tim for the first time, combined with moving boxes, furniture, and endless junk from the guest room took its toll on the two women. Tracie was glad that she hadn't had to stop in the middle of their project to pick up the boys at three. It helped her and Dani stay focused on the work they'd needed to get done.

Like he did nearly every Thursday, David had left work early to pick the boys up from school. He took them for ice cream and then to the park. Not only did it allow Dani and Tracie the time they needed to get the house ready for company, but this week, David's playdate with the boys also allowed him the opportunity to relieve some of the anxiety he'd been feeling since his call from Tim only three days earlier.

David wasn't sure what to expect. Was Tim coming to vent his anger? Was he coming to try to reconcile their relationship as brothers? Did he simply want to meet his family? David truly had no idea why his brother was coming to see him after all these years. David had to admit to Tracie the night before as they lay in bed—Tracie on the verge of sleep, David reading his Bible, unable to let go of the uneasy feeling that had consumed him all week—that he was afraid. "I'm afraid that Tim coming back into my life—our lives—might bring back all the old stuff," David had confessed. "He never said it, but I think Tim might have blamed me for dad leaving and even mom's death."

Tracie had curled up next to David and sprawled her arm across his chest. Without a word, she kissed him gently on the mouth as he pulled her closer to him. As they laid next to one another, for the very first time in their marriage, David began to open up to her about his childhood and his parents and his relationship with his brother.

"Tim was only fourteen and I was sixteen. Mom and dad were always fighting. They fought about everything, especially us kids. Mom didn't like the way dad disciplined us. But instead of putting a stop to it, my mom would scream at him while he beat us until we were black and blue. She'd start drinking until she passed out. When she'd wake up, it would be another day, and I think in her mind, it had all been more of a dream than reality.

"She'd ignore the bruises, and Tim and I would stay home from school for days at a time so our teachers wouldn't suspect what was going on." David had chuckled cynically. "But they knew. Child Protective Services even showed up at school and at the house a couple of times. Mom had always told us that if the police came, we were to tell them that everything was fine; that we had fallen off our bikes or something. So they'd come. We'd answer their questions just like mom had instructed. They'd look in the refrigerator to make sure there was food to eat. Mom always kept the house immaculate—that was the one thing that she really cared about, making sure the house was spotless when dad got home from work...or the bar...or wherever else he had been—so they never questioned whether we were being neglected." David ran a nervous hand through his hair as he remembered back. "If they'd only known."

"Anyway, I started acting up. They caught me smoking a couple of times. I was even suspended from school for bringing a bottle of Vodka to campus one day. As usual, mom and dad fought and I got beat. One time when mom found some dope when she was cleaning out my bedroom closet—she was *always* cleaning—she showed my dad." David shook his head with a confused look on his face. "To this day, I can't figure out why she did. She knew what would happen."

Tracie had looked up at David's face. For a brief second, she saw anger. But his next words revealed only determination.

"I was sick and tired of dad knocking us around. So when I heard him coming toward my room, I told Tim to hide in the closet, and I grabbed an old wooden baseball bat. When he opened the door, I was standing there with the bat raised above my head. First, dad looked like he was scared. Then he started toward me and said, 'Put that thing down, you no good druggie!' When I raised the bat even higher and swung, he ducked and it slammed full force into the wall. The bat broke in half and the top half went flying. It ricocheted off dad's arm, but it didn't hurt him." Tracie had only known David to be a gentle, kind man who didn't have a violent bone in his body. Listening to him recount what happened sent a chill up her spine.

"I stood there with the broken bat in my hand. I could tell by the look on his face that dad was afraid. He knew I'd swing it again if I had to. He just stood there speechless. Finally, he turned and walked away. It was the first time I ever stood up to him. It felt good," David recalled. "And it was the last time he ever beat either of us." David sighed loudly. "He was gone by the end of the week…walked out of the door and never came back."

David continued as if recounting the story of someone else's life, or perhaps retelling the scenes of a movie. "Over the next few years, mom's drinking was out of control. She didn't care about anything anymore. Not even us. She even stopped cleaning the house and doing laundry. All she did was watch soap operas and drink and cry and sleep. I truly think she was waiting for him to come back. All day long, she'd sit on the front porch with her bottle of booze rocking back and forth in the wicker swing and staring down the street as if he was going to show up any minute. Like she expected him to skip up the stairs holding his lunch pail and a dozen roses and sweep her off her feet."

As an afterthought, he'd continued, "I don't know what was worse on her mental state, the booze or the soap operas." He shook his head with a combination of disgust and sympathy. "Either way, she lived in her own little world. And Tim and I weren't a part of it anymore."

David looked sad. Tracie squeezed him closer to her as she gently outlined a scar on his chest that served as a constant reminder to David each time he looked in the mirror of his loveless, volatile childhood.

"Did your mom ever get better?" Tracie had asked. "I mean did she ever stop drinking. Or get over your dad leaving?"

"Not really. My uncle called about two years after dad left and told us that he'd been killed in a motorcycle accident. He hadn't crashed his bike or anything. They just found his Harley on the side of the road with the kickstand up. He was sitting alongside of it and looked like he had just stopped to take a rest. They said he'd had a heart attack." Even with all the abuse the man had inflicted upon him and his brother, David had still loved his father. The news of his death had been hard for David to take. It was even harder on his mother.

"Mom hit rock bottom after that. Within the year, her liver went. We didn't even have money to buy a headstone for her grave. Tim and I and a couple of neighbors were the only ones at her funeral," his voice cracked at the realization of how lonely his mother must have been throughout her life. It made him sad to know that even her children had not been a source of happiness for her.

Tracie's eyes filled with tears as she listened to her husband share his innermost secrets. She hurt for David and all that he had gone through. "What happened to you and Tim? You were just boys," she asked, almost pleadingly.

"By that time, I was nineteen and Tim was seventeen. Tim enlisted in the Navy. I found an apartment and worked odd jobs to get by. But mostly, I just drank and did drugs." David had raised Tracie's hand to his lips and gently kissed each finger as if she were a porcelain doll.

"I'm not sure how I ended up in Glenbrook, but I did. I was high on meth when I met Amanda."

This wasn't the first time David had told Tracie of how he'd met Amanda and spiraled downward after that. But she knew he needed to talk about it again.

"I ended up in jail for like the third time on drug charges." David wiped the tears from his face with the back of his hand.

"I really thought I was going to prison because, this time, they got me with intent to distribute. Before, I'd only been arrested for possession and pretty much got a slap on the wrist. But this time was different." Tracie could feel David's pulse begin to race.

"I remember walking into the courtroom that day knowing that when I walked out, they would be sending me straight to prison. For the first time since I was a boy, I was scared to death." David paused for what seemed like an eternity to Tracie, but she waited patiently for him to find his next words.

"I'd never really prayed before…not like I was really talking to anyone anyway. But all of a sudden, I felt calm. I closed my eyes and talked to God as if He was standing right beside me. I asked Him to please give me another chance. I told him that if He allowed me to go free, I would change my life. I would make better choices. That I wouldn't let my past dictate my future. I promised Him that I would do everything in my power to learn about Him and who He really was." David persisted, "What's crazy is that I really meant it."

Shaking his head as if coming back from a distant place, David continued, "Then, the judge called my name. My public defender and I stepped up to the defendant table and stood there. The judge looked at me for the longest time. It was really uncomfortable. Even my attorney was kind of wriggling around. I remember that he looked at me and shrugged his shoulders like he didn't know what was going on either."

David continued unrelentlessly, "You could hear people in the courtroom whispering and even some chuckles. Then the judge says to me, 'Son, I realize you're here for sentencing today. However, I'm feeling compelled to refrain from rendering my decision at this time. I would like to postpone adjudication for two weeks.'

"I wasn't sure what to think. My attorney thought it might be a good thing. That maybe the judge wasn't ready to send a twenty-two-year-old kid to prison for ten years. I was sure hoping he was right.

"So, that night when I was laying in bed, all alone in my cell, I started thinking about the promise I had made to God. I remember thinking, 'I wonder if God is just testing me to see if I will keep my word.'

"Later when the officer came around to do a head check, I asked him if I could get a Bible. He called me down a few minutes later and handed me a book called *Celebrate Recovery*. It was a Bible, but it also had notes for people recovering from different addictions that help them relate to and understand what the Scriptures are saying. It gave me a real-life application to my own life and the things I had experienced.

"Two weeks later, I showed up at court with no idea what was going to happen. When the judge said he was sending me to rehab instead of prison, I couldn't believe it." Humbled, David had said, "It was the best thing that ever happened to me."

"I had just completed the program when I met you." David kissed Tracie's forehead. "And you know the rest."

They made love that night with the lights turned off. Touching, feeling, loving—as though it was the first time.

CHAPTER FOURTEEN

She'd been in an exceptionally cheerful mood since she awoke to a ray of morning sunshine warming her cheeks. The pain in her leg had kept her awake during part of the night, so instead of her usual early morning run before church today, Dani decided to bring her Bible down to the massive maple tree that stood as a masterpiece at the top of the rolling hills in the park below her bedroom window. She used to do that a lot; spread out a blanket and read and observe the people as they strolled through the lingering gravel pathways that intertwined throughout the park. She'd watch as a daddy hoisted his baby girl up into the air and captured her in his embrace as she came ascending back down to the safety of his arms. She'd smile at the sight of childhood friends playing hide-and-seek among the trees and shrubbery that landscaped the park. She'd daydream of a love that she hoped she would find one day, as a young couple strolled hand in hand along the paths, stopping only to embrace or look passionately into each other's eyes. Retrievers out for their daily walk. Squirrels frantically in search of their next meal. Birds singing a familiar melody. Those were just some of the reasons Dani was drawn to the park. Those were the things that caused her fast-paced life to slow down, if only for a moment. All that those people and things stood for—joy, contentment, love, family—that's what Dani wanted.

So she would go there to read and watch and daydream and hope and pray. Only eventually to be forced to pluck herself away from the glimpses of a world that she so desperately desired.

An hour later, sitting crossed-legged on the sprawled out quilted blanket and mesmerized by Scripture, Dani was oblivious to anything or anyone around her. While she'd been reading in the book of Philippians, chapter 1, as it had done so many times before, her mind kept wandering back to verses 3 through 6:

> *I thank my God every time I remember you. In all my prayers for all of you, I always pray with joy because of your partnership in the gospel from the first day until now, being confident of this, that he who began a good work in you will carry it on to completion until the day of Christ Jesus.*

Dani knew that God was speaking to her through that Scripture. He had been for a long time and on many different occasions, especially throughout the past two years. But what was he trying to tell her—besides the obvious? What *good work* had He begun in *her*? To Dani, her life had been a series of mediocre self-fulfilling accomplishments and relative minimal success in her career, filled with short-lived relationships and insignificant encounters. "Not much *good work* there," she said, unconsciously revealing her thoughts aloud.

Dani pondered the enthusiasm she'd possessed as a teenager. At sixteen, Dani was sure that one day she would revolutionize the world. Make it a better place. Witness to people in far reaches of the deepest jungles and driest deserts who, otherwise, would never know what Christ did on the cross for them. She was going to touch lives and change hearts. Her imagination was boundless then. She was certain that God truly was going to use her in mighty ways. But this morning, with the mediocrity of her life staring her in the face, those youthful dreams seemed, to Dani, completely unattainable. She wasn't even certain fulfilling those dreams was what she wanted anymore. She didn't know *what* she wanted. And so she prayed.

Dani prayed for God's direction in her life. She prayed for forgiveness in the areas of her life where she knew she had failed God. She prayed for discernment to make the right choices. She prayed for contentment. She prayed for Mason. She prayed for God to ignite a fire in her that couldn't be squelched by obstacles or hardship or life itself. She prayed for someone with which she could share her life and raise a family. She prayed for humility. She prayed for boldness to share Christ's love. She prayed that she would honor and glorify God in her everyday life. She prayed for David and Tracie and Tim and the children. She prayed for Uncle Buck. She prayed for Jacks; he was gone, but she still prayed.

He who began a good work in you will carry it on to completion. The words reverberated in her mind over and over. In the next moment, it hit Dani like a brick. It was true, Dani didn't know what *she* wanted, but she realized that God was adamant about what *He* wanted for her. Though she didn't quite know yet what His plans might be, Dani understood, beyond that of any understanding she'd had ever before, that God truly did have a plan for her life; that God had placed her on Earth to fulfill a purpose—His purpose. Her heart literally jumped at the excitement of the opportunities that lay ahead.

Moments later, Dani jumped up, grabbed her belongings, and headed back to her cozy little condominium with a regenerated fervor for life. From now on, Dani decided, she would begin living her life focused not on what *she* wanted out of it, but rather, on what *God* wanted for her. She looked forward with anticipation to what He had in store.

CHAPTER FIFTEEN

Dani was just removing her world-famous double-fudge-chocolate-chocolate-chip cake from the oven when the telephone interrupted her franticly hurried pace.

"Hello," she said as she grabbed the receiver with one hand and stood holding the just-out-of-the-oven scalding hot cake with her other oven-mitted hand.

"Dani, when awe you gonna get hewe?" It was Mason. As usual, he sounded excited in his inherited impatient way.

"Mason?" she announced, though it was more of a statement than a question. "How's my little man this morning?"

"Gweat!" he exclaimed. "Chuch was weally fun. We got to do fingew painting. I painted a pictuew of Jesus on a fishing boat. Miss Ali told us a stowy about Jesus and the fishewmen." Dani couldn't help but smile as she listened to Mason's uninhibited enthusiasm in describing his morning adventures. He always seemed to revert back to his pre-speech therapy way of speaking whenever he was excited.

"I can't *wait* to see your picture," she exclaimed with almost as much enthusiasm as Mason. "I'm sure it's a masterpiece. Can I hang it on my refrigerator?"

"Well...I was thinking," he began, sounding like a little adult. "You alweady have lots of pictuews fwom me." He continued, "And Uncle Tim doesn't have any. So I gave it to him. He said it's the best pictuew of Jesus he evew sawed." Dani could envision Mason on the other end of the telephone bouncing up and down with pride in his creation. She had to chuckle.

"You mean he said, 'it's the best picture of Jesus he ever *saw*'," she corrected in her usual journalistic perfectionism. As quickly as she said it, Dani silently admonished herself for raining on Mason's proverbial parade.

"Uh, huh, 'the best picture of Jesus he ever *saw*'," Mason corrected, emphasizing the *r* in the word picture and slowly and measurably drawing out the word *saw* as he spoke.

Unaffected by Dani's need to rectify the idiosyncrasies of a seven-year-old's language habits, Mason continued, "Uncle Tim's weally nice, Dani. He dwives a big motocycle. It's weally loud and weally cool, and it's bwight wed just like youw Jeep!" Mason barely took a breath between sentences as he talked about his uncle Tim who had obviously become Mason's new best buddy in only a matter of hours.

The heat of the cake pan was beginning to penetrate the oven mitt, and Dani nearly dropped the cake on the floor as it crashed to the countertop. "Wow, Mason, your uncle Tim sounds pretty neat." Dani licked a melted chocolate chip from her thumb as she tried to form a mental picture of Tim. She wondered to herself if he looked anything like David. Was he tall and slim like his mother had been, or stocky like his father? Dani wondered if Tim had inherited the Fowler trait of long, slender fingers. Did he have those big blue eyes like his older brother? *Those eyes. Those eyes.* But as Dani's mind began to drift, all she could see was Jacks. His piercing green eyes. She remembered how he'd looked at her as though he could see right into her heart. Dani fought back the memories of her short time with him. As she had done so many times over the past few months, she silently asked God why He would bring Jacks into her life, only to take him away in some senseless tragedy. Was He simply giving her a glimpse of what He has in store for her one day? Allowing her a bit of hope? Perhaps that was it. But even in the short time she'd had with Jacks, Dani knew the love she felt for him would be embedded in her heart forever. She was in love with a man whose body lie buried deep beneath a mound of rubble. She needed to forget. She had to move on and not let the memories—as few and short-lived as they were—consume her. She had to take the love she had for Jacks and cling to it, shape it, and mold it in a way that maybe one day she could share that love, only deeper and stronger, with the man that God has planned for her. She had so wished that man was Jacks. But, once again, God had other plans for her. Dani knew she had to put that chapter of her life behind her.

Finally, Dani's thoughts began to drift back to the present. Maybe God was writing a new chapter. Was it possible that Tim might be a part of this new beginning? She wondered. She closed her eyes as she tried to create an image of the man she was going to meet in less than an hour. It wasn't difficult to imagine what her potential knight in shining armor might look like as she closed her eyes.

Earlier in the week while they were getting the guest bedroom ready for Tim's arrival, Dani had asked Tracie why there weren't any pictures of Tim.

Tracie had said that when David and Tim had their "falling out," David couldn't bare to see Tim's photos. It was as though pictures of the two of them together brought back so many bad memories for David—memories of experiences that he felt were the core reason Tim had severed his relationship with his older brother. Tim must have blamed David for everything. David was the older brother. Hadn't it been his job to protect Tim? It ate away at David.

Tracie had tried to explain it to Dani, "It's like…if he didn't see the photos of Tim…he didn't have to think about him. Where was he? What was he doing? Was he all right? Or was he even alive."

Dani had seen the pain in Tracie's eyes that day as she described how David, during their move from Southern California, had gone through every photo album and tore out all the photos of Tim. The framed family portraits, which were few and far between, a picture taken of David and Tim as children riding their bikes down a gravel drive, a picture of Tim in his dress whites that was taken during naval basic training, Tim and Christine on their wedding day—all of it—boxed up and packed away in some far corner of the attic.

Since Tim had called out of the blue last week though, David was determined to find that box of sealed up memories before Tim showed up at their door on Sunday. David didn't want Tim to know that he had all but erased Tim from his life during those years he was away. David was ashamed that he had so easily tried to dismiss the inherent bond that two brothers had formed over a lifetime of shared experiences. Never again, though. Tim was coming home. And if David had anything to say about it, his baby brother would become a permanent piece of the family puzzle that had been missing for far too long.

"Da-ni. Aren't you listening to me?" Mason asked exasperatedly, his rate of speech slightly dawdling.

"I'm so sorry, little man. I guess I was thinking about something else. What were you saying?"

"I sa-id, Uncle Tim said it was our secret—but I can tell *you*—that I'm his favorite oldest nephew!" Mason shared his secret with Dani in a hushed whisper as to not hurt his little brother and sister's feelings. After all, it's not every day that your brand-new, best-buddy, uncle tells you you're his favorite.

"Of course, you're his favorite," Dani assured. "Just like you're my favorite oldest cousin too!"

Mason laughed his sweet little belly laugh. "That's silly, Dani. I'm your *only* cousin!"

"Oh, that's right," she teased. "I forgot!" causing them both to laugh even harder.

"What's Tracie doing? Is she busy?" Dani asked Mason when his sweet little laugh finally subsided.

"She's making dinner. You know that, Dani. She always makes spaghetti on Sundays!" Mason exclaimed, still excited, but more conscious of his speech.

"I know, kiddo. Can I talk to her for just a second though?"

"Okay, but hurry. I want you to meet Uncle Tim!"

Dani heard in the distance, "Tracie, Dani wants to talk to you," as the Fowler's phone went crashing to the ground. Dani cringed at the ringing in her ear.

"Sorry about that, Dan, he slid across the kitchen floor and munched it. The phone went tumbling under the table," Tracie explained in annoyed amusement.

"Is he all right?" Dani asked, only slightly concerned because she hadn't heard any crying on the other end of the telephone.

"He's fine. As tough as always." Tracie continued, "He's a little trooper. He's already back in the living room wrestling with Tim."

"So," Dani asked, "is he as great as Mason says he is?"

"He's pretty terrific," Tracie admitted. "He's clean and sober and looks healthy. Don't know much more than that. since Dave last saw him?" Tracie couldn't help but wonder.

"I don't know. David doesn't want to push it. He figures Tim will tell him when he's ready. They've only talked about real surfacy stuff so far. I can tell they're both a little nervous," Tracie admitted.

"You can't blame them. It's got to be pretty awkward," Dani returned.

"Yeah, it's a little awkward. But they were so happy to see each other. When David answered the door this morning, they both just stood there for a few seconds, then threw their arms around each other and embraced for the longest time," Tracie's voice cracked. "We all cried.

"You know what's really great though? He went to church with us this morning and seemed to really like it. He even knew most of the songs. I think he might be walking with the Lord," Tracie said with a hint of giddiness to her tone. "He's darling, too, Dani. I think you're going to like him."

"That's what Mason said." Dani closed her eyes as she tried to will herself to open her heart to the possibility.

"Come on, Dan. I know things have been hard for you," Tracie said with complete sincerity. "Please just don't shut yourself off to the idea."

Dani exhaled a sigh of resignation. "I'll try," she said.

"Dani, please *really* try," Tracie pleaded. "Promise me you will."

"I will. I promise," she said, knowing how difficult it was going to be to keep that promise. A half hour later, Dani was out the door, leaving a trail of chocolate glaze behind her.

-- -- -- -- --

The traffic was unusually heavy for a late Sunday afternoon. In her typical impatient style, Dani was driving way too fast and tailgating way too close to the car in front of her. She was already late for dinner, and she knew how anxious Mason was for her to get there. Although, truth be told, Mason had probably forgotten all about her the second he dropped the phone to resume his roughhousing with his uncle.

Dani darted in and out of traffic in her hurried pace. "Come on. Come on," she said exasperatedly—to no one, to everyone. She took the final turn onto the Fowler's street a little too fast, which sent the chocolate cake rolling and finally plummeting to the floorboard. Dani's futile attempt to catch the cake before its final descent left her covered in chocolate glaze.

Exasperated by her own carelessness, Dani came to a screeching halt in front of the Fowler's house. Becoming more irritated by the minute, she reached for the tousled cake that now looked as though it had been created by a five-year-old. By now, Dani looked, she imagined, as unkempt as the neglected cake. Removing the plastic wrap that now covered only half of the chocolate blob, Dani attempted to reconstruct some semblance of the masterpiece she had left her house with only fifteen minutes earlier. She licked some of the sticky glaze from her fingers and unwittingly left a chocolaty smudge on her cheek. Looking at the cake in its final state, Dani was relatively pleased with her damage control endeavors. It didn't look great, but Dani knew the kids wouldn't care, and David and Tracie were far too polite to mention it. Tim, though,

Dani thought, was sure to think she was challenged when it came to baking.

"What do I care anyway?" Dani asked herself aloud. "Why would I want to impress some guy I've never met before?" she continued, hypothetically as she headed toward the front steps. She was still mumbling to herself when the front door flung open and Mason came catapulting out, throwing his tiny arms around Dani's waist. "Dani, you're finally here!" he exclaimed.

Dani lost her balance and nearly dropped the already disheveled cake as she attempted to steady herself. "Whoa, little man," she said, trying to hide her irritation. "You almost knocked me over."

As she knelt down on one knee to return Mason's hug, he gave her a great big kiss on the cheek and began to giggle. The jovial sound made Dani's heart melt and erased any hint of irritation that remained. Mason was such a precious and loving little boy; one couldn't help but instantly fall in love with him…over and over again. Dani could never resist his innocent little charms. "What's so funny?" she asked, gently tickling Mason on his belly.

"You have chocolate on your face!" He laughed even harder.

"Do not!" Dani teasingly argued, knowing that she likely did, in fact, have the sticky goo not only on her face, but everywhere else on her body as well.

"Uh, huh!" Mason insisted. "Right here." He licked his thumb and tried to wipe away the chocolatey mess from Dani's cheek, just as Tracie had done to him and the other children so many times before.

"Yuk!" Dani teased as she pulled away from Mason's clutches. "I'll clean it off with a wash rag when I get in the house. Thanks for taking care of me though." She chuckled. Mason's attempt to wipe away the chocolate smudge only made it worse. Now the unsightly blotch looked like a mud smear.

Mason grabbed Dani's hand and dragged her toward the front door. "We're st*aaa*rving, Dani," Mason whined. "We've been waiting for you for hours." He still did not understand the concept of time, only that in his eyes, they'd been waiting far too long.

She apologized, "I know, little man. I'm sorry." In her usual way, she affectionately ruffled the hair on the top of Mason's head.

As she and Mason entered the foyer, Dani could see Tracie in the kitchen stirring a pot of spaghetti sauce and, as usual, Kylie resting on her hip as though she were a superfluous extremity. Tracie was unconsciously rocking back and forth when she noticed Dani and Mason come in to the room.

Tracie had to laugh—first at the disheveled cake then at the smudge on Dani's cheek. "Rough afternoon, Dan?" Tracie tried to sound sympathetic, but found it difficult to hide her amusement.

"Thanks for the concern," Dani jokingly countered. "And you better not say a word about my cake!"

"Your cake?" Tracie acted as though she hadn't noticed the heap Dani was carrying. "It's beautiful, as always." She winked at Mason as she took the cake from Dani.

Dani could hear laughter and squeals coming from the living room. Tracie rolled her eyes. "They've been at it all afternoon. All of them—Tim, David, Mason, Samuel—you would think David and Tim were a couple of little boys themselves. Even Kylie had to get in on the action."

Dani could see partially into the living room from where she stood—a heap of bodies entangled together as they rolled across the carpeted floor. She could hear growls and uncontrollable giggles. She hadn't even noticed Mason leave her side, but his bright red dinosaur shirt was clearly visible among the scrambled web of bodies.

He's good with kids, she thought, admiring Tim's ability to be so comfortable in what could have been an awkward situation. *That's a start*, Dani ascertained to herself. *But apparently he hasn't matured past adolescence*, as she listened to the animal sounds and giggles coming from the adjoining room. Almost instantaneously, she silently admonished herself for already making judgments about a man she had yet to meet—a man about whom she'd promised Tracie she would "keep an open mind."

Tracie eyed Dani inquisitively. "I know what you're thinking, Dani." In a hushed whisper, she continued, "He might be acting like he's a six-year-old, but wait until I tell you what he's been up to. He's a catch!" Tracie hurriedly reached to turn off the burner as the boiling spaghetti sauce began bubbling over the side of the pot.

"Here, Dan, take Kylie for a minute while I put dinner on the table." Handing the baby to Dani, Tracie leaned into her and mischievously whispered, "I'll tell you more after dinner!"

Kylie wrinkled her nose with her now-famous flirty little smile as she reached for Dani. "Come here, you little monkey." Dani kissed the baby's ringlet-covered forehead before resting her on her hip. "You just get bigger by the minute." Fascinated by the shiny metal, Kylie grabbed hold of Dani's cross necklace and instantly put it to her mouth.

"Yucky, baby girl." Dani pulled the charm away from Kylie's hand and reached for the teething ring she'd been chewing on over the past few days. But before Dani knew it, she felt a tug around her neck and heard the necklace fall to the floor. She bent down to pick up the necklace, but only the chain was in sight. Her eyes began to scan the floor for the glistening charm. It wouldn't be difficult to find— the cross was nearly an inch high and a half-inch wide. It must have slid under the refrigerator. But as quickly as the thought occurred to her, a chill ran up Dani's spine. She glanced down at the little bundle she was holding, now silent, arms flailing.

"She's choking!" Dani screamed frantically. "I think she swallowed my charm!"

Pasta went hurdling across the dining room table as Tracie dropped the bowl she was preparing to set on the table. She grabbed the baby from Dani's arms.

All at once, the unruliness that had been taking place in the living room subsided and chaos ensued in the kitchen. There were bodies everywhere. Everyone was in a panic. Even the boys were frightened by the commotion, although neither of them was quite sure what was happening.

"I'll call 911," Dani shouted and ran to retrieve the telephone from the den.

Just then, Tim, calm and composed, as though he had done it a hundred times before, gently took Kylie from Tracie's arms and inserted a finger into the baby's mouth searching for an obstruction.

Unable to hear above the confusion that was taking place in the kitchen, Dani stayed in the living room talking to the 911 dispatcher. Tim's back was to her, so Dani was unable to see what was taking place, only that he had placed Kylie face down on his upper thigh and had begun giving her firm back blows.

Then, as quickly as the charm had managed to lodge in her throat, it came hurtling out. From the living room, Dani could hear a welcoming wail coming from Kylie's lungs. Still trying to communicate with the dispatcher what had occurred, Dani listened as Tracie's cries turned to relieved sobs. Though she remained calm and collected on the telephone, now, Dani could no longer hold back her tears. Even the boys were crying, overwhelmed by the chaotic scene.

Finally, Dani set the receiver down with shaking hands. She heard David's soothing voice, "She's fine. She's fine. It scared her more than anything," he assured Tracie.

Though it seemed like a lifetime, all the chaos had begun and ended in a matter of ninety seconds—the longest ninety seconds of their lives.

Dani couldn't bring herself to go to the kitchen and face Tracie and David. After all, it was *her* fault Kylie had choked. *Her* carelessness could have had devastating consequences. Dani's knees began to buckle beneath her. She collapsed onto the oversized ottoman, put her face in her hands and began to cry uncontrollably.

Even through her own sobs, Dani could hear David in his soothing manner. "Her airway was only partially obstructed. She was still getting small amounts of air into her lungs." His familiar, comforting voice seemed to have a soothing effect on Dani as well.

Her sobs subsided, though Dani's hands still cupped her face as she listened more intently to David's reassurances that Kylie was going to be alright.

Strangely, it occurred to Dani at that moment that David was exceptionally knowledgeable regarding a medical emergency involving a choking baby. How did he know Kylie was going to be alright? Shouldn't they take her to the hospital? Wouldn't most fathers be frantic? Dani was confused.

In an instant, Dani realized it wasn't David's voice she was hearing. It was similar. It was familiar. But it wasn't David's. She'd heard the voice before. Been soothed by it before. Comforted by it. Then it came to her as the blood drained from her face.

She felt a light tap on her shoulder. "Awe you okay, Dani?" asked a shaking little voice. Dani looked up to see Mason's quivering bottom lip and tear-filled eyes.

Dani gently pulled Mason into her arms, squeezed her eyes closed and held on for dear life. In that moment, Dani realized that her need to embrace Mason was as much for her sake as for his.

As the sound of footsteps approached, Dani slowly, reluctantly opened her eyes.

-- -- -- -- --

Tim froze when he walked into the living room; Samuel plowing into the back of his legs. The color drained from her face as Dani's eyes met Tim's.

Tim's knees were weak. His heart felt as though it would beat right out of his chest. Dani was simply numb. She didn't know what to think; how to feel. *Could it really be Jacks?*

She had watched the building crumble around him. He'd been buried in a pile of rubble. *This can't be*

Jacks, she thought. He's dead. But, as quickly as the thought crossed her mind, she knew. It *was* Jacks. Those eyes—she could never mistake those eyes. The man standing before her was Jacks all right.

Her mind became a jumble of confusion. Her thoughts kept flashing back to snippets of that moment; the explosion, the noise, the ensuing chaos, then the darkness. She remembered Buck's words, *"I'm sorry, Dani…no one has had contact with him…it doesn't look good…the debris is too dense…They've barely penetrated the surface…There are hundreds missing; most presumed to be dead, buried beneath the ruins…he's gone, Dani."* All she had left of a man she had barely known, but had come to love was a battered tin box with the tiny metal Jacks and red rubber ball safely protected inside. It was the only tangible thing she had left to remind her of Jacks. Maddie had mailed it to Dani the week after she returned to the United States. She had found the tin box while rummaging through what remained of the medical clinic. When it came in the mail, the package had contained only the box, with its metal and rubber contents, with a sticky note attached. The note read simply,

"He would have wanted you to have this — Maddie."

Since Jacks' death, Dani had often held that precious box to her chest, felt its cold metal on her cheek as she'd close her eyes trying to remember every feature of his face. The outline of his jaw. The angle of his nose. The fullness of his lips. The color of his eyes. She had promised herself she was never going to forget.

Dani kept playing Uncle Buck's words over and over in her head. She'd had a difficult time accepting that Jacks was gone. Her heart had never allowed her to believe it. But her mind had told her it was simply her inability to let him go.

She'd convinced herself that her life in Uganda had been more of a dream than reality. It was a world away; a lifetime ago. But all this time Dani had known, somehow deep inside, that Jacks was alive.

For a brief moment, both Dani and Tim were oblivious to the reaction of the others in the room. Her traumatic experience all but forgotten, even Kylie seemed to feel the tension and confusion that had permeated the room as she wriggled to free herself from her mother's arms.

"Jacks," Dani mumbled in barely a whisper. "Is it really you?" she managed.

Before Jacks could respond, both boys simultaneously, and as if on cue asked, "Who's Jacks?"

"His name is not Jacks, silly, it's Uncle Tim," Mason insisted matter-of-factly, charging his uncle in a playful manner; the drama of Kylie's choking overshadowed by the newly unraveling events.

Without thought, Tim reached down and lifted Mason into his arms, his eyes never leaving Dani's. Oddly, Dani thought at that moment, Jacks—or was it Tim—looked so natural, so comfortable holding Mason.

Tracie knelt to the floor, less to allow the antsy little Kylie to find her footing on the plush carpet, and more because she didn't think her legs could hold her own weight at the comprehension of what she was witnessing. The adrenaline that had shot through her body like a bolt of lightning from Kylie choking was beginning to subside, only to be replaced by a sense of bewilderment at what, she realized, was unfolding before her. She looked over at David. He appeared dumbfounded, his mouth slightly ajar, his eyes full of confusion and understanding all at once.

Tracie looked at Tim, then at Dani. It was all beginning to make sense. *But how was it possible?*

"Danielle?" It was more of a confirmation than a question. The color in Jacks' face was beginning to return. He had thought about her every day since that smoldering afternoon the first time he saw her standing across the hospital courtyard, her hat flapping in the wind.

He hardly knew her; their time together had been so brief. Yet, he felt that he'd grown to know her in that short time better than he knew himself. He cherished each moment as if those days held a lifetime of memories…experiences… moments that consumed his mind, betrayed his senses. That's why he'd had to leave Gulu and the children he loved behind. That's how he knew he was no longer doing the work he was called to do. Dani had distracted him in a way that had thrown his life into turmoil. That's why he hated, yet somehow loved her at the same time.

Dani had completely manipulated Jacks' thoughts, his reasoning, his sensibilities. He hadn't wanted to love her, but he had. He didn't want to grow to hate her for it, but he did that too. He loved her passion, her intelligence, her enthusiasm for life, her feistiness. He hated…he hated… *her*…for making him love her. For making him love her more than his work. Even more than the memory of Christine. How could he have allowed Dani to steal *that* from him? When Christine died, he had known he'd never love another woman, at least not the way he loved *her*. But then Dani walked into his life. Quietly, gently, softly…and all the sudden, she was there. As if she had been a part of his life all along. She had taken him by surprise, without warning. She hadn't meant to, but she had nonetheless. And it rattled him to the bone.

"Uncle Tim...Uncle Tim..." Taking Tim's face in his tiny hands, Mason forced Tim's gaze away from Dani and his thoughts back to the present. "What's wong, Uncle Tim?" Mason asked.

Tim was speechless. His mouth moved, but nothing came out. Almost in slow motion, he leaned down kissing Mason on the forehead before planting him in the middle of the room. He stood there in silence, simply staring at Dani in bewilderment. The room was silent.

Tim turned and bolted out the front door. The sound of the door slamming broke the silence of the moment.

"Why did Uncle Tim leave?" Mason pleaded with tears in his eyes. "He said he was gonna play dinosaurs with me and Sam."

Shaken at what had just happened, David jumped in, "Uncle Tim had something very important he had to do." His voice was strained. "I'm sure he'll be back soon."

Swooping Mason up in one arm and Samuel in the other, "Why don't you two go out back and play in the sandbox for a little while."

Squealing with delight, Samuel whined, "Daddy, you're squeezing my belly too tight!"

"Me too." Mason giggled.

Then, with an unbridled excitement, Samuel hollered, "Mason, let's go build a jungle in the sandbox with tunnels and secret hideouts for our dinosaurs. I'll bet Uncle Tim will never be able to find them!"

"Yeah!" Mason scrambled to get to his feet. "Let's hurry before Uncle Tim gets back!"

Both boys headed toward the back door, all the drama behind them.

Still kneeling on the carpet trying to settle a riled-up Kylie, Tracie's voice was shaky, "What just happened?"

Confused, David appeared less than composed. "*Tim* is Jacks?" he asked, not waiting for an answer from Dani. "I don't get it. He said he's been working out of the country, but it's been like pulling nails trying to get any information out of him. He's been so private and vague about everything. But I didn't want to push him. I figured he'd tell me everything in his own time, when he was ready." David shook his head as if in disbelief.

Dani's legs were quivering. She still could not speak. A single tear cascaded down her left cheek as an indescribable mix of emotions invaded her. *Confusion. Excitement. Bewilderment. Panic. Joy.* She still couldn't believe it. How could she comprehend something that was nearly impossible? But there was no doubt in her mind that it was Jacks who stood before her only moments before. She turned to David. "Did you know?"

As baffled as Dani, David's surprise could not be concealed. "Know what? I still don't know what's going on! Is *Tim* really *Jacks*?"

"Yes," Dani whispered. "I don't know how, but Tim *is* Jacks."

Dani had so many questions. With her arms folded in front of her, Dani began to pace back and forth. How had he made it out of the explosion? They said he'd been killed—or had they? No, they said he

264

hadn't been found. They said it didn't look good. They said all hope was lost. Then they'd whirled her away, out of the hospital, away from the line of fire. And she had been so willing to go—to run from the memories of a man who had, in only a few short days, changed her life forever.

Now he was here. Not only alive, but in Glenbrook of all places. In David and Tracie's home! It all seemed so unbelievable.

Where had Jacks been all these months? Why hadn't he come for her? Maybe their time together meant far more to Dani than it had to Jacks. Maybe he hadn't even given her so much as a second thought after she'd gone. Or maybe the explosion somehow altered his memory—like in the soap operas. But no, that couldn't be. Jacks had clearly recognized her standing in the living room. Anything was possible. He'd said her name, *Danielle*. His mind had not been altered, she assured herself. In an instant, Dani's bewilderment and confusion quickly turned to hurt and anger.

She and Jacks had connected in Uganda. She knew Jacks had felt it too. Their walks, that day at Murchison Falls, their time at the hospital—it had all been so intimate. They'd spent so little time together, knew hardly anything about each other's lives, yet it was as though they had known one another a lifetime. What she knew of Jacks was all she had needed to know. They had traded their hearts during those few short days in Africa. Jacks still had hers, but had he taken his back? Her anger grew by the moment, by the memory, one by one.

"Tim looks nothing like he did as a child. My goodness, the last photo I have of him is fourteen years old. It was taken just before Christina's death." David was beginning to put the pieces together.

"It's ironic," David said. "As a kid, Tim always talked about becoming a doctor someday. He said he was going to change the world. He wanted to help people who were poor and neglected and didn't have anything or anyone to care for them." Tears came to David's eyes. "Just like Tim and me. Even though mom was there, she wasn't ever *really* there."

As if in a distant world, he continued, "He talked about going on missions and finding cures for AIDS and malaria and all the other kinds of diseases that people in third-world countries die from." Remembering his brother as a pretentious, wide-eyed little dreamer, a smile came over David.

"He'd had so many aspirations. He was on his way to reaching his dreams when Christina died." David's smile faded. "Then everything went downhill from there. When he lost Christina, he lost everything. Then he was just gone. He disappeared off the face of the earth."

David leaned forward, rested his elbows on his knees, and began wringing his hands. "I looked everywhere, called everyone he'd ever known, but no one knew where he was or what had happened to him. Even the Navy wouldn't give me any information about him or even if he was still enlisted." David was reiterating most everything Tracie had already told Dani earlier in the week when they were preparing the guest room for Tim. But voicing his thoughts was helping David—and for that matter, Tracie and Dani—compute the events that had lead up to that moment in time.

For the first time in Dani's memory, Tracie was speechless. But Dani could see in Tracie's eyes that the wheels were turning. Still flabbergasted, Tracie asked, "Dani, do you know what this means?"

Dani hesitated for a moment. She looked at Tracie. She looked at David. "Yes, I know what this means," she said. She turned around to face the window and absently gazed out as if lost in thought. "This means Jacks…or Tim…or whatever his name is has been out there for months getting on with his life while I've been sitting here with my heart broken, barely remembering to take my next breath."

Without giving David or Tracie a chance to respond, Dani turned around and looked toward David. "I don't get it. How do two people make a connection like Jacks and I did, and it mean nothing?"

"Dani…," Tracie rushed to comfort her.

"There's nothing you can say to make it better, Tracie," Dani said. "I don't know how I let myself fall in love with him."

Wiping the tears away, Dani said, "I really believed God had brought us together for a reason. Then I thought he was dead, even though it didn't *feel* like he was gone. Now, for some inexplicable reason, he's back in my life. Then," she cried, "he can't get away from me fast enough. He ran out that door like he'd seen a ghost."

"Dani, he's got to be just as shocked to see you as you are to see him," Tracie tried to reason. "He probably didn't know *how* to react."

"That's just it," Dani resigned. "When *I* first saw him, I wanted to run into his arms - *he* just wanted to run."

"Maybe he—" But Dani interrupted Tracie before she could continue.

"I have to go." Dani reached for her keys. "Tell Mason I'm sorry and that I'll call him later," she shouted over her shoulder just before slamming the door behind her.

"David," Tracie looked at him pleadingly. "Stop her. She's too upset to be driving."

"Let her go. She's not going to listen to anything we have to say right now," he implored. "She just needs some time to absorb it all. Don't worry, she'll be back."

"What about Tim, she said. "What if he doesn't come back? What if we never see him again?"

CHAPTER SIXTEEN

It was after midnight and the house was silent when Tim finally returned home. The front door unlocked, he snuck past the living room and made his way through the kitchen to the guest bedroom. He'd spent the last six hours trying to absorb the improbability of his and Danielle's paths crossing again. It made no sense. It was nothing short of a miracle. In fact, that's exactly what it was—a miracle. There was no mistaking that God had His hand in this. Of the billions of people in the world and the millions of places and circumstances, God had brought Tim and Dani together in a single place in time, and then, a world away, had brought them together again. It was unfathomable. Yet Tim knew that anything was possible with God; He had no limits, no boundaries.

What began as pandemonium and confusion just hours before had now turned into resignation and acceptance— perhaps even hope for Tim. Emotionally exhausted, he sat on the bed, laid back on the plush feather comforter, and covered his head with a pillow. The cotton was cool and inviting against his flushed face.

Tim was in that oblivion between wakefulness and sleep when a knock at his door startled him to his feet. "Come in," he announced before silently reprimanding himself for being so loud.

David opened the door, quietly closing it behind him.

"You okay?" He looked at Tim with compassion.

"Yeah," Tim said. "I'm sorry I ran out of here earlier."

"We were all stunned," David shook his head in disbelief again. "It's just all so unbelievable." The two men, in unison, sat down next to one another on the now disheveled bed. "What happened Tim…or Jacks…or whatever? I don't get it." There was no judgment in David's voice, only trepidation.

"I'm sorry, Dave," Tim said with sincerity. "It's just all so convoluted that I don't even know where to begin."

"How about starting with what happened to you after Christina died." There was a hint of anger in David's voice. "Where did you go? I called everyone I could think of who might know what happened to you. I went looking for you. You disappeared off the face of the earth." Though not meaning to, David sounded accusatory and harsh.

David's voice cracked, "I was afraid you were dead."

"I wanted to be," Tim admitted. "*Dead* that is."

"Christina was my life," he said lowering his gaze. "I loved her with all my heart. You know how you hear people say they don't know how they can survive after someone they love dies? Well, that's how I felt. I had no reason to live after she was gone." A tear rolled down Tim's face. "Did you know she was pregnant?"

David swallowed back a lump in his throat that had begun to form hours earlier.

Tim continued, not waiting for a response from David. "That morning—before the accident—I was running late for work. I was in a terrible mood because I had woken up late, and I was irritable with her."

Then, remembering with a half-smile, Tim said, "She was always so happy in the mornings…and you know how pleasant *I* am in the mornings," he added sarcastically. Both men chuckled as their minds simultaneously, and for only an instant, drifted to their boyhood days when David would intentionally rile Tim up in the early morning hours before school. A fight would inevitably ensue with David coming out the victor every time, serving only to irritate Tim even more. The morning taunting and invariable battle had become a daily event. In a weird way, the interaction, though dysfunctional, helped to foster a bond between the two boys.

The smile faded from Tim's face. "She'd made me breakfast as usual. Two eggs, over easy…two pieces of whole wheat toast…orange juice." His voice was monotone, robotic.

David didn't speak. He only listened.

Tim stood and walked to the window. He stared out as though looking at something, but seeing nothing as his memory took over. "I took a few bites without even sitting down at the table," he said. "It's funny how you don't appreciate something until it's gone. I loved that she made me breakfast every morning, but I never told her that. I just took it for granted," his voice beginning to break again. "I took *her* for granted."

David didn't know what to say. An awkward silence permeated the room. Then Tim continued as though he were the narrator of a book that he had read a hundred times—a narrator who needed no props or even words to tell his story. One who could recite the chapters of his book simply by closing his eyes and remembering.

Then, as if returning from another world, Tim continued, sharing the details of that fateful morning. "I grabbed my computer and the hundred other things I'd bring to work with me every day, kissed her on the forehead, and told her I'd be home late."

Tim grinned again. "She grabbed my arm and pulled me to her and kissed me hard on the lips." He could almost taste the sweetness of her kiss as he remembered her lips against his. "Then she handed me a small cardboard box with a white bow on top. She wanted me to open it right there...before I left for work." He lowered his gaze again as if in shame. "But I didn't. I just grabbed the box and told her I'd open it when I got to work.

"I could see she was disappointed, but I was already running late. What was I supposed to do?" he asked rhetorically. "She was always leaving me little notes in my lunch box or surprising me with some little gadget she thought I'd like. I didn't realize how important this one was to her."

Tim's slow, monotonous rendition of what took place that day took on a new fervor. "So I get in my car, toss the box on the seat next to me, and pretty much forget about it.

"The next thing I know, my sergeant comes in to my office and tells me Christina's been in an accident and that I need to get to the hospital," his voice softened again. "He hadn't told me that she was already gone—that she'd died instantly.

"It wasn't until about a week later—after the funeral; after her family and all of our friends all left to go back home—I was sitting in my living room in the middle of the day with the shades pulled closed. I was exhausted and numb. I hadn't even let myself cry yet; not even at her funeral. It was as dark as night except for a narrow ray of sunshine that shone through opening in the curtain. I'd taken the box out of the car and had set it on the coffee table a few days before. The light was shining right on the box. All I could do was stare at it. I couldn't bring myself to open it." Tim could feel his own pulse racing as he told David his story.

"I have no idea how long I sat there before I had enough courage to open the box. I'm not sure why I was so scared. I think it was sort of a combination of things. I'd felt guilty for not opening it that first morning. It was the last thing she ever gave me. It was like...opening that box would somehow mean closing my life with her."

Tim's face paled as he continued, "When I finally opened it, I went nuts. I went off the deep end."

After several moments of silence, in almost a whisper, David asked, "What was in it?"

Tim took a deep breath. "It was a pair of yellow crocheted booties with a sticky note that read 'Congratulations, daddy'." He was visibly shaken. "She tried to tell me that morning, but I wouldn't listen. To me, it was just another hectic day. To her, it was probably one of the most important days of her life, and I couldn't stop for just one minute to open that box when she handed it to me."

David struggled to find the right words. "We all take the people we love the most for granted. It never occurs to us that it could be the last time we'll ever see them." He thought about the last time he saw their mother. "Guilt can destroy you, Tim."

"I know. And it did," Tim admitted. "I didn't think I could live without her...and our baby that I never had the chance to meet—that she never had the chance to meet."

"I tried to get on with my life, but everywhere I went and everyone I knew reminded me of her. I'd see a baby in the grocery store, and it would paralyze me. I couldn't function. I'd go to work, but just sit at my desk and stare out the window all day."

David's heart broke for Tim. He had been through so much and had isolated himself from everyone. David remembered that after the funeral, he had to get back home right away—back to work and his own dysfunctional life. David had felt guilty for not staying longer, but Tim had told him he needed some time alone. So he'd left. David had tried to call Tim a dozen times a day in the weeks after Christina died. Tim had refused to answer his phone or return David's calls.

Tim continued, "It didn't take me long to pick up all my old habits. I didn't want to be a part of anything or anyone I ever knew. Anything was better than having to think about what I had lost and asking myself what I could have done to change what happened. I ended up doing some really stupid stuff one night when I was high." Tim shook his head back and forth in disgust with himself. "I was court-martialed and spent thirty days in the brig."

"That's where you were? I came out to look for you about a month later because you wouldn't return my calls. I needed to know what happened to you. The Navy wouldn't tell me anything. They said your status was confidential." David remembered how his heart sank when "the brass" would not even tell him if Tim was alive or dead. They'd said that Christina was listed on the next of kin notification, and they could not release any personal information about Tim to anyone who was not listed on the notification. David had begged for information, but still they had refused.

"I know, man. I'm sorry for so many things. I knew you were looking for me, but I just didn't want to be found." Tim squeezed David's shoulder. "I was really self-absorbed... and ashamed."

Tim went on, "Then when I was in the brig, I promised myself - I promised Christina - that I wasn't gonna go back to the drugs and booze. My mind was clear, and I was able to deal with a lot of the things that had brought me down. But by then, it was too late to call you. I didn't know what I would say."

"You could have called, Tim. You *should* have called. I would have been there for you. You're my brother." Swallowing hard, David said, "I thought I would never see you again."

The two men embraced; neither concealed their emotions. It was as though a dam broke loose. Both felt as vulnerable in each other's arms as they had so many years ago when they were abandoned first by their father by choice, then by their mother in death. Back then, they only had each other. Now, they knew they had each other again, but so much more.

David gathered himself. "It's been so many years, Tim. Where have you been? How did you end up in Uganda...and a doctor?"

Tim let out a loud sigh. "Long story short, when I was in jail, I had a really compassionate therapist who thought I had potential. He pulled some strings, and I ended up reenlisting. Within six months, I finished all the premed stuff that I had nearly completed before Christina died. I worked my way through med school and earned my PhD within three years. I was driven by a mission to prove something to myself. I'm still not sure what. Then I did my fellowship in Boston. I became good friends with the chaplain at the hospital. He helped me with some issues I'd been holding on to for a long time—like from when we were kids.

"Anyway, he invited me to his church." Tim laughed. "Man, I was pretty hesitant at first 'cause, you know, I've never been into the whole 'God' thing, but this place was incredible. From the minute I walked in the door, I felt like I was home." He laughed again.

"I know it sounds corny, but the people welcomed me like I was part of their family. They didn't judge me even after I got involved in a Bible study where I told them all about my life…ya' know, when we were kids, the drugs, the booze, Christina, my court-martial. All of it—they just accepted me the way I was. It was shortly after that, that I gave my life to Christ."

"The rest is history. You know, I had always said I was going to change the world. Well, I figured there was no better place to start than in Africa. My church was planning a mission trip to Uganda. I went with them and never left." Tim ran his hands through his hair like he had done so often as a child. "Until now."

David was crying again. Although He'd learned to break some of his walls down over the years, he had never cried as much as he did this night. "I've prayed for you every day for all these years, not knowing if you were even alive."

"Well, your prayers worked. It's been almost two years since He changed my life. Ya' know what's crazy?" It was more of a rhetorical statement than a question. "I've been praying for you for the past two years too. Although He's taken a lot of the shame and guilt away from me, I was afraid to get in touch with you, or even if I should. I was still feeling guilty about abandoning you after Christina died. I did the same thing to you that mom and dad did to us." A hint of remorse lingered in Tim's voice.

"Why now, Tim? Why after all these years?" David asked pointedly.

"I don't know. I can't explain it," Tim began rambling. "After the explosion, the devastation in Uganda—they needed us more than ever. Some of the other doctors and nurses were killed in the explosion so we were short-handed. I thought Danielle had been killed along with them. I'd barely known her, but it was like losing Christina all over again, but somehow it was even worse."

During the weeks and months following the explosion, Tim had tried to return to the normalcy of his work in Uganda. The makeshift clinic designed from the rubble of what was left of the hospital had been sufficient to meet the basic healthcare needs of the community. Those patients with more serious conditions were shuttled off to surrounding community hospitals. Jacks continued his work with the children, though many had perished in the explosion. While few of his young patients remained, those left needed him then, more than ever. Many of those who had not died in the blast had been left with disfiguring injuries from flying metal and other debris. A four-year-old girl lost both legs. A young boy already afflicted with cerebral palsy had his right arm blown away. Several patients lost their vision as a result of the shards of glass that rained down upon them immediately following the blast.

After the explosion, chaos had erupted throughout the city. Buildings that had once adjoined the hospital were now piles of rubble. Orange flames protruded from various mounds of wreckage. The sky was filled with thick gray smoke. People were unrecognizable as the descending soot and dust masqueraded their faces.

The death toll continued to rise as rescuers and towns-people alike delved through the vestiges. In some cases, it took days to find the remains of the hundreds of innocent victims; some were never found. The memories of the aftermath still haunted Tim.

"I couldn't do it anymore." Tim's voice was calm, "So I just walked away."

He continued, "I stayed in Africa for a few more months driving my dilapidated truck from one town to the next. I would sometimes come across a family with a sick kid or an older person in failing health. I'd do what I could to help them. Occasionally I would stop at a run-down clinic offering my services. But my heart just wasn't in it."

"I don't understand, why did you think Dani was dead?" David was trying to comprehend and absorb it all.

Tim cleared his throat. "Apparently, I was knocked unconscious during the explosion. The day after, I came to as a couple of townspeople were pulling me from the rubble. I asked them about Danielle. I described her long silky dark hair, her bright green eyes." Tim's face, his eyes took on a faraway look.

"One of the men who rescued me spoke broken English, but enough to tell me that Danielle was dead. They had found her body the previous day. At first, I didn't believe him—I couldn't believe him." Tears began to sting his eyes. "But the week before, I had given her a cross necklace that I carved out of a piece of petrified wood and put on a braided macramé chain. She hadn't taken it off since the day I fastened it around her neck." Tim struggled to form his next words.

"The man reached into his pocket and pulled out Danielle's necklace. He said he had found the necklace lying near her body. When he handed it to me, I turned it over."

His next words were barely audible. "It was Danielle's necklace. I had inscribed 'Jeremiah 1:5' on the back." That faraway look returned. "It was hers." Tim turned away from David to hide the tears that flowed from his eyes.

David sat in silence trying to absorb it all. Tim stood at the window, remembering.

David's voice broke the silence. "They told you she was dead?" It was more of a statement of understanding than a question.

He shook his head in continued disbelief. "I don't know who the woman was that your rescuers think they found, but Dani was found beneath the rubble with massive injuries to her eyes and head, and she had a fractured leg. They flew her to a hospital in Kapala. She was in a coma for four days. When she woke up, they told her Jacks...er, *you* were dead," David said.

"As soon as she was well enough to travel, they whisked her back to the United States. It almost destroyed her, Tim. And after all she's been through over the past two years, I was worried it was going to send her off the deep end."

"What do you mean?" Though he felt he had come to know Danielle in the short time they had spent together, better than he'd ever known anyone before—even Christina—at that moment, he realized he really hadn't know her at all. Her heart—he knew...her life—still a mystery to him.

"She didn't tell you about her parents…about Mason?"

"No. As much as we shared together, she always seemed to be holding something back," Tim said, surprised at his own realization. Then as an afterthought he said, "What about her parents? And Mason? You told me yesterday that Mason came to live with you after his mom died." Completely confused, he continued, "What does that have to do with Danielle…or her parents?"

It was David's turn to talk. He told his brother everything. He told him about the death of Dani's parents, his relationship with Amanda, and how Mason had come to live with them. They talked about their childhood, about their mother, about their father. They talked about Tracie and the kids. They talked about Dani. Tim had so many questions about Dani. Some, David could answer; others could only be answered by Dani herself.

The two men shared their stories of how they had come to accept Christ. When the sun was beginning to rise, they prayed together. Thanking God for their lives and for the paths wrought with pain and suffering that had lead each of them to Him.

When David finally left Tim's room, both men were emotionally and physically exhausted. But sleep was the last thing from Tim's mind. He didn't know what he would say to Danielle, but he knew he had to find her.

CHAPTER SEVENTEEN

After a sleepless night of thinking, pacing, praying, and thinking some more, Dani waited impatiently for the first hint of daylight so she could take her anger and hurt out on the paved paths of Big Oak Park.

It was an unseasonably cool, crisp morning as Dani double knotted her running shoes. Though her leg was getting better by the day, the ache that remained could be felt mostly in the early morning hours. She stretched in her attempt to will the pain away.

Mason. Dani felt guilt tug at her heartstrings as she thought about his terrified little face when Kylie was choking and the ensuing chaos that followed. She had stormed out of Tracie and David's house last night, leaving a wake of confusion behind her. But she couldn't go back there yet. She wasn't ready to face Jacks. And he clearly wasn't pounding her door down. The anger began to build again. She braved the coolness of the morning and locked the door behind her, determining to call Mason when she returned from her run.

When Dani finally arrived home an hour later, out of breath from her uncharacteristically zealous run, she found herself more frustrated than when she'd left. The fresh air hadn't cleared her mind; it only served to convolute her thoughts even more. For the past twelve hours, Dani had asked God for clarity, for discernment, for understanding, but none had come. She wanted to see Jacks, talk to him. But as she thought about the questions she wanted answered, she realized there existed none that would satisfy her. In Dani's mind, there was no reasonable explanation for why he hadn't come for her. Why he hadn't looked for her. Why he let her believe he was dead for all these months. Still, she and Jacks *had* connected in Uganda—it was undeniable. She knew he had felt it too.

Dani never missed her mother more than at that moment. She needed her—her comfort, her encouragement, her advice. Britta had always known the right thing to say. She had known just how to encourage Dani; how to make her feel better. Dani knew how to blow things out of proportion; Brita always knew how to bring Dani back down to reality.

All the sudden, Dani knew what to do. *The river.* She could think there. Whenever she went to the waterfall, she could almost imagine her parents there with her—laughing, swimming, and basking in the sun. When she stood below the cascading water, she felt closer to heaven—to Jesus—than when she was any other place else on earth.

Dani's clothes were changed and she was out the door in a matter of minutes, forgetting to call Mason.

Fifteen minutes later, Dani's little red Jeep—nearly identical to the one she'd totaled last spring—was winding its way down the potholed highway leading to the river, cascading further into the depths of the canyon. Surrounded by billowing pine trees and blue skies, each hairpin turn revealed a glimpse of the trailing river below as Dani neared the ravine floor. Simply seeing the pristine water below gave her an immediate sense of reprieve.

Gradually approaching the canyon bottom, glimpses of Dani's childhood invaded her mind. She remembered summer days spent basking in the penetrating sun—jumping from the cliffs into the cool, crisp water below. She had always been a daredevil.

"Dani, you're going to be the death of me," Britta would holler as Dani climbed another granite wall for her umpteenth jump of the day.

"*Daddy*," Dani would shout breaking the water's surface after ascending from the river depths, "*what was my score that time?*"

As had become their father-daughter custom, Randy would give Dani's jumps and swan dives a score as though she were an Olympic diver.

"Eight point five," Randy would announce. "Score would have been higher, but your legs were bent!"

Time after time, Dani would jump and perform until she heard the words she had been working for all day long. "A perfect ten!" Randy would finally proclaim when he knew Dani had reached the point of exhaustion.

Dani's mood relaxed as she cherished the summertime memories. She laughed aloud as she recalled her uncompromising obsession for the river. She exhaled as if releasing the pressures that had threatened to overcome her recent hours. She envisioned herself tiptoed on the cliff's edge, arms secured against her body, ready to take the plunge.

Often, before plummeting into the glassy waters, Dani would stare out at the obscure landscape before her. Even through her child's eyes, Dani's appreciation for the majesty of God's creation extended way beyond her years. The billowing trees, the crystal water, the granite slabs that served as a foundation for the vegetation-covered mountains, the flecks of gold that shimmered from the river floor, the breeze that sent a fleeting chill over her petite frame—all were miraculous to Dani. She would fearlessly stand on the granite ledge pondering the intricate details of God's creation. In her eight-year-old mind, the river and all that it encompassed was what Dani had imagined heaven would be like. The feelings that it evoked always gave her a sense of peace and security. Plummeting into the water, then breaking through the glassy surface emerging to the penetrating sunshine and warm breeze gave Dani a feeling of being reborn. She once told her parents on a sleepy drive home after a long day on the South Fork that the rhythmic descents into the water and subsequent emergence was like being baptized over and over again. *Jacks had said that too.*

Though superficially childish, Dani's childhood confession had been theoretically intuitive. Her insightfulness never ceased to amaze Dani's parents. As they often did, Randy and Britta had exchanged a knowing, grateful glance that summer day.

A speeding car approaching from the opposite lane startled Dani back to reality. What had started out as a cool morning was quickly proving to be one of the most blistering days of the summer yet.

-- -- -- -- --

Tim could hear the doorbell sounding inside Dani's condo, but there was no answer. Maybe Dani was simply refusing to answer the door knowing it was him. "Danielle, I know you're in there. Please talk to me." He pounded on the door again. Still, no response.

The front door of the adjoining condo opened and a pint-sized shih tzu came running toward Tim, barking and growling as though Tim were an intruder. "B," shouted Miss Cilla. "Come here!" she ordered.

B turned around, rejoined her master, and then stood staring down Tim while wagging her miniature tail.

"May I help you, young man?" she asked.

Slightly embarrassed by his actions, Tim asserted, "Yes, ma'am." He continued, "Do you know the woman who lives here. Her name is…"

"Dani. Yes I know. You must be Jacks." Miss Cilla gave him a knowing grin. "You're just as she described." Reaching toward him, the old woman grasped both of Tim's hands, clutched them in her own as though the two had known each other a lifetime. "My name is Priscilla Gordon." She gave his hands an inviting, affectionate squeeze. "My friends call me Miss Cilla." Directing her gaze toward the antsy little canine at her feet, she continued, "And this is my Beatrice. *Her* friends call her B."

"Actually, my name is Tim, Tim Fowler," he corrected. "It's nice to meet you, ma'am." Tim instinctively bent down and patted B's head.

Miss Cilla looked at Tim with simultaneous confusion and understanding. Dani had describe Jacks to the tee— from his disheveled sun-bleached hair to the dimple in his left cheek and the barely noticeable scar above his right brow—Miss Cilla was certain the man standing before her was Jacks. Why he was calling himself Tim was a mystery to her.

Miss Cilla invited Tim in and offered him a cup of hot tea as was her custom whenever she entertained guests. "No thank you, ma'am," Tim said anxiously. "I just want to find Danielle."

Tim looked at the peculiar little woman with a mix of curiosity and anticipation.

"Nonsense," Miss Cilla avowed, clutching his arm and escorting him to her quaint sunny breakfast nook. Somehow, Tim instinctively knew not to argue with the kind, but assertive gray-haired woman.

Miss Cilla motioned for Tim to sit on one of two paint flaked metal chairs with olive green padded seats. Tim breathed in deep as a mixture of fragrances flooded his senses. Was it the sixties-style décor or perhaps the vague smell of the woman's face lotion that made Tim think of his mother? For a moment, he was back in his childhood Michigan home, sitting at the breakfast table with his mother—in one of her rare moments of lucidness—and big brother. A fleeting sense of nostalgia overwhelmed him. It was Miss Cilla's voice that regained his attention.

"She thought you had died you know?" The woman declared matter-of-factly. "I knew differently. When she would talk about you, I felt your presence." She laughed aloud at the awkward look on Tim's face. "Don't worry. It wasn't in the 'crazy neighbor lady' sort of way. God was telling me.

"You remind me of myself when I was young—always in a hurry," she said, motioning for Tim to have a seat.

"I don't know how to explain it, but I knew you were alive," Miss Cilla continued. "I trusted what He was telling me, but I didn't trust enough to tell Dani what I knew in my heart was the truth." There was a hint of shame in Miss Cilla's words.

"Dani always talked about you in the past tense," she said. "I wanted to tell her 'he's alive, go find him'," she said with remorse. "I don't know why I didn't. Then," Miss Cilla said in a defeated tone, "she stopped talking about you all together. I think it just hurt too much."

Tim sensed that Miss Cilla had more to say. He sat patiently waiting for her to continue.

She reached for Tim's hand with a maternal instinct. "Do you know that everything we do, every choice we make, every breath we breathe has a purpose?" she said, not waiting for his answer. "It all leads to a specific moment, a specific event that was executed precisely according to God's plan."

Tim had heard the term according to God's plan more times than he cared to remember throughout his life— especially after Christina's death. What did that mean exactly? It seemed to Tim that it was simply a person's response when there seemed to exist no appropriate words of comfort.

Tim sat in silence as Miss Cilla stood and poured herself a cup of tea.

With her back still turned toward Tim, she continued, "Every childhood memory, every decision, every action, every person that enters your life plays a role in His plan." She returned to the small Formica table, this time sitting across from Tim. She peered into his eyes. "Meeting Dani in Uganda, the connection the two of you made, the time you've been apart, even your life before—as a boy, as a man—it was all deliberate."

"Even Dani's belief that you were dead, Jacks. It was all part of the path that lead you here to this middle-of-nowhere little town." Miss Cilla nodded her head as if in disbelief. Her curiosity getting the best of her. "How did you find her, Jacks?" she asked. "How did you know where to begin looking?"

The two newfound friends shared an oddly personal glance. Tim ran his hand through his hair in his uniquely nervous way. "The truth is, I thought Danielle had died in Uganda."

As though he had something to be ashamed of, Tim admitted, "I wasn't looking for her. I came here wanting to put the pieces of my life back together—trying to start over. Right some of my wrongs in a sense. Then all of the sudden, she was just there." Tim's pulse began racing again, as though saying the words aloud made it all real for the first time.

Cilla didn't begin to understand the events that had led up to that moment, but there would be time for that later. Right now, all she knew was that the young man before her needed answers. First, he needed to find Dani.

"I'm afraid I can't help you. I don't know where she is," Miss Cilla confessed. "But I do know that *God* brought the two of you back together. You didn't just find her once, but twice. And it wasn't by accident or coincidence. It was part of His plan."

Miss Cilla's voice took on a softness that penetrated Tim's core. "Search your heart, my love. You know where to find the answers you've been looking for." Their eyes locked. "You'll know where to find Dani."

As he and Miss Cilla exchanged hugs, Tim couldn't help but feel a sense of gratitude for the wisdom the silver-haired stranger had bequeathed upon him. In the brief moments he'd spent with her, Miss Cilla had transformed herself from stranger to trusted friend.

A short time later, Tim waved good-bye as he headed for his motorcycle, not knowing which direction he would go.

Miss Cilla began to pray. At that very moment, Tim began to pray too.

Sitting on his motorcycle and with his head still bowed, a warm breeze propelled over Tim. His mind took him to a far off place. He vividly recalled his trip with Dani to Murchison Falls National Park. Tim would never forget that day. He would never forget the moment he realized he was in love with her. Standing at the base of the falls that late afternoon, Dani had stared in wonder at its beauty, speechless, for what seemed like an eternity. Tim remembered watching Dani in awe as she engulfed the breathtaking sight, admiring her the same way that Dani was admiring the natural wonder. But to Tim, the splendor of the waterfall and its tropical surroundings paled in comparison to the beauty that permeated from Dani. Her beauty, though, was more than physical; it penetrated deep within her.

Tim could recite nearly every word Dani spoke that day, envision each smile. Her laughter echoed in his mind every day since. Dani and Tim had shared an undeniable connection in Africa. Beyond the brief stories of childhood antics though, both had spoken very little about their past. But in Tim's mind, having had months to ponder the time they had shared together, perhaps it was each of their subconscious method of attempting to leave the past behind and anticipate only what the future held for them. Tim recalled their time together as if it were yesterday.

His thoughts, it seemed, were louder than the hum of the idling motorcycle, as memories of Dani flooded over him. Tim felt hopeless. He felt lost as he never had before. Panic began to set in. He couldn't let her go again. He had to see her—had to explain what had happened, why he'd stayed away, and more than anything, how he felt about her. But where was she?

Where could she have gone? Then, in an instant, it came to him. The falls. *Her* falls. The ones she'd known as a child. The ones where she would go to think—to escape. The ones where she felt most at peace—closest to Jesus. She had to be there! But would he be able to find Dani's secret heaven? That day at Murchison Falls, she had described them in such detail that even then, Tim was certain he would be able to find his way as if he'd driven the twisted highway, walked the dusty, overgrown trail a thousand times. He revved his engine and was gone.

Miss Cilla peeked out her window as Tim sped off in the direction of the river. She reached down with a smile on her wrinkled face. "I knew he'd figure it out B," she said, patting her devoted little friend on the head. B excitedly leaped around as if in anticipation for what was to come.

-- -- -- -- --

Cars were parked up and down both sides of the highway as Dani reached the South Fork Bridge. Teetering on a shoulder of the road, Dani finagled her Jeep in to a compact space between a lifted Silver Chevy pickup and a sixties era orange van with tie-dyed curtains blocking the view of its inner workings from passers-bys. The back bumper of the nostalgic van displayed a myriad of peace-promoting stickers: Make Peace, Not War; Give Peace a Chance; Coexist. A faded magnetic rainbow clung to the rusted metal bumper. On the back right corner of the window, there appeared a hand-painted marijuana leaf.

Dani looked at the untarnished, pristine pickup in front of her, then back at the unpretentious, history-on-wheels with its unassuming memorabilia and message of peace behind her—both telling a story of someone's life and the dogma of their convictions, of their status in society, of their place in an otherwise faceless existence with too numerous members to count.

It occurred to Dani that even in this small community, people lived worlds apart. Those she encountered today would likely never cross her path again. Yet, a man she'd met half-a-world away and what seemed like a lifetime ago had shown up, out of thin air, at her proverbial front door. She still could not fathom the possibility of it all. Her heart was telling her what she already knew; only God himself could have construed a plan so intricate, so precise, wherein He chose two people among the billions that occupy the earth to meet in a specific time and place, inexplicably tear them apart, and, in an entire world away, lead them back to one another again. That's what her *heart* was telling her. But her mind was telling her something completely different.

Probability was at odds with reality. *Probability* told her that it could never happen. Jacks had died in Uganda. He was gone forever. Only his memory existed in Dani's mind. *Reality* told her Tim was really there; he was alive and had returned to her. It didn't make sense, but somehow it was real.

Lugging her backpack over her shoulders, Dani headed toward the well-worn footpath leading to the river's edge. But rather than take the descending routes that lead directly to the shallow waters below, Dani selected a barely identifiable path less traveled, ascending higher up the mountainside through brush and overgrown vegetation. The further away she ventured, the more foliage that obstructed her path.

Beads of sweat began to trail down her back as the temperature rose at a rapid pace.

Dani encountered only one other person along the way to her private respite. "Hey man. Peace," he said in a slow, lackadaisical tone. The man's long dreadlocks and the pungent smell of marijuana told Dani she had just encountered the owner of the orange van. The two strangers stopped briefly to exchange the usual pleasantries.

"Be careful up there," the man warned. "The trail's pretty gnarly."

"I will," Dani assured. "I used to come up here when I was a kid. There's no place like it on earth." Though Dani knew differently. Murchison Falls and the brief memories it held had grown to mean as much to Dani as had her childhood utopia.

"So you've been to the falls, huh?"

"Yes," she admitted. "Back then, hardly anyone knew about it. I hope it's still fairly secluded," she hoped aloud.

"It usually is. A few people know about, but there aren't a lot of people who are willing to hike all the way out there." The man continued, "I was just there. Not a soul in sight."

Dani silently thanked God. She needed to be alone. She needed to be where she felt safe. "Thanks!" Dani exclaimed, returning to the dusty path with a new fervor.

"See ya' around," the man shouted as the distance between them widened.

Dani turned and waved, "Probably not. But it was nice meeting you!"

"Right, man. You too," the man hollered. Then, as an afterthought, "The name's Jess." But Dani was already out of ears distance.

-- -- -- -- --

Tim scanned the parking area for Dani's Jeep. He'd never seen it before, but he knew that the vibrant color would stand out like a sore thumb. It couldn't be too difficult to find. But it wasn't there.

Glancing across the bridge a hundred yards up the highway, Tim could see a red bumper peeking out from behind a plush manzanita bush. It was sandwiched between a silver pickup and what, from a distance, looked to Tim like an old beat-up orange van.

Tim parked his bike in a small clearance at the head of the trail leading down to the river. The space was too small for a vehicle to park, but just large enough for his motorcycle.

He removed his helmet and tossed it over the handlebars, leaving it dangling. He couldn't move his feet fast enough as he started down the compacted dirt path. He'd barely gotten started when he came to a fork in the trail. *Up or down?* Which path had she taken? There was probably dozens of trails she could have taken. What if he chose the wrong one? He might never find her.

Tim stood at the trailhead panicking. To the right of him, he heard a noise. From the shrubbery ascended a barefooted man with a small piece of a broken branch hanging from his hair. The man nearly plowed down Tim as he bent over brushing the twig from his head.

"Hey man, sorry about that," the disheveled man announced. With a muted chuckle, he said, "You're the second person I almost knocked over today."

Without acknowledging the man's apology, Tim asked, "Do you happen to know the way to the falls?"

The man hesitated. He knew that the woman he had run into—literally—nearly half an hour before had been hoping for some privacy. He was hesitant to give Tim directions to the "secret" falls. But, in reality, the falls were not secret at all. Plenty of people knew about them. He considered his dilemma. *Who was he to prevent someone from experiencing the peace of mind that the falls could bestow upon a soul?*

"Just follow that path." The stranger pointed toward the brush from which he had just ascended.

Tim could barely make out the semblance of an unkempt walkway. "Are there any other falls around here?" he asked, hesitant to believe that Dani would have hiked the foreboding trail alone.

The eccentric-looking man studied Tim's face. What he saw was desperation in his eyes. "Are you looking for someone?" he asked curiously.

"Yeah. A young woman—really beautiful. Long auburn hair and incredible green eyes. She—"

The man interrupted Tim mid-sentence, "She had the same look in her eyes…I mean you both look kinda lost."

"You saw her? Was she all right?"

"Yeah, she's there. But I'm not sure she wants to be found."

Before the man could say another word, Tim was off and running.

-- -- -- -- --

Thirty minutes after leaving the nature-loving stranger, Dani finally reached the sloped clearing that framed the inviting pool of crystal water below the cascading falls. As she timidly approached the sun dried earth above the water's edge, a light mist masked her face. She stopped, closed her eyes, inhaled the fresh air, and listened. The sound of the falls cascading into the crystal-like pool caused her heart to skip an extra beat. It was surreal. She'd heard the mesmerizing sound in her mind hundreds of times over the past two years, but simply standing within driving distance of the water at that moment, the noise was deafening.

As she stood on the ridge of the gigantic granite boulder overlooking the pool of water below and absorbing the plethora of senses that threatened to vanquish her, Dani was overcome with emotion. Falling to her knees as if in a scene from a movie, Dani buried her face in her hands and began to sob.

Raising her face toward the heavens, she cried out, "I don't understand. What are You trying to teach me?" She screamed. "Haven't I been through enough already?" Dani didn't hold back. All the anger that had been growing was suddenly loosed upon God. "Haven't You taken enough from me? You've taken everyone I've ever loved," she accused. Then, she heard the doctor's words that had echoed in her mind a million times before, *You'll never have children of your own.* In quiet resignation, Dani's cries turned to a hushed whisper, "You've even taken from me the joy of ever becoming a mother." A tear fell from her cheek, leaving a glistening liquid trail on the granite slab beneath her.

Then, in a strange instantaneous change of emotion, instead of chastising God, Dani began to plead with Him. "I know I've lost my faith in You lately. I'm sorry." She wept. "I'm so sorry." She sat in silence as she waited for an answer from God.

"I don't know why You brought him here or what Your plans are for us, but You brought Jacks back into my life for a reason, and I don't think I could survive if you took him from me again," she beseeched God.

Still waiting to hear His voice, Dani listened intently. When His words did not come, Dani lowered her head in defeat.

At that instant, a balmy breeze began to blow, yanking half-withered oak leaves from branches and twirling them back and forth as if a ravishing tornado had passed over. *Dani, you need only to have faith.* The voice was barely audible, intertwined among the sounds of the vigorous breeze, but Dani had heard it. She's heard the words innumerable times before, yet this was the first time she truly *heard* them: *Dani…you need only to have faith*, the utterance echoed in her head…*you need only to have faith.*

At that moment, an inexplicable peace washed over Dani. The scorching heat that had been present all morning finally began to penetrate her sun-drenched body. The numbness that had consumed her since that moment she first laid eyes on Jacks the previous evening began to dissipate, and a sense of hope and anticipation came over her. What was she running from? Why was she so angry? There must be an explanation for why Jacks had not come for her. Was she simply afraid of being loved? Perhaps, Dani thought, I'm running in the wrong direction.

She slowly opened her eyes to the cascading water and, as if seeing it for the first time, was overwhelmed by its splendor. She kicked off her sneakers, leaving them next to her backpack as she rose to her feet. She noticed for the first time the blistering heat illuminating from the granite slab. Dancing around to avoid the burn, she tore off her shirt, securely tightening her bathing suit top around her neck, not bothering to remove her shorts before teetering on the edge of the rock platform.

Raising her arms above her head in a precise vertical pose, Dani closed her eyes readying herself for the plunge into the glistening pool below.

"Danielle." It was the voice again, this time calling her name. "Danielle." It came again. Then, instead of plummeting into the water, Dani stopped, dropping her arms to her side. In that instant, she knew the voice was familiar, but it wasn't the voice she'd heard only moments earlier. Her heart began to race as the realization took hold. Staring straight ahead, Dani was afraid to turn around.

-- -- -- -- --

Seeing her from behind only, Jacks knew it was Dani. A night had not passed when Jacks had not dreamed of Dani. He'd memorized her every feature—her muscular shoulders, the curve of her hips, the small of her back, the slender legs that extended gracefully downward to the pretty little feet that held her upright. Every part of her was unique. Jacks had determined never to forget her, and he hadn't. Rather, time had solidified his memories of her—made them more distinct, more vivid.

Moving closer to the edge of the rock, Jacks approached the statuesque Dani from behind. Reaching forward, he smoothed her long flowing hair to one side causing it to cascade over her shoulder. Though she had yet to see him, to feel him, Dani knew Jacks had finally come for her. He reached around her, leaving the carved wooden cross dangling high on her chest as he clasped the notch behind Dani's neck.

Instinctively, Dani reached for the necklace that had haunted her dreams since the moment he'd given it to her. She clutched it in her hand, holding on for dear life.

Still unable to move, Dani stood breathless. After a silent eternity, his touch finally came. It was his hands first; they grazed her tanned shoulders and trailed down her satiny arms until both hands reached hers. Dropping the necklace free, Dani's fingers instantly intertwined with Jacks'. His touch sent shivers through Dani's body. All the previous anger and hurt vanished; Dani suddenly forgot what it was that had caused her to run. Now, unable to resist his closeness, Dani's body molded into him, her back resting securely against his chest. Hands still interlocked, Jacks moved their conjoined arms around the front of Dani's body and simply held her. She felt safe. She felt secure. She felt alive. Jacks smothered his face into her ebony strands of hair, inhaling her fragrance. Dani felt the tickle of a tear trailing down her back.

A lifetime passed before either of them moved, before either of them spoke. Finally turning to face him, Dani's eyes met Jacks'. There was so much to say, but at that moment, no words were needed. Then, reaching around her miniature frame, this time face to face, Jacks lifted Dani from her feet and secured her body next to his. He took one step forward and hurdled their united bodies into the river below.

The force of the breaking water separated their bodies, if only for a moment. Ascending to the surface, they frantically scurried to return to each other's arms. The waters depth kept Jacks emerged to his mid-chest. Holding her to him, Dani's feet swayed freely below the water's surface; she was completely at his mercy.

He leaned forward and began kissing the glistening moisture from Dani's face. Her forehead, her eyelids, her cheekbones, her jawline, then—her lips. At first, his kiss was sweet and gentle. Then it was hungry and passionate. Then it was sweet and gentle again. Dani returned his kisses as eagerly as he had offered them and with the same conflicting passion. Then, Jacks pried his lips from hers. He carried her toward the water's edge and rested Dani's feet carefully on to the gold-flecked sandy shore.

Tenderly brushing away a loose strand of hair from Dani's face, Jacks reached out his hand. "Hello," he said. "My name is Tim Fowler. My friends call me Jacks." Dani smiled.

Taking his hand in hers, Dani offered, "I'm Danielle Shaw. My friends call me Dani."

Epilogue

The wedding was small and intimate. Uncle Buck served as Dani's fill-in daddy, though he wasn't the one to give her away; she wasn't his to give. Dani and Jacks had belonged to each other from the start. Separately, they had given their lives to Christ; together, they were committing their marriage to Him. Mason held the rings as he stood alongside Pastor Nick on the familiar granite slab. The water cascaded over the falls to an eurythmic tune as Miss Cilla's angelic voice sang the last lines of the song to which Britta Shaw walked down the aisle at her and Randy's wedding nearly thirty years before. Samuel at David's feet and Kylie in Tracie's arms, the couple tearfully watched as Jacks and Dani promised to share their love for eternity. Together, they vowed to make God the center of their marriage and never to let anything—not time, nor distance, nor man— separate them from Him or from each other. Dani knew in her heart, without reservation, that God had brought them together. Jacks knew it too. Everything in their lives—every laugh, every heartache, every memory, every step—had led them to this moment. It wasn't coincidence, nor was it fate, but rather, it was God's perfect plan.

-- -- -- -- --

Dani and Jacks spent the first six months of their marriage living and working in the States. Dani had earned national recognition for her piece on the plight of the Ugandan children. The article had been directly responsible for a number of new medical clinics and health programs currently being planned and established in the northern district of Uganda and surrounding communities. As a permanent employee of *The Humanitarian*, she wrote mostly about nonprofit organizations, promoting the work they were doing, while Jacks practiced at a community clinic for next-to-nothing wages. But the money didn't matter. They were both in love with their work, with Jesus, with each other.

Dani's job was rewarding, but her heart told her that it was all just temporary. She knew God wasn't finished with her yet. She was certain that He had unimaginable plans for her. It wasn't just Dani, though. Jacks felt it too.

They had lain awake until the sun began to peek over the snow-capped mountains the morning following their wedding night, learning about each other in ways they had not known before physically and emotionally. They made love. They talked about the path that had led them to one another. They laughed. They cried for the love they shared. They made love again. They talked about the future and what it might hold. Only God knew the answer. But they both knew, unequivocally, that God was calling them back to Uganda.

-- -- -- -- --

Today, under the African skies, Dani reminisced about that night as she prepared for her and Jacks' first anniversary dinner. One year ago to the day, they had lain awake dreaming of returning to the grounds on which they first met, but neither of them could have imagined that it would happen so soon. Yet it had been a whirlwind.

Dani had planned weeks in advance, spending a good part of the day traveling nearly three miles on her prized run-down motor scooter for the fresh fruit and other supplies she would need. Tonight, Dani planned to prepare the same meal she and Jacks shared during their first trip to Murchison Falls nearly two years before—glazed carrots, dried fruit chutney, green mealie bread, salad with delectable chunks of fresh rock lobster, and Klappertert for dessert. She had much to do before Jacks returned from his work at the clinic. Scurrying around the three-room bungalow, Dani gathered together all the items the children would need for the night. Tina would be expecting them soon.

Todd and Tina Gibbs were American missionaries who lived down the road from Jacks and Dani. From the moment she met the woman nearly twice her age, the two women shared a special bond; in part because familiarity breeds friendship—they were among very few Americans who lived in the vicinity—and partly because Tina, too, was unable to have children of her own. It helped both women to have someone to talk to about the pain their respective infertility caused. Dani and Tina shared a certain melancholic and strangely private resignation about their childless providence. Yes, they could talk about it with their husbands, share their greatest fears and the insecurities it evoked. Even then though, for the women, being able to share their emotional ups and downs and the unimaginable emptiness made it more tolerable. Even more, it was Dani and Tina's overt way of easing the burden that Jacks and James had so unconditionally and lovingly bore for their wives.

Returning to the moment, Dani realized she had just enough time to bring the children to the Gibbs's bungalow, come back, get washed up, and then begin preparing her anniversary surprise.

Excited as she was about her and Jacks' rare night alone, Dani was anxious about leaving the children with the Gibbses. Not because it was the Gibbses—after all, they had become like family, and Dani and Jacks trusted them with their lives—rather, it was because the children had not spent a night away from Dani and Jacks since coming to live with them last March. Dani wasn't sure how they would handle the short separation. The day that began as a day of celebration gradually evolved into a day of nostalgia and reminiscence. Dani's thoughts drifted back to an unforgettable moment nearly four months before, shortly after she and Jacks arrived in Gulu.

-- -- -- -- --

Inya had been only five months old, Tafari had just turned two. Their father had died of AIDS only three days after Inya's birth. Their mother, Kamaria, had struggled to feed her children. The single mother spent many sleepless nights on the dusty streets, her children by her side, refusing to beg, but accepting any small offer of help that was offered—a dish of rice, water to quench their thirst, a torn blanket to soften the ridges of the sharp rocks that pierced their backs as they lay on the noisy, crowded dirt alleyways that served as their transitory beds. Kamaria had been proud, but not too proud to accept the things that were necessary for her children's survival.

That's all they were doing when Dani found them; surviving. She recalled that day with vivid clarity. She had been taking a shortcut through an alley on her way to the vegetable market after giving a writing lesson to her students in the one-room, dirt-floored shack when she nearly stumbled over a large bundle in the middle of the unofficial walkway. Nearly plummeting to the ground, Dani scuffed the palm of her hands trying to prevent herself from tumbling face-first in the dirt. Brushing the hair out of her face, Dani had looked down at a sad set of chocolate brown eyes gazing up at her from under a tattered blanket.

A filthy tear-stained face provided the only glimpse of life beneath the disheveled heap.

Dani knelt down in front of the awkward bundle and spoke softly to the scared little person whose face appeared unusually small beneath the obtrusive package. "Are you all alone?" Dani quietly asked in what she assumed was the child's native language. She caressed the mud-stained little face with her smooth thumb. Without a word, the tiny person slowly shifted its weight beneath the otherwise motionless bundle.

After learning of the many tragic stories of children and women and even entire families left to die in the streets in the aftermath of the GCP violence, Dani feared the worse. The heap surrounding the child was far too large to encompass simply a small person.

Dani gently pulled back the tattered blanket, exposing a thick black head of hair and thin, bare shoulders depicting a nutrition-starved little frame. The contrast of the white of the child's eyes surrounding the deep brown color and bronze facial tones, to Dani, seemed inappropriately beautiful at that moment.

"Where is your mother?" Dani had questioned, pulling the blanket off the child's shoulders and letting it drop to the ground, revealing the little boy's nakedness.

The boy's wide, scared eyes pierced Dani's as they filled with tears and a single drop trailed down his stained face.

Again, Dani asked, "Where is your mother?" this time making a greater effort to articulate her words.

The fragile boy's eyes trailed downward to two frail fingers with dirt-encrusted nails extending from a pale hand barely visible at the edge of a corner of the torn blanket.

Dani's heart sank. Even with all the death and mayhem she had witnessed over the past years, the weight of her own imagination was almost too much a burden for her to bear. She swallowed hard trying to dissolve the lump that was quickly forming in her throat as her mouth went dry.

The small boy lifted his arms toward Dani, but remained seated on the dusty ground. Dani gently lifted the boy to her and cradled him to her chest. The boy clung to Dani's clothing with an unbreakable fierceness.

As she looked back down at the ground, the lightweight covering slipped to the side revealing a woman's lifeless face. Dani shielded the boy's eyes from the sorrowful sight. She began to back away from the chilling scene when she noticed a slight movement from beneath the blanket. Startled, Dani allowed herself a glimmer of hope that this child's mother might still be alive. She reached down and tossed the blanket from the woman's body. But hope quickly turned to a mixture of grief and surprise. What Dani found was a tiny infant cradled in the dead woman's arm. The baby stretched soundly as though waking from a rest-filled sleep. She was plump and appeared healthy and well cared for as she smiled up at Dani. That was the day Dani, unofficially, became a mother.

-- -- -- -- --

"Mama!" The angelic squeal of Tafari's voice jolted Dani out of her reminiscent dream world. Hurdling himself into her arms, Tafari howled, "We go see Tina?" Dani had been preparing Tafari for his sleepover at Tina and James's bungalow for the past week. At first, he was hesitant, but quickly warmed up to the idea after discovering that Tina was a master storyteller.

"Yes, Tafari, we're going to see Tina." Dani squeezed her son lovingly. The adoption process had been relatively simple; it had been finalized the previous week, but Dani had decided to wait until her and Jacks' anniversary celebration to tell him the good news.

When Inya woke from her nap twenty minutes later, Dani and the children were out the door and on their way to the Gibbses. Kissing the children good-bye and leaving Inya in Tina's competent arms, Dani assured Tafari that she would be there in a matter of minutes if he needed her during the night, then thanked Tina for taking care of the kids for the evening.

Noticing the look of concern on Dani's face, Tina assured, "They'll be fine, Dani. I promise."

"I know they will," she said, tightly embracing her friend and kissing Inya on the forehead one last time.

As Dani turned to leave, Tafari's innocent little voice stopped her in her tracks, "ISDLY, Mama."

A myriad of emotions overwhelmed her as thoughts of Mason invaded her mind. Dani twirled around, and for a brief instant, she envisioned Mason as she looked at her son. "ISDLY too, Tafari," then she blew him a kiss.

-- -- -- -- --

That evening, full from their nostalgic meal, Dani and Jacks spent hours reminiscing about their trip to Murchison Falls—the day Jacks admittedly first knew he loved Dani. Together a year, they still had much to learn about one another. They talked, they laughed, they cried for the miracle of God bringing them together through such an astonishing chain of events. They missed their family— those in America, and those who had long since passed. But they were grateful to have each other. They toasted to their anniversary, the life they shared and to an eternity together.

Encased in each other's arms, Dani and Jacks sat in a comfortable silence momentarily consumed by their own thoughts. Dani kissed Jacks passionately before rising to her feet.

"Where do you think you're going?" he teased.

"I've got a surprise for you," she said. She walked to her bedside table and pulled out a folded piece of paper.

Returning to Jacks, she handed him the document before snuggling against him, burying herself in his arms.

"What's this," he asked, curiously inspecting the crisp paper.

"Open it and find out," she said mischievously.

Jacks unfolded the paper. Instantly, he knew what it was. After catching his breath and kissing Dani gently on the forehead, Jacks whispered, "Congratulations, Mommy," his voice cracked as he said it. They held each other as their tears freely flowed.

When she was finally able to speak, Dani confessed, "There's only one problem."

Though her tone revealed nothing, Jacks was confused and momentarily frightened, "What kind of problem?"

Still in his arms, Dani twisted her body around to face Jacks. "Our family really won't be complete for six months still."

Scrutinizing the adoption papers again, Jacks argued, "That can't be right. It says right here that the adoption became final last week".

"Don't worry, Tafari and Inya are ours," she confirmed, hesitating for a moment. "But our baby isn't due to arrive until December!"

Dani squealed like a child, seeing the shock of realization in Jacks' face and feeling, for the first time, the faint fluttering of the miraculous life just beginning to form inside of her...God's perfect plan.

ABOUT THE AUTHOR

Born and raised in the Sierra Nevada Foothills of Nevada County, California, Lori's roots are deeply ingrained in the landscape of the local community. She draws her inspiration for writing from the ups-and-downs of her walk with Christ, precious family and experiences living in a small, tight-knit community.

Made in the USA
Lexington, KY
06 September 2018